WHITES CAN DANCE TOO

KALAF EPALANGA

WHITES CAN DANCE TOO

Translated by Daniel Hahn

faber

First published in 2023
by Faber & Faber Limited
The Bindery
51 Hatton Garden
London EC1N 8HN

Typeset by Faber & Faber Limited
Printed in the UK by CPI Group (UK) Ltd, Croydon, CR0 4YY

Translation © Daniel Hahn, 2023

First published in Portugal in Portuguese by Editorial Caminho
in 2017 as *Também Os Brancos Sabem Dançar*.

A CIP record for this book
is available from the British Library

ISBN 978-0-571-37142-6

MIX
Paper | Supporting
responsible forestry
FSC® C171272

Printed and bound in the UK on FSC® certified paper in line with our continuing
commitment to ethical business practices, sustainability and the environment.
For further information see faber.co.uk/environmental-policy

10 9 8 7 6 5 4 3 2 1

For my family

PART I

NORWAY

9 AUGUST 2008

When the guns turn meek
Kuduro will still speak
'Cause a voice can make bullets seem weak.

—Bruno M, 'Já Respeita Né'

I

I guess I must have got distracted by those Bruno M lines, because I didn't even register the bus slowing and parking on the side of the road, amid an exuberant green. I didn't notice when we crossed the Svinesund canal, separating Sweden from Norway, over the new bridge built across the Iddefjord and baptised with the same name as the old one beside it: Svinesund. I would have liked to have seen it, this being my first time visiting the northern lands, but couldn't help falling asleep. We're 113 km south of Oslo and 180 km north of Gothenburg, where last night at the Way Out West festival a crowd of well mannered blond Swedes danced frantically to our blended Kuduro, house and tropical techno, as if it were the last August of their lives, and as if the cities of Luanda and Lisbon were not so distant and unknown.

The door opened and two police officers, both in plain clothes, with badges round their necks, boarded the vehicle. The man, tall and blond the way only a Viking can be, introduced himself to the passengers. I don't recall his exact words, but my mind immediately went back over the reply I'd practised dozens of times just in case I were to come across border officers at any point on the three and a half thousand kilometres I had covered since Lisbon. I was travelling without a passport, having lost it somewhere in a hotel in Paris, a few weeks earlier. A nightmare which, at the time, had forced my band Buraka Som Sistema to cancel a series of engagements, because in addition – since misfortune always brings a plus-one to the party – I am an Angolan citizen. When you are an ordinary Angolan citizen, the last thing you want is to lose your papers. I'd give anything for it to have been my phone, or the suitcase with my clothes, my laptop, just not the passport, as this meant travelling to Luanda, finding a handler, paying an expediting fee and then praying to Kianda, our Saint Iphigenia, for her to bless the computers of the Angolan Migration and Foreigners Service for the system not to fail.

And I prayed now, I prayed to Saint Elesbão and to Saint Benedict that I would not falter, I prayed for my voice not to fail me when my turn came to present my papers, for the lie I'd prepared for the occasion to come out convincingly. But it did not. I showed my residency card and the blond man looked at it suspiciously, asked for my passport. I lied, saying I had it in my suitcase. The other officer, a brunette who looked like she might be a professional judo player, joined us. Apparently I was the only person on the bus with a suspect document – I'm sure no other foreigner with a residency card issued by the Portuguese Immigration and Borders Service had ever crossed that border before.

The blond man, who could easily have been in our audience the previous night, asked me to go fetch my passport, instructing the driver to open the luggage compartment. The two officers escorted me to my suitcase, and in those few metres I even considered turning back and telling them the truth: confessing that the passport I had to show them was an old expired one, so devastated by time that nobody in their right mind would ever allow me passage with a document in such a condition. Not only had it expired back when the Angolan revolutionary Jonas Savimbi was still alive and wreaking havoc, but the space for a photograph was occupied by what now looked more like a painting by the impressionist master Willem de Kooning.

My legs trembling, but with the most confident attitude I'd ever boasted, I held out the passport, just like that, 'rotten-faced', as the Angolans say, and my bold and irresponsible gesture must have set off every alarm in those two officers' heads. Only a madman – or a really first-rate criminal – would attempt to cross the whole of Europe by bus and train with the threadbare excuse that he's a musician in a Lisbon band and that he was due to play a concert that night at one of the continent's most iconic festivals of electronic music. I wouldn't have believed it myself if I had been in their position.

The officers invited me to retrieve my luggage and accompany them to the nearest police station for questioning. I didn't say a word, I felt the sweat forming on my brow, my mouth dry, heart pounding. I was sure any sudden movement would make me throw up.

Nobody had asked me to turn missionary, to travel the world from the slums of Luanda like a Mormon Elder, spreading the gospel of kuduro – a musical genre born in the intersection of house, techno and kizomba in the late 1980s, when the Angolan civil war was at its peak and the youth desperately needed something that could help make sense of the chaos surrounding them.

The two officers hadn't exchanged a word since they had got into the car, and with so much silence, I did consider explaining myself, somewhere between begging for my freedom and telling them the truth, the whole truth. But what truth? What good would it do for me to explain kuduro to them? In any case, I'm sure the two officers would not have been interested in my truth. I kept my mouth shut and fixed my eyes on the landscape – this might be my last chance to see Scandinavia. I would give anything to be alone, able to lose myself in that green and think freely.

II

Everything will be OK. I repeated this mantra to help me bear the silence inside that car. I will be able to prove I'm a musician, a 'cultural agitator' – as the Portuguese journalists like to characterise me. Travelling without a valid passport is not wise, but I'm not trying to fool anyone. I'm just a non-musician musician, a singer-poet, trying to make it to Oslo. If I start my statement with this confession, they might set me free, on time to make it to the festival. History is crammed full of musicians living on the edges of the law, who use their careers as a front, and get up to all sorts behind the curtain. I didn't want to give in to the paranoid thoughts that were forming in my head, but the possibility of being mistaken for a drug trafficker was starting to seem likely. To what other activity could African musicians arrested crossing a border without papers be applying their talents? Everyone knows how hard it is to make a living from music. My own mother, however happy she is to see her son following his dreams, if asked about the sort of life she'd like me to lead, I'm sure would give a reply involving a desk and a nine-to-five schedule. That's what mothers are like, always wanting the best for us.

The moment I realised I was being taken to an airport, my heart began to beat easier. I thought I was going to be deported. 'Rygge', I read in the neon that hung from one facade. The blond Viking man hurried to open my door, reached over and pulled me out. I offered him no resistance. I was too tired to struggle and I allowed him to exercise his authority over me as if I were a child, or maybe even a criminal. He put his hand on my head so that I might avoid hitting it on my way out. And I would have appreciated his care, had I been brought there under any other circumstances.

At that moment, all I wanted was to put an end to that humiliation, and I turned to the police officers to ask about my belongings. 'Don't worry, just keep walking,' was their only response. It was immediately after my question that I felt the touch, a light push to my back, the first of several that would be repeated whenever I slowed down. I still don't know whether the touch is to maintain speed or whether it is common procedure for the police whenever they are escorting suspects to the station. People were watching us and, as a way of showing you're doing your job, nothing beats a little shove to make a point. It must be protocol, one of those protracted guidelines fulfilled to the letter, which was repeated over and over, even after we had walked through the door to the building, and even inside the station, a place so sterile it looked more like a tax office.

The faces of the officers we walked past were almost as grey as the walls. I was led briskly to a door, where I was asked for my papers. I handed them to the blond Viking at the same moment the judoka was opening the door to a room, and, employing the same pleasant gesture they'd used to convey me from the car, with a push to my back, she invited me to go in. I ignored it, I knew that brusqueness of hers was part of the game. They wanted to test me, to see how far my air of serenity could go, my haughtiness even, as if I were so sure that it was all just a mistake and I'd soon be free to continue on my way.

The room was just as you would expect: grey, no windows and a chicken-coop light on the ceiling. It smelled new, like a building only recently completed. The floor was the same colour as the walls, in a material I was unable to identify. It didn't matter to me. My eyes were fixed on the single piece of furniture against the far wall, whose ends connected the two side walls. It might have been a desk, and was too hard to be a bed – I nonetheless, since there were no chairs, decided it would be a bed and lay down. There was nothing else for me to do. My fate was now in the hands of the Scandinavian gods and, since I was well aware that divine interventions are never particularly speedy, I closed my eyes.

But my mind refused to shut down. I couldn't avoid running through answers in my head in case the officers asked me what had brought me to Norway. I can start by saying I'm an artist. An Angolan expatriate, an artist-expat, and what makes me jump out of bed and travel the world, cross borders, even without valid documents, at the risk of running into the police and landing up in a Norwegian jail, is a need to meet the other. It's the only exercise I know how to undertake that will allow me to materialise into words, not too many of them if possible, what I know about myself. My name, for example, says more about me than any adjective, and I didn't even know its exact meaning. Imagine what it's like for a five-year-old kid to accept that they have a strange name when the other members of his family had, for the most part, names inspired by Catholic saints. At a moment when most kids were obsessed with finding out where babies came from, all I wanted was to be told the origins of my own name, given an explanation as to why I hadn't been assigned a simple, neutral Gustavo or Felipe? I never got an answer. Some old guys back in the day used to tease me, singing a song by this guy called Luís Kalaff, a merengue singer from the Dominican Republic.

I only know how to whistle one refrain from my double-f namesake, the one they'd assault me with whenever they heard my name. 'La Mecha, La Mecha, Ai Maria . . .' And that's it. But whatever the old guys in Benguela thought, I know that the 'La Mecha' we knew is actually performed by Tabito Pequero, the second vocalist in Luís Kalaff's Los Alegres Dominicanos – The Happy Dominicans – and it's the track that opens the record *El Rey del Merengue*, released in 1962. To this day, I wonder whether my ending up in music was influenced by the name I bear. I'm not one of those people who believes in destiny, but I can't help smiling at an odd coincidence. The old Kalaff was a prolific composer, who put his name to more than two thousand compositions, some of them covered by giants of Latin music, like Fernanda Villalona's *El Niño Mimado*, as well as by the most romantic ex-goalkeeper of all time, Julio Iglesias. Not bad for the son of a humble Dominican woman, Dona Bernavelina Pérez, and Juan Kalaff, a Lebanese merchant who, at the age of fourteen, when he was working as a carpenter, made his first guitar out of the remains of an instrument he'd found on the street. A trajectory almost biblical in outline, since it was on this guitar that his son began to spread the gospel of merengue, of mangulina and of bolero from Santo Domingo to the world.

III

The Viking and the judoka came into the cell, him two steps ahead of her. I stood up and he gestured for me to sit back down. I obeyed. The judoka watched my movements and only when she saw my backside at rest did she move away from the door, leaning back against the wall. That woman intimidated me. I didn't expect, I didn't need her to smile at me, but after I'd surrendered without a fuss, she really could loosen her shoulders a bit and grasp that I didn't represent the slightest threat to the national security of the kingdom of Norway.

'We can't find anything on you,' said the Viking. I suspected he wasn't anticipating any response from me, so I kept quiet. 'We tried to consult the Portuguese police and there's no record of your name,' he went on.

'I've never committed a crime,' was my reply.

'We think it's strange there's no record of you any-where,' he continued. I thought it didn't seem so hard to understand that if the Portuguese police had no record of me, that could only be a good sign, surely? I chose to say nothing, and just asked: 'Can I go?' The judoka joined the discussion with a categorical 'No'.

The Viking and I both turned towards her, both surprised, though not for the same reasons. What had surprised me was the fact that she'd spoken at all, finally! 'Since we don't have access to the Portuguese Immigration and Borders Service database, we can't let you go,' the Viking added.

I brought my hands to my head, and the judoka, sus-pecting that I was about to lose my shit, flip out, kick the furniture, launch my closed fist in the direction of the Viking's imposing jaw, rend my garments, shout, cry, or whatever – I have no idea how far her imagination could have gone – peeled her back off the wall and positioned her feet diagonally, slightly further apart than the breadth of her shoulders, her arms down, the heel of her back foot raised just a few millimetres off the ground, her knees slightly bent and curved chin pointing at her chest. If I got up, or made any sudden movement right then, I was sure I'd get a thump in the mouth.

But there was no need, the Viking's words had already caused more damage than any blow the judoka could have inflicted. If she'd touched me, I suspect I wouldn't even have felt the impact, so numb had those words left me.

'I'm booked for a concert in Oslo, I need to get onto that stage,' I told them. The stage, that inhospitable planet I learned to call home.

I turned back to the two officers, who were still just standing there gawping, waiting for the true confessions of an illegal immigrant. Maybe my calm was giving me away. I couldn't stop thinking my performance might be lacking in drama, kind of like when we get up onto the stage and address the crowd with lines like: 'You're the best audience in the world, nobody parties like you guys,' the kinds of words that every audience in the world is tired of hearing, but that doesn't stop them applauding and yelling for more. Besides giving them details of the festival in Oslo, I didn't know what else to say to the Viking and the judoka that hundreds of other illegal immigrants hadn't said before. Please let me call my tour manager or take me to the festival. They looked at each other and moved towards the door. It crossed my mind to invite them to come up onto the stage with me, even though I know it's not the best place to watch a concert, but it's where I feel safe. I have nowhere else to be. *You could even shackle my ankles if you think that's appropriate, if it brings you some peace of mind. Then I'll be all yours, I promise. Arrest me, throw me out of your country, send me back to Africa if you think that would be the outcome that would satisfy you. But for now, release me, so that I can go work.*

The officers left the cell without even looking at me. Maybe I should have done more than profess my innocence. I could expand on what kuduro is about. Present the right story, with a better introduction, something like:

'And in the beginning was the ndombolo.'

That was how this story really ought to start.

Just ask the Langas, the Zaïkos, as we call the Congolese people who migrated to our country, bringing a high sense of fashion and fantastic music. Music from Franco Luambo Makiadi, the king of the Congolese rumba, who along with Zaïko Langa Langa and under the leadership of the great Jossart N'Yoka Longo, would come to inspire the birth of many of our musical groups, like Os Jovens do Prenda and Os Kiezos, round about 1960 in Angola. And I discovered it all in one of Africa's largest open-air markets: Roque Santeiro.

Pepetela once wrote: 'If they haven't got it at Roque, it's because it hasn't been invented yet.' Those words from one of the fathers of Angolan literature summarise what for me, and for many of my contemporaries, is the essence of that most fascinating and yet most intimidating of spaces in the city of Luanda. Ever since its establishment in the mid-1980s, Roque Santeiro has always been more than a market, it was the heart that pumped life into Luanda's economy and, up to a point, the country's.

My own baptism into Roque happened thanks to my cousin Tininho, my first idol. To this day I hold him in the same regard as my most esteemed philosophers and poets. He was responsible for my discovering a taste for mixtapes. BASF cassettes were our favourites. We spent afternoons on end sitting beside the radio, recording the perfect selection that, as a general rule, we would give to friends or girls. 'Never underestimate the power of a mixtape in the game of seduction,' Tininho used to say. Then he would add, 'A cassette with just the right selection, nowadays, is worth as much as Shakespeare's sonnets and, like photographs, songs perpetuate moments whose shelf life is not defined by time.'

One sunny Saturday afternoon in 1989, we went to Roque to buy BASF cassettes and, as soon as we had got out of the car, my eye was caught by the sea of people spreading out as far as the horizon. 'Welcome to the biggest open-air store in Africa,' my cousin said to me. 'Within these five hectares, under zinc sheeting, something like five football pitches, there's about seven thousand registered stalls and loads of others operating "illegally",' he said, regaling me with those stats he always liked to share. 'You know how many people work here?' he asked. I wrinkled up my nose and tossed the number 'two thousand' into the air. He laughed and asked me to pay attention to the sound, to the noise that covered Sambizanga hill, a sound of which I'd never heard the like before, the sound of a giant pressure cooker on the boil.

'That's the noise of thousands of traders and customers keeping the wheels of the economy rolling,' he said. As we passed through the food area, the smells of just-made manioc funge and moamba palm oil were dancing into the sky. Around the stalls, everything was for sale: home furnishings, household appliances, shoes, French perfumes, sex, cars, car parts, stereos, school textbooks, medicines, building materials, Scotch whisky, designer clothing, made-to-measure clothing, coffins assembled while you waited, Brazilian weaves, Indian weaves – everything. The video clubs were screening the latest American action movies. And between the stalls, the sea in Luanda bay. 'Awesome sight, huh?' Tininho sighed.

Roque was strategically positioned just a few kilometres from the port of Luanda, and it was widely known that the containers destined to supply the city's trade never ended up going through customs. At the height of the civil war in the early 1980s, even those products intended for humanitarian aid used to end up at Roque. The market mirrored a post-colonial Angola. It did have a picturesque side, festive and colourful like any local market in an African city, but it was also the stage for racial, political and regional tensions brewing in silence within our society. Boavista Popular Market was the official name, 'Roque Santeiro' was the nickname coined after a Brazilian TV soap that livened up Angolan family evenings in 1985. With all his knowledge about our history, even my cousin couldn't explain why the name stuck. 'Perhaps people wanted to forget what happened here, and a new name associated with more joyful memories was necessary,' he said, knowing that I would immediately ask him what happened here. I did, and he fell silent for a minute and looked over his shoulder as if the people around us were listening. He moved closer, lowering his voice. 'This place was the stage for mass executions that followed a split inside the MPLA government in May of 1977.' Tininho tapped my shoulder and added, 'It's still an open wound. Avoid talking about 1977 in public.' And then it was my turn to fall silent.

Being in that market was like being in a musical. At first, everything seemed chaotic, but once inside, everyone knew their choreographed steps and the only way to survive it was to dance along to ndombolo like your life depended on it. This music genre and dance style from the Democratic Republic of the Congo (DRC) – present in our culture thanks to the large community of Zairians, who, for decades, helped to make Roque Santeiro what it is – are believed to be the staple cassava meal, the central pillar, the foundation that serves as the basis for all kuduro's other dance steps, starting with the ndombolo walk which took me forever to master.

In the ndombolo, the whole body dances, in a swaying of smooth and gentle hip movements in women, quick and irregular ones in men. Kuduro's ndombolo steps flow from the Congolese's footwork, accelerated to match the rhythmic and theatrical demands of our genre. We call it the ndombolo walk, and I learned its basics from the dancer Heráclito Aristóteles, better known as 'ATM', a reserved man who didn't talk much, and who insisted on telling jokes only the Angolans in the group would understand. We did two concerts with him, at the start of 2007. The first was in Lisbon, at the Musicbox, a small club where the people who had come to see us filled the place beyond the legal capacity. That concert served to refine some of the details for the launch tour of *Black Diamond*, our debut album, before the first date in London, at the Hoxton Bar & Grill, the very next day. I remember ATM showing up at Lisbon Airport dressed all smart as if he were going to mass, his trousers starched, shirt buttoned up to his neck, and a black blazer that was a couple of sizes too big for him. He had even brought along a family-size suitcase, which weighed more than anything else in the backline. When we asked what he was transporting, he admitted he was carrying food – sausages, hams, salt-cod – at the request of some Angolan friends living in London. We had to pay for excess baggage.

On arrival in London, Branko, Riot and the crew headed for the queue for EU citizens, leaving us non-Europeans behind. The first person they checked was Andro, Blaya followed, and ATM and I were seen at the same time at different desks. After the customary questions – 'And what do you do?', 'And how long do you intend to remain in the United Kingdom?', and all that – the border officer welcomed me to London and, just as I was about to retrieve my documents and head down to baggage reclaim, I saw ATM looking downcast and being sent to wait in a side area reserved for passengers in irregular circumstances. I felt for him. More than anyone else in the group, I knew that desolate feeling well.

I walked over to try to find out what was going on, but I was intercepted by a policeman who informed me I wasn't allowed to be in that area once I had crossed the border. I pointed at ATM and said we were travelling together and that I was just trying to find out why they weren't letting him through, seeing as we had the same kind of visa. The policeman nodded and turned around. An embarrassed ATM admitted that he had been prevented from entering because they'd spotted an item on his record involving some situation with the police in Northern Ireland. A young Heráclito Aristóteles, who at the time had migrated to Ireland, had once got involved in a bar brawl and was arrested, spent the night down at the station and, the following day, still stunned from the previous night's events, decided to leave the realm of Elizabeth II and move to Lisbon. Ever since, each time he has travelled to the UK, he has been stopped at the border for questioning before being allowed in. And that was what had happened. Thanks to the gods of ndombolo, ATM was not deported. Later on that evening, when we finally got on stage, he was another person. Knees slightly bent, moving his legs from outside to in, in a syncopated fluctuation, alternating the weight onto and off his planting foot, at a rhythm of 140 BPM in a movement that created an illusion that ATM's legs had an extra elasticity and could flout the very logic of motor coordination. His dance was cathartic to him and us. He brought great joy to the crowd of partygoers who filled Hoxton Bar & Grill to watch Buraka.

IV

I knew from the start that our role would not be merely to showcase our individual talents to the world. Alongside that, we would need to cast a light on the musical genre itself, and on the city that bred it – Luanda. But also on the city where we were based and which, owing to historical circumstances and geographic location, represented the ideal place for absorbing, processing, transforming and disseminating kuduro like nowhere else – Lisbon. However, we realised the world turns much more slowly than our senses are able to grasp. There weren't many journalists willing to embrace a narrative divided into four separate points: Buraka–kuduro–Luanda–Lisbon. They asked us to simplify, to disseminate the narrative's strongest points, which means, briefly: talent, a genre and one city. Lisbon was the weakest link, at least to the foreign journalists we encountered in the early years, when we were still trying to sell them the idea of Lisbon as the most African city in Europe. They frowned and spat, preferring to buy Luanda instead. So much more exotic, mysterious, dangerous, even sexy to some, than the worm-eaten old city of seven hills.

Hearing kuduro at a party for the first time is an experience that leaves no one indifferent. From child to old man, from humble monangambé to lofty governor, passing through the civil servant, the emigrant in the diaspora, mothers from the Organization of Angolan Women or local women hawking their wares on the street. Hear a kuduro playing and there's no way for you not to tap your feet. Even the actor/musician/comedian Jamie Foxx agreed. I saw a clip of his stand-up special *I Might Need Security* on YouTube describing the moment he heard kuduro for the first time. While he was in South Africa filming the Muhammad Ali biopic with Will Smith, he went to a club. The locals warned him that around midnight, the dance floor would be overtaken by something he'd never experienced before. A liberating beat that would bring everyone into the middle of the room, entirely stripped of any prejudices, surrendering themselves to kuduro, as if it were the day of the Last Judgement. I used to show that clip of Jamie Foxx to everyone sceptical about buying my enthusiasm towards kuduro. To me, it was the best dance music ever made, something that was saving the lives of the youth of my country, and if an Oscar and Grammy-winner was impressed by it, how could the international press turn a blind eye and fail to understand just how revolutionary that genre was? I felt responsible. I could have been serving in the military but made it out of the country before I was called up. I wanted to use that privilege and shout – Angola had something to say. We couldn't just be ruled out of the dance music culture. And when *Pitchfork*, *The Fader* and the British *Fact Magazine* decided to look into what was happening in Luanda and Lisbon by writing about kuduro and my band, alongside the great names of the global electronic music scene, it meant the world to us. I felt we were not invisible any more.

V

But I can't talk about kuduro until I've told these officers about Luanda, the city that created it. The war and the resilience of its people. For me, kuduro is a by-product of all the dramatic events that took place in the city and shaped the country, ever since the civilians rebelled against the Portuguese colonial power on 4 February 1961 in what was later called the 'Katana Revolution' – among them a priest called Manuel Joaquim Mendes das Neves, from the archdiocese of Luanda, who helped and blessed the revolutionaries. Neither did the group assigned to the uprising pass up the blessings from the witch doctors who washed them with roots and mystical ointments. Many of the participants believed that such rituals sealed up their bodies, making them unbreachable by bullets. The rituals didn't have this effect, but they did fill the men with courage and confer a spirit of brotherhood on them. As legend has it, hours before the attack, the group chosen to carry out the action swore an oath after swallowing a fifty-centavo coin: those who survived the offensive would look out for the families of the deceased once the revolution had succeeded. An oath that many still complain is yet to be kept.

The close to two hundred revolutionaries, led by Neves Bendinha, Paiva Domingos da Silva, Raúl Deão, Domingos Manuel Mateus and Imperial Santana, left Luanda's poor musseque neighbourhoods early in the morning of a Saturday, with katanas in their hands, ready to free Angola from the oppression of the Portuguese colonisers. One of these groups ambushed a Military Police patrol, neutralising the four soldiers and taking their guns and ammo. They attacked the São Francisco Fortress, but their attempt to free the political prisoners failed. Other targets included the PIDE prison in the São Paulo neighbourhood and the prison of the 7th Squadron of the Public Security Police (PSP), where more political detainees were being held. They likewise attempted to occupy Angola's official broadcaster, a radio station emitting state propaganda. Forty Angolans died in these actions, and the Portuguese side lost six police officers and an army corporal. The priest Manuel Joaquim Mendes das Neves was arrested shortly after that Saturday and sent to the Aljube prison in Lisbon, where he remained until the place was closed in 1965, finally dying in 1966. At first, the Portuguese state believed the 4 February uprising to have been an action orchestrated by Patrice Lumumba, prime minister of the newly independent Congo-Léopoldville. But however sympathetic he might have been to the idea, and however much he might have dreamed of an Africa freed from European rule, Lumumba could not have masterminded the revolt, as he had been killed in January of that year in Lumumbashi, at the hands of a rifle squad under the command of rebel leader Moïse Tshombé, with the involvement of Belgium, the United States and the United Kingdom. The 1961 attacks were actually organised by Angolans linked to a variety of fledging political movements who were then taking their first steps.

Sambizanga, Cazenga and Rangel were the neighbour-hoods out of which the 4 February uprising was born. The kingdom of red earth, on the far side of the 'border' – the name given to the limits of the tarmac city – was the cradle of the 'Katana Revolution', and it is no surprise that those are the places where the most exciting kuduro music is created. Art made by the descendants of the fifty-centavo revolutionaries, people who should be benefitting from the promises made to their forefathers who lost their lives to the cause. Those artists' goal is not to hear their music played on the radio or in the most talked-about clubs of the day. Their sound is too raw for that, too wild, and they have no intention of polishing it up and making it more accessible. It is music for consuming out of informal 'open window' kiosks, at yard parties or via YouTube, in the candongueiro minibuses painted in white and blue, which circulate the city, covering for the country's chronic lack of public transport.

VI

'The best way of drawing the true portrait of Angolan society is sitting inside a candongueiro,' my aunt Beatriz used to tell me, who was herself a candongueiro driver, described by a TPA journalist as 'the only woman in a world dominated by men'.

My mother's youngest sister, Aunt Beatriz – who we called Tia Bia – was always a woman ahead of her time, or perhaps just another Angolan woman who was a mistress of the art of survival. In the 1980s she was a soldier and a police officer, and in the 1990s she became the owner of a snack bar. In 2000 she took the wheel of a candongueiro.

It was she who told me that the candongueiro business had started to become fashionable around 1986, when Luanda's traditional public transport was in decline – caused by poor management, maintenance problems and progressive deterioration of the streets.

As the civil war in the country's interior intensified, Luanda became a place of refuge for those who were more affected. The city grew dramatically. The musseques were expanding seemingly arbitrarily, in total disorder, and the existing transport networks didn't cover the whole suburban area. Immediately, in obedience to their entrepreneurial spirit, anyone who had their own vehicle saw a business opportunity.

Unlike most of the city's candongueiros, in which you could only hear kuduro and kizomba, the speakers of the HiAce driven by Tia Bia only played sembas from the olden days. Ruy Mingas, Artur Nunes, David Zé. Singers who gave voice to the Angolan people's aspirations, who sang our pain and our yearning for freedom.

'Blessed be they who sacrificed themselves and fought for change,' I remember hearing my aunt saying, as if in prayer, when I was accompanying her on her favourite route, from the airport to Baleizão.

A lot of the candongueiros would drive packed to impossibility, with the radio full volume and disrespecting all the traffic rules defined by the highway code. 'Benguelense, d'you know that the history of transport here in Luanda is a perfect metaphor for understanding the Luandan people?' she asked me, but gave me no time to reply. 'First came the owners of light vehicles, who'd gotten tired of giving people lifts and so started charging five hundred kwanza per ride, those old kwanzas, the ones from back in the days of the one-party regime. But their cars, just like Luanda itself, started to get too small with the arrival of so many people and so then came the flatbed trucks – still an Angolan classic today – where it's best we don't even count how many people get on them. They're a menace! It wasn't till the 1980s that you started to see nine-seater minivans in circulation as taxis, the ones that came from Belgium, from Holland and West Germany. You hearing me, Kalaf? After those, it was almost the end of the 1980s before our Toyota HiAces started to invade our roads – or those things we optimistically think of as roads – becoming the official vehicles for business. This thing can handle whatever you throw at it, potholes, dirt tracks, the lakes of rain and, most of all, the beatings you take on the roads. There's no motor better suited to Luanda than a

Toyota HiAce. It's like the Luandans: however worn out everything's gotten, and with the road no better than a beaten earth track, they keep on going.'

My aunt's story amazed me. Not for the analogy or for the facts in themselves, but because I don't think I had ever heard her speak so much while she was driving. Like a lot of the candongueiro drivers, my aunt Bia used to drive her routes without showing the least facial expression, almost in a meditative state, seemingly pure and oblivious to all the day-to-day tensions of the Luandan traffic, a Zen mistress, immune to the questions that afflict regular mortal drivers.

It's the conductors who do have a voice, shouting the taxi's destinations with the effectiveness and volume of the most committed broker on the Wall Street Stock Exchange. But they don't call 'buy' or 'sell', they're shouting 'Going to . . .' your destination yelled with lungs full of air, wherever, always announced quickly and twice over: 'AIRPORT AIRPORT'; 'MUTAMBA MUTAMBA'. It's the conductors who take the kwanzas for each route, folding the banknotes in half, between index finger and ring finger, beneath the middle finger, thus forming a wad of bills that is neatly ordered, by value. The conductor doesn't have a designated seat. Well, actually no one does. The van, which was designed by Japanese engineers, was conceived for carrying nine passengers, but the 'Angolan engineers', in order to maximise profit, transformed it into a vehicle with sixteen seats, all of them intended for the customers, leaving the young conductor contorting himself in the space between the back of the front passenger seat and the knees of those passengers in the row behind.

In addition to playing semba, my aunt's candongueiro was also an exception because its windows didn't contain any writing. It didn't have any popular wisdom, religious sayings or references to the crew she belonged to, as you usually see in those vehicles.

It's a given that, for the development and expansion of kuduro, at a time when that kind of music wasn't welcome on the radio or at bourgeois yard parties, the Roque Santeiro market and the candongueiros that drove around the capital played a crucial role, not only in keeping kuduro alive but also in elevating it to the category of official soundtrack to the city streets. Except in Tia Bia's candongueiro.

VII

The officers entered my cell again. I stood up and looked at them without fear, ready to risk everything for the love of music. It had crossed my mind before that something like this was bound to happen one day. I've challenged festival security guards in the past, real bruisers, who would have broken me in half in other circumstances. Still, since I had a microphone in my hand, I disrespected their authority and shouted at them to let the most over-excited fans up onto the stage.

The officers changed their line of questioning. They asked me if I was seeking asylum in Norway. I shook my head. They asked me when I arrived in Europe. I smiled. '1995.'

On the list of my greatest torments, the troubles caused by the police hardly register compared to those provoked by consulate employees. Now, them I *am* afraid of, it gives me a chill just thinking about them. Whenever I need to request a visa, on the night before a trip to the consulate or embassy I have nightmares. In the morning, I always put on sober clothes, the kind nobody who saw them would think belonged to someone who lives off kuduro. I always show up a couple of hours before my appointed time, with the bearing and the outfit of a worshipper at his first communion.

My friends tell me to marry and put an end to my embassy visits. But getting married for papers? The idea had occurred to me, of course, and there was even one candidate, Sofia, with golden hair and the loveliest sway to her when she danced. If I didn't know she had been born in the Lisbon suburbs of Rio de Mouro, I would have said she was one of those Benguela women, Angolan but of Portuguese origin, who when independence finally came on 11 November 1975, had simply forgotten to return to Portugal. But that wasn't how I had always imagined it . . . And in these matters I'd like to be as tackily old-fashioned as possible. Take my future bride off to someplace beautiful, get down on one knee, pull the engagement ring out of my pocket and ask her to take my name and put up with me until our final breath. These words or others, improvised in the moment, with pauses, hesitations, hands sweating, voice serious and legs wobbling. (That's why we kneel, lest the devil steal away our balance.)

'Let me go – please – I've got to go work.'

The Viking shrugged and left the room without giving me an answer. The judoka went with him. But before the door closed she turned and said, 'Well, you should have thought of that before crossing the border without a passport.'

At that moment everything became clear. The look in the judoka's eyes said it all. The problem wasn't really my having hopped from Sweden to Norway without a passport, the problem was my sheer nerve. I wasn't fleeing from a country at war, even if it was suffering great deprivations after one war of independence and another civil one. Our civil war, to a certain extent, had ended on the afternoon of 22 February 2002, near Luio village on the banks of the Lungwebungu, in the south-west of Moxico province, when Brigadier-General Simão Carlitos Wala, Angola's youngest general at the time, commanded the troops that defeated Jonas Savimbi in what would come to be known as Operation Kissonda.

At no point did I raise the fact of being a war refugee, which must have led them to think I was pompously posing as a cultural ambassador trying to come in through the back door. I didn't pay some pirate to carry me across the Mediterranean, I paid for my trip using a Visa card with my name on it.

'I know my freedom troubles you,' I shouted. And even if nobody heard me, it felt good to clear the lump in my throat; the same lump I had felt the first time I faced a border officer.

'What is the purpose of your visit?'
    'Vacation.'

'Where are you going to be staying?'

'At my father's house.'

'How much money have you brought with you?'

'It's enough for the cab, I think. Around fifty thousand escudos.'

It was 1995 and I'd just arrived in Lisbon. The border officer stopped leafing through the pages of my passport and looked up, fixing his eyes on mine. I gave him a smile. He looked back down at my visa, set my passport to one side and asked me, while he had a word with the inspector, to wait for him next to a wall, where there were already some other passengers from my flight, along with two Eastern European women and a Brazilian lad, maybe in his twenties. At that moment it didn't occur to me that I was running any risk of being denied entry and sent back to Luanda. I didn't even think that, in the eyes of those border police, a seventeen-year-old guy who'd just landed in Lisbon with a tourist visa almost certainly would not be going back to his country – he'd have to be crazy. News of the civil war in Angola must have been making headlines in all the papers. I was not a refugee, I had not come to claim political asylum, but right there in my tourist visa, those must have been the words that shouted the loudest. That was the moment I realised that there's nothing scarier than an African crossing European borders. 'Hide your money, hide your daughters, the blacks are invading our backyard!' When they see us approaching the window, I can hear their thoughts as we hand the border police our third-world passports. Those were my first hours in Portugal. I lost count of how long I waited before I was taken to a windowless room where I found a police officer behind a desk, leafing through the empty pages of my passport with the impatience of someone who'd seen hundreds that morning alone. When he finally turned his eyes on me, I was already sitting down. He repeated the same questions the border officer had put to me. He asked my father's profession.

'Doctor.'

'Is he coming to meet you?'

I nodded and he, looking at the page with my tourist visa, made a sound, a long *hmmmm*, as if he already knew what my answers to his next questions were going to be. That sound was a way for him to find his balance, perhaps courage, to make me one more number in the growing stats of African immigrants who were arriving every day at the borders of the European Union. If they had some way of locking the borders, they'd do it, I have no doubt. From my perspective, at that moment, they could go ahead and lock them. I would have given anything not to have had to leave Angola. It would even have been a relief to get sent back. I knew I wasn't welcome. It would have been a relief for everyone, even my father. I'm sure he would have preferred me not to be in Portugal. We barely knew each other. Ever since he left Benguela for Coimbra, the news I received from him was in letters and occasional phone calls. The letters were always addressed to my mother, who, after reading in silence through the things that related only to the two of them, would then read the few paragraphs addressed to me. I don't remember when I received or sent the last letter; I must have lost interest, and he stopped bothering.

The inspector picked up one of the stamps, paused for a second and then hammered the page. I was free to enter Europe.

I walked briskly through the Arrivals terminal and spotted my father near the automatic glass doors, where I could see the 'Exit' sign. I was taking broad strides but it felt as though I were running, not into my father's arms, but out of that place. I had just arrived in Europe and already all I wanted was to run away.

But I kept on going towards my father, towards the faint picture I retained of him. I had always wondered if I'd know how to react at that reunion. I even wondered, during the journey, if we would recognise each other. Maybe it would be easier for him to recognise the features of mine that were, or had once been, his own. I would have to make a much greater effort, since the only image I had of his face was from my parents' black-and-white wedding photographs, from 1975, a time and country that no longer exists. The access I had to these few photographs was limited too. Only occasionally, in the most acute phase of my childhood curiosity – a phase in which I inundated my mother with questions about 'When is he coming back?' – my father – and 'What did he look like?' – did she, in an attempt to calm me down, go to fetch the photographs. She used to do this when she no longer had the patience to explain my father's absence. Off she'd go to fetch the album of their wedding photos and tell the story of the family and of the characters who appeared in those pictures.

Thirteen years had gone by since I had seen him. I felt

doubly foreign, not only because I'd just landed in a foreign land but because between me and my parent there
was a gulf like the Strait of Gibraltar, where you could
only hope to glimpse the opposite bank on an occasional
cloudless day. I smiled when he saw me. He then lifted his hand and pointed to the end of the Arrivals corridor, away from the crowd holding signs and flowers
and the folks waving gleefully to their relatives coming
out through the door behind me. We both dashed, trying
our best not to stumble on the pieces of luggage crossing
our path. Then he paused, opened his arms, and I threw
myself at him. My heart was drumming fast. He grabbed
my shoulders and held me away. I wished it could have
been longer. Thirteen seconds more, at least, for the number of years we had stayed apart. He touched my head,
and I noticed we were the same height. His lips stretched
slightly, but not enough to expose his teeth to me. He
then wrinkled his forehead, took a parking ticket out of
a pocket and grabbed my trolley. As we sprinted to the
exit, he kept rambling about what he would have to pay
for the car park and that he could have filled the tank
several times over with that small fortune. 'This is not
Angola, where a litre of gasoline is cheaper than a bottle
of water,' he said, and I wondered where the Angola was
he was referring to, because the country I had just left
was far from affordable.

Just outside the airport, apropos of something I no
longer remember, my father said, his two hands firmly on
the wheel and eyes on the road, with the banal expression of somebody describing the state of the weather to

break the silence in a group: 'My days in Lisbon are just home-work-home. I don't have friends.' I wondered how a man could live without friends. What sort of relationship could he and I hope to build? Bearing in mind that, in my almost eighteen years of life, I had no memory of having lived under the same roof with him at any time, this admission made me shudder. I felt sorry for us, for the chasm there was between us, which neither one of us had had the patience, or the courage, to cross.

Maybe I gave up too quickly. I didn't try all that hard, I wasn't planning to stay on Portuguese soil very long. In my mind, I'd be hanging around only until Jonas Savimbi and José Eduardo dos Santos came back to the negotiating table and were persuaded that peace was more beneficial to them both. As soon as the guns fell silent in Angola, I wouldn't stay a minute longer. Europe was not for me. Who would want to live there when you had a country like Angola at peace?

In those first two years, such questions troubled me. I couldn't believe how we – us Africans – preferred to waste the best years of our lives in Europe, putting up their buildings, cleaning their houses, frying their burgers. Wouldn't it be better to take that strength to a place that, even if it weren't our own, was the one that first saw us come into the world, that was at least inhabited by – and belonged to – a majority of blacks like us? Of the fifty-four African countries, I thought, there was surely one that would shelter us for as long as the rival forces of MPLA and UNITA failed to reach an agreement. A country that didn't live under the constant threat of a civil war, one that, however small, would be grateful to take us in and would give us the opportunity to contribute to their economy. Any one of them, anywhere but the countries in Europe. These were the thoughts that occupied my mind in those first two long years in Portugal. I developed such a great aversion to the country that I didn't even unpack the suitcase I'd landed with.

There I was, feeling like a refugee, an exile, an emigrant . . . All words whose meanings I hadn't known until Savimbi became convinced that there had been fraud in the 1992 elections and my mother – who had seen Angola gain its independence and who knew the hearts of the warlords better than I did – fearing for my life, took the first opportunity to send me to Lisbon. I don't blame her, she's a mother: I suspect any Angolan mother would have done the same in her place. I can't imagine how agonising it must have been for a mother in a situation like that, seeing her son growing up with the certainty that one day he'd have to go off to war, not knowing if he would ever come back.

VIII

Like a lot of Angolan teenagers in the diaspora, I received my musical education in a kizomba disco, though calling it a disco hardly does the place justice. For years, those clubs had fulfilled the role of cultural centres, the only location that allowed us to be ourselves. Within those four walls, until the sun rose, we stopped being immigrants, we stopped being scholarship students with our annual uni fees in arrears, stonemasons' assistants, busboys, night-time security guards or simply unemployed people malingering on some distant relative's sofa. We were just Angolans dancing to songs that were made by us, for us and about us.

In the late 1990s, Lisbon was living through the dawn of electronic music, with raves pretty much everywhere, the epicentre of the movement being the area that stretched from Avenida 24 de Julho to Alcântara. For us, the Angolans, who'd always been given to running wild, it was more than evident that we were not going to be satisfied just with our kizomba nights. It was only a matter of time before we would set foot inside Alcântara-Mar – in those days Portugal's cathedral of dance music, with endless queues at the door – where the actor Robert de Niro was once denied admittance, and from where the Formula One driver Ayrton Senna, grabbed by the trousers, was almost thrown out for bad behaviour. That's what the 1990s were like. Music and the way we consumed it were changing. Perhaps to compensate for the fact that they weren't offering the BPM needed to seduce their audience, the architects of the African nightclubs tried to supply what they understood to be the African response to the rise of house and techno, which dominated a large part of the country's nightspots.

The kizomba clubs became the cradle of kuduro, the only place you could hear the music genre that Toni Amado baptised with his song 'Amba Kuduro', since there was no radio station that dared play it. In Lisbon, no DJ or

dance music producer took any interest in the genre. The
retailers refused to distribute it; most of the city's cool DJs
only stocked up at stores like Bimotor and Question of
Time, and I'm certain that none of the cool kids of electronic music in Portugal would ever have considered, even
under the influence of drugs, buying music in the Praça de
Espanha market, which until very recently was the only
place you could acquire kuduro records.

As far as I recall, even the DJs of African origin who
were surfing the wave of techno and house weren't interested in what was happening in the universe of kizomba,
not even when they played records by the New York duo
Masters at Work, who fused their Puerto Rican origins
with Chicago house music. Our local African DJs and
producers in Lisbon looked at our own rhythms, at the
African ones closest to them – from Duo Ouro Negro,
Bonga and Dani Silva, the beats from the Sintra Line, from
the dishes of muamba and cachupa – and did nothing with
them. Despite those rhythms being familiar, they didn't
feel they could bring them to the dance floors of Alcântara-Mar, Kremlin or Kadok. However, there was space
for house and techno in the African clubs. The DJs were
not shy about playing house music there. They made it
work in their sets alongside kizomba, zouk and batida.

I'm sure I still have one of the Ku Mix series, with classics
like Sebem's 'Felicidade' and Snap!'s 'Rhythm Is a Dancer'.
Out of that series, it's the third volume that is DJ Amorim's
masterpiece. The first was released in 1997, and, if it hadn't
been for kuduro, the DJs of the African music universe
probably never would have ventured into releasing projects

like these. DJ Amorim was the pioneer, and the success of these compilations helped to solidify his status as god-of-the-booth at Mussulo, the most important African disco in Lisbon in the late 1990s and early 2000s. Their 'ladies' night' Wednesdays were legendary, as were Sundays, the hardest night to get in: that was the favourite night of all those famous Africans who lived in Lisbon, whether footballers, musicians, politicians, businessmen or building developers. Sunday was the big day at Mussulo.

The first time I went into the basement of number 5d Rua Sousa Martins, in Picoas, it was thanks to DJ Beleza, a short, pot-bellied man from Amadora, a white guy, or rather, a 'bollycao', like the sweet bun – that's what we call whites who are into black culture: white on the surface, chocolate-black on the inside. Born and raised in Amadora, a municipality on the outskirts of Lisbon famous for its large African community, dating a light-skinned black girlfriend from Benguela, what else would you expect?

I had just moved to Lisbon, and was in that difficult adolescent phase, when I went to do a few odd jobs at another African disco in Marquês de Pombal to earn a bit of change. Beleza was the resident DJ. There was nothing extraordinary about the place; it's not even there any more. It was a modest sort of space, where the old Angolan guys used to go to drown their nostalgia in whisky, to the groove of Paulo Flores's 'Cherry', in the arms of some of the most beautiful women Lisbon had ever seen.

In my country-mouse innocence, I was constantly so entranced by those daughters of the moon that I took to hanging out in the space even on my days off.

'Dude, don't give yourself away,' said the always sensible bartenders, those in-house psychologists, keepers of the most awkward secrets that the small hours in Lisbon produced, secrets which, if ever told, would have made the devil himself blush. Those women, in my eyes, took on the same prominence as a monument erected in the middle of a roundabout. They were beautiful, but it wasn't only their beauty that hypnotised me. I rarely heard them say more than half a dozen words: 'Whisky and Coke,' when I was taking their orders, 'More ice,' or 'Got a light?' What I was very familiar with were widely smiling lips and their teeth gleaming like mirror-balls. That and the swaying of their hips when they danced the kizomba. And how they danced!

We Angolans all know that discos aren't the best place for dancing. It's yard parties and weddings that you go to if you really want to show your moves. But that club wasn't just the sanctuary for our African fifty-somethings shipwrecked in Lisbon on a sea of whisky and dazzling women, it was also the place where the best kizomba dancers Lisbon had ever known chose to dance before going to end their nights, inevitably, at Mussulo.

Of all the women I saw blessing that dance floor, the one who danced best was neither black nor African; it was Sofia, the blonde from Rio de Mouro, the one who suggested we get married in order to resolve my passport drama. My fellow bar staff never tired of calling me a fool for having turned her down. 'Man, she's so pretty,' they'd tell me, as if I were blind. To me, it wasn't Sofia's physical beauty that made her special. It was the way she danced, like a goddess, capable of making men who were the most mediocre of dancers, like me, look like Mateus Pelé do Zangado. Memory allows me a little exaggeration, but the truth is that she, in her fathomless generosity, did me the honour of having her in my arms while I lost my way in even the most elementary of steps. Sofia made the simple base in two seem a moment of magic.

DJ Beleza must have noticed how entranced I was by that blonde girl and, out of solidarity, or just curious to see where my entrancement would lead me, invited me to Mussulo, because that's where Sofia and the most gorgeous African women in town would be headed. He knew Sofia was way out of my league, and I was bound to come out of the story with my heart shattered into little pieces.

I suspect I must have disappointed him, because the moment I found myself inside Mussulo, Sofia automatically stopped being my focus and I concentrated on the musical journey DJ Amorim was laying on for me. The African nights were no longer reduced to just the sweet beats of the kizomba; there was another, nervier sound that demanded space on the dance floor, and no one remained unmoved. People would be gripped by a euphoria, a feeling like a birthday or New Year's Eve. A circle would open up in the middle of the dance floor and the most gifted dancers took turns, each flashier than the one before them. The 4/4 hard-hitting disjointed beat coming out of the speakers, raw and fast-paced, was infectious, and got every living soul in the building moving to the groove.

Mussulo was the sanctuary for musical celebration,

where Angolans would make their pilgrimage every blessed weekend, to restore old friendships and retrieve, through dance, the cultural identity of a people haunted by a civil war that had amputated our lives and our ability to dream.

Mussulo was to transform my relationship with music forever. At that moment, some time in the first half of the 1990s, the decade when Lisbon became my nation-city, hearing kuduro was a discovery. For the first time, my fear of the foreigner's stigma stopped being so serious and I came to accept it, just the way one might come to speak a second language – the language that, besides the one we use to communicate with the world, exists and rests within us, manifesting itself only when we dream. Kizomba, and everything that existed in its universe, was this internal language, something I kept inside me and shared only with those who, like me, lived between worlds. Jazz, rock, electronic music and hip hop – these were all the musical languages I adopted in Lisbon, and which I added to the one that had already resided within me for as long as I remember existing.

I discovered myself through music; it was with music that the colour of my skin came to be a predominant factor in my self-affirmation. Prior to that awareness-raising, the term 'black music' didn't even exist in my lexicon. It took my settling in Lisbon to begin the journey through what I thought I knew about myself, and what others thought they knew about me. Identity came to be synonymous with survival, and kizomba and kuduro were its secret soundtrack.

IX

My first months of 1997 (the year the Colombo mall opened) were spent standing in queues for the SEF – the Foreign and Borders Service. I had come into the country on a tourist visa, but, as a return to Angola was proving impossible, I had no option but to wait through the small hours outside the SEF in the São Sebastião da Pedreira neighbourhood, the first Lisbon address I ever memorised.

The year 1997 would prove to be unforgettable. Not because Lisbon unveiled those hundred and twenty thousand square metres of commercial property in Benfica, but because it was the year Portugal's true colours became visible to me. The severe, serious tone the inspectors used for addressing us no longer impressed me. That year I stopped being afraid of getting deported, being ashamed of the stigma of illegality, and with this, I began to notice the people around me and, in a way, to respect and cherish the tragic condition that united us. We were all foreigners, mostly black, Africans who spoke other languages, possessors of different customs and experiences, different stories.

I also earned my first wage in 1997, doing the same thing all the lads of my age and from my ethnic group were doing: working in construction. Working as a bricklayer's mate is slave labour and only served to provide an honest wage for my most urgent needs.

I felt like the song 'Letter from the Labourer' by Dog Murras was my biography. Murras humorously recounted the mishaps experienced by Angolans who worked construction sites in Lisbon, grappling with the difficulties of managing the high cost of living in Portugal and helping the family back in Angola, and whenever I held a shovel, his verses played in my head.

The construction work was hard, badly paid, and the first chance I got, unable to bear the humiliation inflicted on me by an illiterate racist foreman any longer, I traded it in for the kitchen of a restaurant in a shopping mall. Carrying buckets of cement up scaffolding and frying chicken teriyaki for less than four euro an hour gave me a very real perspective on Europe. The kind of integration African immigrants were experiencing still makes me wonder about the extent to which Portugal has come to terms with its colonial past.

What made me hopeful was seeing the way the shopping malls were changing the cultural fabric of the big urban centres. Without those places, we probably wouldn't have the kizomba we have today. A quick lap of the food court of any shopping mall is enough to confront us with the number of young people of African origin working in restaurant chains. And what do they listen to? Kizomba, kuduro, hip hop. Thereby turning spaces like Colombo, whether it likes it or not, into something that more closely resembles the diverse cultural and social realities that inhabit the suburbs of greater Lisbon.

Aside from the African clubs, part of my own musical education happened in Bairro Alto in the old Lisbon. During my first years in the city, I placed myself, day in, day out, on the corner of Travessa da Espera with Rua da

Barroca, a place where I ended up meeting the people I established most of my musical complicities with, when music became more than a hobby. Firm as infantry soldiers on the battlefield, united by a single cause, the struggle against a common enemy: boredom. The younger ones, out of respect for those before them who had fleshed out the manifesto, were the first to arrive, filling up the main arteries of that small neighbourhood, which not only presented itself as a place for good nightlife but was an incubator for many ideas and projects from this urban culture in which my life is now totally submerged. The older ones did not witness the emergence of this youth with a huge amount of indulgence. The neighbourhood, while democratic, respected the idea of class and naturally had well-defined hierarchical divisions. We, the younger ones, while we did feel we could speak, also knew you need to grow in order to show up and have a voice.

At that moment, the city was getting ready to host Expo '98. As a result, Lisbon nights exerted a gravitational pull, attracting people of all kinds. Everyone was seduced by the city's potential, which was apparent from the way a considerable number of preppy-boys from Linha were there cheek by jowl with tourists and youths from the suburbs. It was irresistible. We were welcoming in Expo '98. Everything suggested that the city was going to be the next (and maybe better) Barcelona, facing out onto the Atlantic and speaking English with a better accent. From that moment, the city has only continued to become more cool. The preppy-boys no longer wear the same fringes that used to give them away at several kilometres' distance.

Today they sport the same haircuts as the suburban lads, and dress the same way too – courtesy of the cool shopkeepers on Rua do Norte. They use the same slang and take an interest in the same things. The foreigners I see today aren't tourists; they speak Portuguese and behave like friends come to visit from far away, a legacy of the Erasmus programme. The weekdays in Bairro Alto were my favourite. The DJs mostly played records they enjoyed to a handful of listeners like me, who barely could afford more than one drink at the bar but were loyal to the music. We never approached the booth, requesting a song and a genre, like the weekend clientele. We simply accepted whatever the selecta was willing to serve us, and every time we walked into a bar and saw DJ Johnny behind the turntable, we knew it would be a feast. He was in his early thirties and was considered a Bairro Alto living legend. A five-foot-three Bantu god, with small eyes and dreadlocks tied at the nape of the neck. With his signature red Gauloises dangling out of his mouth and wholly immersed in the groove, that's how we would find him: unaware of the long ash hanging on the tip of his cigarette, dancing like a child who has just received a new toy.

We became close around the time he was evicted from his shared apartment and moved back in with his parents. He asked me to help out with the move, but instead of taking his belongings to his folks', we drove around the city, dropping the sofa, TV, the Technics turntables and Vestax mixer at friends' houses. They all shrugged when they looked at his record collection. 'More than five thousand pieces of vinyl are not something to be taken lightly,' he said, adding that his parents made it clear that he wasn't allowed to bring more than a suitcase with him. I offered to be the custodian of the collection, which also came with a good handful of books and music magazines like *Straight No Chaser* and *DownBeat*, and records, lots of records of all genres and for every taste. Johnny is an old-school type of DJ. While a large share of the records was electronic music, a lot of drum and bass, a lot of reggae, some house, techno, there was also quite a lot of jazz from all eras, and a respectable collection of hip hop, as well as (and hence perhaps one of the reasons for our friendship) an admirable collection of pre-Independence Angolan music. During that time, I spent hours in libraries searching for anything Angola-related, and at record shops, listening to and reading the liner notes of the rare vinyl records I couldn't afford to buy. Still, I felt the urge to study those songs. To me, they were pieces of a big puzzle, the coded language that would allow me to understand the place and the people that gave birth to me. Just try to imagine what it's like to live thirsty for this kind of information, and suddenly you get handed such a diverse and eclectic library of sound. What more could you wish for? One day, browsing through the jazz section of Johnny's collection, I came across the New York Art Quartet album released on ESP-Disk in 1965. The cover caught my attention because the art chimed with José Rodrigues's illustrations for the anthology *Poesia de Angola*, the only book that travelled with me to Portugal. At the time, free jazz was foreign territory for me, until Amiri Baraka appeared reciting the poem 'Black Dada Nihilismus'. He sent me travelling from that bedroom

on the Costa do Castelo de São Jorge to Harlem, there to
stumble upon James Baldwin and see my life changed for
ever.

Johnny was the first cosmopolitan black man I met in
Lisbon. Through him, I gained access to people and places
and was respected – or at least looked at with curiosity.
I had just turned twenty-one when he first took me into
Lux, the trendiest disco in the city, opened the previous
year, in Santa Apolónia, just by the Tagus river. The fact
it was the first time I went into that club would barely be
worth a mention, were it not for that day having started at
the beach. On the way back – since Lisbon summer days
are long! – we went to enjoy the last rays of the sun at
the Adamastor viewpoint in Santa Catarina, the ultimate
meeting place for hedonistic Lisboetas. Many were just
heading off to get dinner. Others, committed bohemians
like us, were leaving the viewpoint for a bar crawl through
the narrow streets of Bairro Alto. By the time we'd noticed
the lateness of the hour, the available alternatives were not
very convincing, and that was when Johnny suggested,
'Let's go to Lux.' If it hadn't been the fashionable venue of
the moment, the place to be, a world-class nightclub created by Manuel Reis, Lisbon's iconic nightlife impresario,
the proposal wouldn't have seemed strange. I asked if he
was sure, pointing at the way we were dressed, flip-flops,
shorts, scuffed T-shirts and with traces of saltpetre around
the edges of our foreheads. Johnny smiled and we got into
the first cab that appeared before us. We arrived to find a
mass of people crowding around the door, and a line to
get in that stretched all the way across the parking lot. We

approached the door, Johnny and the doorman exchanged glances and, suddenly, to my amazement, I saw this sea of people move aside to let two sand-covered black guys, two Angolan monangambés, pass through.

Those were days of discovery, and Johnny, whom I met randomly at Chiado metro station, welcomed me like a distant cousin visiting the city – yes, he was the city-mouse and I, the country-mouse. From my corner I watched his steps, constantly on a tightrope between the sublime and the preposterous. I didn't know many men like that, strange creatures who make it to fifty without ever going beyond fifteen. Who carry with them an eternal childish chaos, at once expansive and taciturn. In my own way, I followed his steps. I didn't talk much, which some people found strange. I was closer to the idea of an acolyte, who sinned only in thought, abstaining from alcohol and other substances, and that must have unnerved people. Johnny, who never relinquished his joint, was one of the few who never made jokes about my squareness. At least not to my face. I think he even respected me for living among so many temptations and remaining unshakeable in my choice not to use drugs. One time, to make me feel better, he showed me a Morgan Heritage song, 'Don't Haffi Dread', and explained that I didn't have to rock dreadlocks or smoke ganja to be part of the pack.

Those temptations never went away. And if, for other people, musical trips called for lighting blunts and doing lines of coke, for me the trip, the real joint, was the sound, the music my band made, the combination of grime dubstep and kuduro. Something I was never great at putting into words but which, when it was coming out of the speakers in a club, sent me soaring.

X

Since poems were not going to pay the rent, I'd gone off to work at a fast-food restaurant in the Saldanha mall in 1998.

My favourite customer was Kalunga Lima, son of the Angolan revolutionary and novelist Manuel dos Santos Lima. He introduced himself as a movie director. I would later learn, in the conversations we would have over the months he spent in Lisbon before leaving for Luanda, that this was his fourth incarnation at the very least. Before this, he had been a soldier in the Canadian army, a diving instructor and literature teacher in Saint Lucia, in the Caribbean. Since it is never too late for a man to learn, he had gone back to school, he told me, while he waited for me to prepare him a chicken teriyaki and some tuna temakis. He enrolled in the International School of Film and Television (EICTV), in San Antonio de los Baños, Cuba, an institution that the Colombian Nobel laureate in literature, Gabriel García Márquez, had convinced Fidel Castro to establish. He'd already heard amazing stories about the place, including about the visits paid by Steven Spielberg, George Lucas, Robert Redford and Steven Soderbergh to that oasis of Latin American cinema. On one of his visits to the School of Three Worlds, or the School of All Worlds as it's also known, Francis Ford Coppola didn't only talk about art and cinema but also made a point of inviting the whole school to eat a *pasta al pomodoro* he'd cooked himself. I asked if he had been there at that point, and Kalunga just smiled. The answer was irrelevant. I was totally fascinated by this man's life, I admired his courage, I wanted to be like him. And he, perhaps recognising in me the same concerns he had felt in his own youth, encouraged my poetic impulses and offered me advice: 'Read five books a week, travel to all the countries you can.' He talked of simple things, but, for a kid who had given up everything to be a poet, seeing a black man who was so worldly, with so much knowledge, and yet still accessible, put my uncertainties to rest. I'll never forget the time he turned to me, very serious, and advised me to 'not make babies too early'. He was telling me to think about how much time I would need to travel the world, alone. Words I carry with me to this day.

It was at number 1, Avenida da Liberdade, on the corner with the Glória funicular, at the Palladium shopping centre, that I met one of the men who taught Lisbon to go out at night: Zé da Guiné.

The year was 2000 and he was visibly worn down, multiple sclerosis having reduced him to a shadow of the great Pepel god I'd heard he used to be, beloved of legions of women of every colour and class, and envied by cultured, powerful men. Zé da Guiné had barely finished fourth grade when he was brought to Portugal by the soldiers fighting in the Guinea-Bissau War, he told me, when we became close, in the long conversations we had when we were practically neighbours. But that evening I met him,

he was still Zé da Guiné to me, the legend! It was Johnny
who introduced us. When we went to meet him, we found
him kitted out like a 1920s golfer: a shirt with a collar,
bow tie, tweed jacket, waistcoat, balloon trousers in the
same fabric as the jacket tucked into knee-high socks. On
his head, an ivy cap, or paperboy's cap. The golf club had
been replaced by a cane to help him move about. We liked
each other at once.

Zé da Guiné was the greatest Lisboeta I've met. His
stories about the city amazed and entranced me. I recognised aspects of Johnny in him, and perhaps the two of
them saw something in me that was pretty familiar too. It
was only years later that I identified what united us, when
Johnny and I were hardly speaking: a sadness as big as the
world, never verbalised, a mourning we each carried out
in our own way. Zé da Guiné, losing the use of his legs
and his friends, barely left the house, some people even
thought he'd died. Johnny shut himself up on the street,
struggling with ghosts only he could see, and I, the orphan
of a living father, wandering adrift, seeking a place to call
home. We recognised this sadness in one another, though
we never exchanged a word about it. Not even when the
three of us, inspired by Johnny's desire to prove he didn't
need 'gatekeepers' to leave his mark on the city, went in
search of a seedy club that needed a new concept. Zé da
Guiné remembered he knew a Guinean impresario who
had a kizomba disco in Alcântera and who, having tired
of quarrels between unruly customers, was prepared to let
the place out. Zé felt the opportunity represented a swan-
song, his last chance to solidify his legacy, to leave a mark

of his own. And I, with nowhere else to be, went along for the ride.

We arrived at the agreed time, midnight. The club was rammed, Guineans and Cape Verdeans were dancing, holding each other tight, lulled by the rhythm of Livity's 'Bia' in the voice of Grace Évora: 'nhá coraçon ta na balance, ê só pamodi bó, Bia Bia Bia, bó tem ki comprende . . .' And before we reached the 'yeah yeah yeah' at the end of the verse, we heard a gun, two sharp terrifying shots. Then screaming, panic. We were all running for our lives, barrelling through anything in our way. Amid the chaos, I spotted Johnny out the corner of my eye, being carried by the current of people pouring out towards the exit, the only one we remembered existed, the front entrance. Nobody remembered to look at the signs identifying emergency exits. Our ears were buzzing with the sound of fear, a sound I was quite familiar with, a sound you never get used to, even when it's happening on the occasion of an Angolan New Year's Eve celebration. The last time I felt it so close was in 1992, when MPLA bullets and UNITA bullets lashed the facades of our houses in what came to be known as the War of the Cities. I remember one lone bullet that for years remained embedded in our living-room wall, an anonymous black spot amid a vast immaculate white. It hardly matters who fired that bullet. As long as it remained in that wall, I saw it as a monument to our shame. Yes, that sound was quite familiar, it would never leave me, and it would always give me chills.

Those two shots took the life of a young man of Cape Verdean descent, the victim of a jealous ex-husband, who couldn't accept the sight of his ex-wife in another man's arms. On the street, our hearts still in our throats, we saw Zé da Guiné appear out of the crowd, grim-faced, as if returning from a battlefield. Neither Johnny nor I dared to ask what he had seen, but his face said it all. He put his hand on my shoulder and, from his silence, I understood that it wasn't just a man's body that lay dead in that space. The dreams of a return to the thrill of nightlife had collapsed onto that floor too. He seemed defeated. Zé da Guiné: one of those musical men who don't come along very often. He wasn't a musician, he was a song, beautiful as can be, whose words not many people know any more, but whose melody many others will continue to whistle, for a long time yet.

It was the last time I saw him on his feet and out of the house.

XI

In the room, the judoka continued to eye me suspiciously, studying my movements in search of some gesture that might tally with the verdict she had already formed about me from the moment I first handed her the lapsed passport. Any movement, however tiny – scratching the back of my neck, rubbing an eye – any sign that, instead of clearing me, might condemn me. We were like two gladiators ready to launch into a fight to the death. Like Chuck Norris vs Bruce Lee in that last bout in the Rome Colosseum, in *The Way of the Dragon*. The blond Viking, meanwhile, seemed more accessible. He might try to disguise it, but his diligent-policeman appearance couldn't hide the fact that he'd surely enjoyed some raves in his free time. The lack of facial hair and a fedora does disqualify him from being one of these hipsters I might see in Shoreditch sipping a macchiato. But with his cheery face and an American Apparel neon hoodie on, it wouldn't be hard to imagine him spending unforgettable summers in Ibiza, attending every edition of the International Music Summit, hopping between Playa d'en Bossa and Avenida 8 d'Agost, swearing eternal loyalty to Pacha's two cherries. The two of them left the room again and, this time, it was for longer.

XII

At the turn of the new millennium, I decided to pursue music full time. Back then, museums by day and concerts at night was my recipe for combatting my status as an illegal African. When I didn't have the correct papers, my destinations of choice were the Serralves museum in Porto and the golden triangle of art in Madrid. As soon as I got off the train at Atocha station, I'd launch myself into the Prado, Thyssen-Bornemisza and Reina Sofía museums. Inside those buildings, surrounded by masterpieces of painting, I was looking not for inspiration but rather for a place where I would feel less of an immigrant. In those days, Madrid was also on the hip-hop circuit, a couple of steps ahead of Lisbon which, up till then, had not been visited by a single international rapper. Only Gabriel O Pensador, the Brazilian, had ever trodden Portuguese soil. I loved the morning bustle in Buen Retiro Park, the Saturday afternoons shooting the breeze in La Latina, dusting off my Portuñol with the locals while sitting on the kerb. I learned how to compensate for my lack of Spanish vocabulary by speaking Portuguese with a Cuban accent from the time when our Caribbean comrades were there helping Angola with the war effort. But my pilgrimage wasn't limited to the capital. Cataluña was the logical destination. At that time, the Sónar festival had already managed the feat of transforming Barcelona into the mecca of electronic music in Europe. The feeling I got on my first visit, in 2004, was of having finally found the city to which I'd like to emigrate.

In 2005, my bandmate Branko and I went to a small presentation at an event organised by the Red Bull Music Academy, who had decided to invite some of their former students to present brief showcases in one of the corridors of Barcelona's Centre de Cultura Contemporània, home to Sónar by Day ever since it was first held in 1994. Some of my musical heroes were going to play in that year's line-up, and the first stop was in fact the festival's opening party, at 122 Carrer dels Almogàvers, the address of the Razzmatazz, one of the city's most iconic clubs, located in the industrial part of El Poublenou. The night was to be opened by the US artist Diplo, who the previous year had released the fascinating 'Florida' on Big Dada, one of my favourite English labels, a sister label to the alternative and innovative Ninja Tune.

The set Diplo treated us to travelled the beaches of Miami and Rio de Janeiro, revealing the first musical signs of what we would come to identify as the 'global dance music' movement. Something that began unexpectedly in the favelas and ghettos around the world but which, up till then, had not found the right ambassadors to present it and defend it in conventions dedicated to dance music. This man, who signs the legal name Wes Pentz, made a point that night of clarifying that sacred genres would no longer exist, everything was going to get mixed up and be transformed. That's what baile funk had done with Miami bass, and freestyle popularised by the 2 Live Crew, 69 Boyz, Egyptian Lover and Trinere. And the 2004 free mixtape *Piracy Funds Terrorism* that M.I.A., the most iconic refugee on the planet, and Diplo made together showed us how big this music movement could be.

The world of music, as we knew it, would not be the same. A few years earlier, Napster had been sued and lost millions of dollars in the courts against the giants Metallica and Dr Dre. Pandora's box was opened and it became hard to identify what was legal and what wasn't, distinguishing the pirate from the legitimate. And M.I.A., with that mixtape of hers, presented most of the vocals of her delayed debut album with a melange of different music genres: reggaeton, dancehall and crunk mashups. She was embracing these dichotomies and showing us the way. The new rule was to have no rules and Ms Mathangi Arulpragasam was now applying guerrilla tactics to seize ownership of everything, even her own songs, which her label was jealously guarding to release on a record. It was pure piracy, and it thrilled us.

I thought I saw M.I.A. on the stage of the Razzmatazz

club, appearing alongside Diplo with her hoodie hiding her black hair, but only for a few moments. Perhaps she had come to check out the audience's reaction to those songs and see if they would be ready for her debut concert at Sónar by Night. Seeing her, a mysterious shape hidden under a hoodie, I remembered 'Banana,' and the thirty-six seconds of music that were the most important for my own understanding of what could be done with the information I had in my luggage when I landed in Lisbon in 1995.

The first two lines we heard in the 'Banana' skit interlude/manifesto that open *Arular* are 'Insha'Allah! Refugee education number one', followed by the syllables 'Ba-Na-Na', thus describing the way refugee children who can't speak English learn the language of the country that receives them. These were the classes that the young M.I.A. began to attend after leaving her father, her childhood innocence and her hometown, Jaffna, the main city in northern Sri Lanka, which in 1619 was transformed into a colonial port when the Portuguese occupied the peninsula, before it passed into the hands of the Dutch and, thirty-nine years later, of the British, in 1796. Later came the bloody civil war, from 1983, between the government and the various separatist groups in the north, including the main one, the Liberation Tigers of Tamil Eelam.

The night at the Razzmatazz, however, had one last surprise in store for us. While the French group TTC, up on the stage, were spouting the lines of their 'Dans le Club', the first single taken from *Bâtards Sensibles*, I ran into Diplo in the middle of the dance floor and congratulated

him on the baile funk tracks that had made up his set.
He seemed surprised to hear me commenting on Brazilian music. At the time, the rest of the world mostly knew
bossa nova and samba, but not funk carioca. I made a
point of explaining the affinity that exists between those
countries who share Portuguese as an official language. We
weren't just familiar with baile funk, we were also able to
identify some of its artists and, of course, understand the
meaning of the lyrics. I talked to him about kuduro too,
which he'd never heard of before. At that moment I felt
compelled to re-enact one of the music industry's most
hackneyed clichés, the moment when a wannabe musician
pulls a demo with his songs out of his pocket. And that's
what I did. Perhaps that gesture of mine seemed forced to
him. Myspace had already come into our lives but I felt
as though repeating that classic move would be the most
natural thing in the world. The CD I gave him included a
few songs produced by our Enchufada label, among them
a rough version of 'Yah!' and some other random songs.
I believed, optimistically, that Diplo might listen to them,
like them and pass them on to Will Ashon, founder and
head of A&R at Big Dada – who would be astonished and
offer us a contract with the label. That wasn't exactly what
happened, but dreaming never killed anyone, and in the
small hours of that Thursday morning, I made my way
down Las Ramblas a happy man.

On the Saturday night, M.I.A. performed at Sónar Park,
with all her subversive euphoria. The young Tamil woman
came on stage ready to conquer the world, and she had
some musical bombs in her arsenal, like 'Galang', 'Pull Up

the People', 'Bucky Done Gun' and 'Fire Fire'. The plan
of attack was to present a minimalist concert inspired by
performances by artists from the electroclash scene and
the Canadian Peaches, with one DJ, one backing vocalist
and a cyclorama backdrop showing graphic motifs taken
from the album cover and other stencils that evoked
images relating to the northern Sri Lanka guerrilla war.
Tanks, weapons, tigers – a lot of tigers – emphasised the
content of the lyrics spat into the mic.

The following year we did not receive an offer from
Big Dada or Ninja Tune. We did, however, get a message
from Diplo and a phone call from M.I.A. I don't know
who exactly had told her about kuduro, but the music had
intrigued her to the point where she picked up the phone
and dialled the number she found on the Enchufada website.
She was working on some new songs and she wanted to
fly to Luanda to collaborate with the kuduro producers,
DJ Znobia especially. Diplo had already written to us via
Myspace, from Rio de Janeiro. He had found a group of
Angolan kids who'd told him about kuduro again and
shown him videos on YouTube, which had reminded him
of our conversation at Razzmatazz. He was ready to meet
us in Lisbon and to have us give him an intensive course in
the music that was about to open the world up to us.

Those first three nights in June resonate within me
still. Barcelona was young and musically more interesting
than Lisbon. The only reason I didn't move to the Iberian
peninsula's most vibrant and international city that very
month was because I noticed something that bothered me:
Barcelona had everything, except black people.

XIII

I was woken, disoriented, by another of the judoka's delight-ful nudges. For a moment, I considered telling my story from the beginning – the extended version – connecting the Angolan diaspora in the Lisbon suburbs with Portuguese colonialism and our civil war involving South Africa, Cuba, the USA and Russia that ended six years ago, in 2002. But I hesitated. They seemed impatient. Instead, prudence led me to offer them the pocket version: 'Buraka Som Sistema, that's what brought me here,' I said, my expression sincere.

I've considered giving up several times already. No one enjoys being humiliated every time they need to request a visa. But I can't stop thinking about my bandmates, Blaya of Brazilian nationality and Andro, Angolan – both of whom share the same immigration status as myself – and the disappointment that Branko and Riot, the two Portuguese members of the group, might have felt. They didn't expect this kind of red tape when all we wanted was to escape the invisibility of creating dance music from that basement in the quiet neighbourhood of Campo de Ourique. I think about the crew who devote all their time – on the stage, in the studio, and on video sets – to shaping everything we make musically. I think about their families, for whom they aren't around most nights because they are with us, giving oxygen to the ideas over which we are conspiring. I think about all the people who fill the concert halls whenever we visit their cities, the ones who buy the records, the ones who pay for tickets to see us. Not being present, not making an all-out effort, is a kind of betrayal.

I'm trying not to be overdramatic. I'm well aware of my privilege. Kuduro artists such as Tony Amado, the kid who saw Jean-Claude Van Damme's *Kickboxer* and had the epiphany to create our music genre, doesn't get to tour Europe, so I shouldn't complain. He was the one who got inspired watching the Belgian actor dancing drunkenly, moving his body without moving his hips, which seemed stuck to the sound of Beau Williams's 'Feeling So Good Today', side by side with a couple of Thai girls. That scene lit some kind of light bulb and, using the rhythmic pattern of that electronic thing we called 'batida', he rushed in inspiration to his synthesiser, producing the song 'Amba Kuduro', practically in a single sitting, giving birth to the genre, and the dance, of kuduro.

For me and my bandmates in Lisbon, apart from Praça de Espanha market, the internet was the place that allowed us access to the latest kuduro. YouTube wasn't all that popular at the time, so we spent hours scouring forums like Canal Angola, and annoying relatives and friends who lived in the country with requests to send us music, instrumental stuff preferably. I say 'annoy' because in 2005, internet in Angola was still coal-powered, and uploading a song took hours. Everything that reached us was in MP3 format. I still listen to them, pretty distorted now, and if one of the Norwegian officers brought me a suitable player, I wouldn't waste my time on verbal explanations, I'd just get them listening to music. Os Lambas's 'Comboio', perhaps.

While they listened, I would ask them to picture a basement in Campo de Ourique with tiny booths, four individuals sharing a computer, a sound coming out of the NS-10 monitors – piercing for being so compressed – seeping through the gaps in the doors and ventilators, climbing the building's walls. I would ask them to pay attention to the vocals of Bruno King and Nagrelha, spitting endless coded rhymes in an obscure slang, twisting and stretching the Portuguese language to its limits, with verbs and adjectives I'd never heard before. The words of the two MCs sound as if they're coming from a sub-machine gun on a New Year's Eve back in 1980. But most striking of all, nothing we hear on this song was made with the intention of pleasing Western dance music listeners. Some might have called it ugly, distorted, or even poor quality, and that was precisely what made that whole package so brilliant. That's what fascinated my bandmates and me. I would ask the officers to watch the video as well. 'Comboio' has the best kuduro video of all time, directed by Hochi Fu, who is to Angolan kuduro what Hype Williams, the US director who defined the visual aesthetic of rap during what were to be its golden years, is to American hip hop. The energy conveyed by the video is raw, urgent and colourful, an accurate portrait of what Luanda was and still is. Something no video director had ever managed to translate into images until Hochi Fu came along. The 'Comboio' video makes us believe that Os Lambas and the director were a match made in heaven.

XIV

After being exposed to so much musical innovation at the Sónar festival, we started working on our first Buraka Som

Sistema album. I took up the mission of flying to Luanda, searching for DJ Znobia, our favourite kuduro producer, to invite him to collaborate on our project. I managed to get his phone number and tried for two weeks, without success, to set up a meeting with him. When he finally returned my calls, it was my last day in the city. The violent March rains fell onto Luanda, cruelly flooding the place, as they still do today, transforming entire neighbourhoods into islands and cutting them off. And Rangel – with its chronic sanitation problems ever since its eucalyptus trees were chopped down in the 1980s to put up the Cubans' buildings – was one of the worst affected areas. For Znobia, who was still convalescing from a car accident that had almost cost him his life, it was impossible to get down to Baixa Luanda to meet me, which left me no choice but to go to his house. Given the state the city was in, the twenty-minute journey separating us could easily be transformed into two hours of travelling, depending on Luanda's chaotic traffic. Every Luandan I asked to give me a ride to Rangel flatly refused, offering, nonetheless, to take me there some other day, when the water wouldn't be camouflaging the holes in the road.

I thought about venturing over to Terra Nova in a HiAce. When I was heading to the streets to take a candongueiro to DJ Znobia's neighbourhood, salvation finally came in the person of a Portuguese journalist, Marta Lança. Hearing me complaining during a visit I paid the previous night to the apartment she shared with a small creative community nicknamed Seven and a Half, she offered to take me to Rangel. The trip to the DJ's house took two hours. At several points, I imagined that the car Marta was driving, or rather, helming, wasn't going to make it. At one moment, we almost lost it. I thought we were going to be shipwrecked in the middle of the highway, on the corner of Avenida Hoji ya Henda and Rua da Vaidade, when we fell into a pothole. But the old Toyota managed to hold out, and we arrived at our destination, the sun already disappearing behind the zinc roofs of the tangle of houses that made up the neighbourhood. Znobia, who signs his name legally as Adalgiso Mário Lopes de Freitas, was waiting for us at the entrance. We immediately caught sight of his bleached hair, which is symbolic among kuduristas, MCs and producers, a mania the origin of which no one knows exactly, but comes from the time of Sebem, one of the kuduro pioneers and icons, and which surpasses all logic. The relationship that people of African descent have with their hair goes beyond vanity. It's intimately connected to our self-esteem. If we neglect it, we are also calling into question one of the most important aspects of our identity.

'You found it!' said Znobia, smiling as soon as he saw us. After all our struggles to set this up, our first interaction dispensed with the usual formalities of first meetings – it felt like I was visiting an old friend. He invited us up to the first floor. After his accident, Znobia had set up his studio in his old bedroom again, in the apartment of his mother, whom we found watching TV with Puto Lipi, the elder of her grandchildren. The kid, aged less than five, had already recorded half a dozen kuduros, the most popular of them, and my favourite, being 'Mama Badjojo', which Znobia put onto a flash drive together with other kuduros he had on his computer and some tarraxinhas, the slow-paced kizomba that was trending around that time. Some of the songs were still in draft form but would later become tracks like 'Luanda Lisboa' and, of course, 'Sound of Kuduro' which M.I.A. voiced alongside Puto Prata and Saborosa, released on our debut album, *Black Diamond*.

To me, the music of that kuduro genius reflected the urgency and the suffocating reality of a Luanda in a process of mutation. He was a true revolutionary who changed the rhythmic construction within kuduro, to the point that we began to identify the genre as being divided into two times, BZ and AZ, before and after Znobia of Terra Nova, as he likes to introduce himself. A neighbourhood kid who greets everyone he passes, children and adults alike. To see the way he interacted with his neighbours, I became certain that, even if we hadn't known his address and had got ourselves lost in those streets, some resident or other would have been able to tell us where to find his studio, the sacred place where he spent most of his time, because everyone in the neighbourhood is a witness to his tenacity and his desire to assert himself as a musician. When I asked him where this passion had come from, he laughed and replied: 'It all started with dance. I wanted to dance like Michael Jackson.' He and every other kid in the area. When he realised he wasn't going to be able to reproduce the more complicated moves of the creator of 'Billie Jean', he tried singing, failing again. The next step was to learn producing, so he spent hours watching how other musicians produced music from a computer. The DJing came out of necessity, to get his music to reach as many people as possible. He understood that if he left that task to some third party, he'd probably fall by the wayside, and so he went knocking on the door of the legendary Rangel club, Mãe Ju. No other club in the city of Luanda contributed as much to kuduro and tarraxinha as this one, in his native Rangel. That was the booth from which people first heard what are now classics: 'Abadja', 'Vai Lavar a Loiça', 'Mono Mono', among other songs from this post-Sebem/Tony Amado kuduro.

After that evening, I returned to Terra Nova a year later with my band. I didn't intend to be away that long. Until the very last minute, we hadn't been sure whether we'd get entry visas to Angola for the two band members with Portuguese nationality, Branko and Riot. At that time, the country that was the cradle of kuduro was considered the future 'El Dorado', and it was practically only businessmen with many millions to invest, and their employees, who filled the consulate's square with interminable queues. For weeks, my music partners went back and forth with their bank statements and letters of invitation as if some doctrine of reciprocity did truly exist, and the Angolan state wanted the Europeans to pay in kind for all the humiliations suffered by its citizens when travelling to the old continent. After much insistence from my bandmates, we came to learn, from a friend of a friend who helped resolve the issue, that nobody ever travelled to Angola to see the landscape, or to listen to kuduro, for that matter.

They went through almost the same ordeal a regular Angolan citizen goes through when applying for a visa to Europe. The line 'We made it, we here', with which we opened the video of our single 'Sound of Kuduro', wasn't just bragging. It was a genuine expression of relief.

That time around, the rain was no longer the issue. Our main objectives in the city were to film dancers and book studio sessions with producers and MCs – nothing that would have been too complicated were we not in Luanda. Whenever we shared our work plan with Luanda friends, we would get the same reaction: a laugh followed by a 'Take it easy now.'

In that city, nobody schedules more than one activity per day – that is, you could never plan, say, filming in the morning with a group of dancers and a studio session to record an MC in the afternoon. Why? Because the equation must always include other factors quite apart from our own intentions, such as a lack of electricity or the Luanda traffic. If anyone arrives late for a meeting, or even never shows up at all, if they say it was because of a traffic jam or a power cut, you have no choice but to accept the fact. From the schedule we'd laid out before leaving Lisbon, we took around two or three days just to set up meetings, and only 40 per cent of them worked out. The others didn't happen because of the traffic, or the power, or some other reason that escaped us entirely.

Our original idea for the 'Sound of Kuduro' video had been to record the group of dancers who usually accompanied Bruno M. From the moment we saw the YouTube footage of a group of skinny kuduristas dancing in a yard beneath a scorching sun, shirtless, to the sound of 'I Am', our decision was unanimous: we all wanted them in the video. If that wasn't possible, then at least Euriko, who to my mind was the best kuduro dancer of all time, and another two or three from his group.

We were in Luanda nearly a fortnight and couldn't set up a meeting with any of them. There were dozens of phone calls, we went in person to the Combatentes neighbourhood, to Última Linha, at the invitation of Bruno M himself, who, when asked about Euriko and his dancers, merely gave a shrug, resigned. It was Senhor Esfilêndio dos Santos who saved the situation – Man Sibas, aka Sebem.

One day before filming, Sebem agreed to meet us at the Lusíada University, on Largo do Lumeji, on the border between Coqueiros and Ingombota. There was no particular reason for us to choose that place to meet, it was just convenient: we'd already agreed to go that morning to customise some T-shirts with the Portuguese visual artist RAM, who happened to be in Luanda for a workshop on urban art and had been invited to paint a mural at the university. Sebem arrived at the agreed time. Before we got down to business, he told us about his desire to produce songs that blended kuduro with rock. We didn't really understand why at the time, but as we would later learn, rock had always been one of this iconic kudurista's great passions. Before the raves, before the meeting with Tony Amado and the creation of 'Felicidade', Sebem had wanted to make rock. And he felt that we, Buraka, would be the ideal people to help him realise this long-held dream.

The next day, we met on the Marginal promenade, next

to the post office. Sebem showed up with his wife, Débora, their chihuahua and half a dozen dancers, a group of young acrobats dancing a style of kuduro inspired by Salsicha and Vaca Louca, and showcasing Angolan youth's desire to express, through movement, all the repressed energy, all the struggle, all the joy. They want to be just like any other adolescents in the world, free to exist beyond the poor average life expectancy, beyond compulsory military service, beyond malaria, and so many other hardships many aren't even aware of. They can't verbalise this, it's just a feeling, and so they dance as if their lives depended on it. Which they probably do.

Without proper permission, filming in the streets could also get us in trouble with the police. Sebem remembered one particular backyard on Ilha de Luanda. Once there, we got the chance to witness the influence he exerted on Luandans. He called the woman who owned the house 'auntie' and explained we wouldn't be taking long, and the lady, without a moment's hesitation, allowed us to film in her yard. Sebem also asked her if she had some bits of equipment – anything, a stereo with a CD player. She went into one of the rooms and reappeared a few minutes later with a boombox. We put on the CD with our song, turned it up to full volume and it wasn't long before dozens of children appeared, drawn by the music and amazed by the dancers. Sebem didn't sit back, but like a general, he shouted out commands to the dancers: 'More energy, more energy,' 'Posture, posture,' and they'd obey, doing whatever their leader told them and much more. They climbed walls, they broke chairs by jumping on them, and we just filmed, me and my old favourite customer Kalunga Lima, from the Saldanha mall days. He was based in Luanda working for Dr Eugénio Neto, the owner of the biggest kuduro record label, LS Productions. I had called him at the last minute to help us out with shooting the footage.

We never got to set up sessions in a studio. Perhaps Sebem himself wasn't sufficiently convinced that that fusion would work, and we didn't have Bruno M's dancers. Still, having Sebem's blessing for the first and only video we would film in Luanda was more than we could have asked for.

XV

From the fifth floor of the Ritz Hotel in Lisbon, you could just see an edge of the dome of green leaves surrounding the Estufa Fria greenhouses, in the Edward VII of England park. I would have shared the park's history with them were it not for the fact that they were both, Kalunga Lima and Dr Eugénio Neto, staring at me, waiting for my answer.

'So how much does it cost?' Dr Eugénio asked me, putting the cup of coffee down on its saucer. I noticed a smile forming on the edge of his lips. This was a test, I thought. I looked at Kalunga, who had said nothing throughout my entire introductory monologue, and sought a word from him, a clue that might help me to decode the question that *the doctor*, his boss, had put to me. But his face was as serene as a little old lady content with her knitting. Not a crease between his eyes, no raised eyebrow, no bug-eyes, nothing. I'd known him for years, since well before Buraka, well before the music, back when writing was the only thing I wanted to pursue. Perhaps Kalunga's silence in that suite at the Ritz was another of his lessons.

Dr Eugénio Neto was a businessman, nephew of the poet Dr António Agostinho Neto, Angola's first president from 1975 to 1979. Besides his interest in the music industry, he was also involved with banking and diamonds. He listened to my speech about the ventures and misadventures of my band. He heard my pitch on the importance of putting Angolan money into exporting kuduro to the world and our desire to sign a distribution deal with his LS Productions. Home to Os Lambas and Bruno M. Since he wasn't saying a word, I couldn't help thinking he was finding my conversation deadly boring. Everyone in the country knew of his love for music. His relationship with music had begun back in colonial times, in my own umbilical Benguela no less, around 1972 or 1973, where musical gatherings were dominated by semba and rumba. 'We brought Bonga to Angola for the first time,' he told me, proudly.

Before we were interrupted by the hotel employee who came into the room dragging the breakfast trolley, Eugénio was telling stories of David Zé, Artur Nunes, musicians who'd shaken the minds of the youth during the early days of our independence, and about Luís Montez, father of one of the leading festival producers in Portugal today. In the 1960s, even before Independence, it had been at old Montez's events that the best Angolan music was to be heard.

His eyes shone as he talked about those old days of his, before Independence and before he set off in the first group of Angolan students for the universities of the former Soviet Union, in 1976. It was there that he had graduated from the Piragova State Institute of Medicine in Moscow, on a course that lasted six long winters. The first year was devoted to mastering the language, he told me. 'When I arrived in Moscow, I only knew three words of Russian.' Today he's a polyglot, speaking Russian, French and English fluently. I wouldn't have been surprised if he'd said he knew a smattering of Mandarin too.

Before the meeting, Kalunga had already tipped me off about our Dr Impresario's trajectory. A member of several different medical societies, like the Portuguese societies of Gastroenterology or Endoscopy, he was also one of the founders of Vida and of the National Union of Artists and Composers, and a senior executive in various firms, among them Tranquilidade, Escom and GE-GLS Oil & Gas Angola. Apparently this gentleman didn't sleep: he was known for being the first to arrive at the office and the last to leave. His two cellphones, which sat on the table, always turned on, rang half a dozen times during our meeting. He interrupted our conversation to take some of the calls, always apologising for his rudeness and justifying his actions with an exclamation of 'It's important' or 'They won't leave me alone.'

The music bug had apparently left him with some irreversible after-effects, because no sooner was he able to, than he set up a music label, LS Productions, that today holds the largest catalogue of modern Angolan music.

Anselmo Ralph and Os Lambas are just some of the artists on his roster. At first glance, it would be the perfect label to release our music in Angola – an old dream, but one which up until that point had seemed impossible to realise. My host asked me to enlighten him about my record label business endeavours, and I didn't play hard to get. I told him everything, blow by blow, our achievements, the internationalisation of kuduro, the stages we'd trodden. He let me speak.

I had wanted to write poetry and prose, I told Dr Eugénio Neto. In 2000, I started reading my poems on DJ Johnny's show on Radio Marginal. One day, Riot and Branko, two up-and-coming electronic music producers from Amadora, stopped by to drop off their demo tape. They called their duo Fusionlab and that encounter happened around the same week I had signed a recording contract with Naylon, an independent music label from Lisbon. We immediately began to produce my first album, but the A&R people rejected the music. We did very bold things that nobody had the nerve to release; at least, that's what we convinced ourselves to help us cope with the setback and use it as a motivation for our revenge of the nerds. I started to spend more time in Porto searching for inspiration, and Branko went off to study music engineering in Madrid. When we finally decided to have another go at making music, we set up our independent music label: Enchufada.

Buraka Som Sistema was formed after the appearance of Andro Carvalho, who, at the time, had a knack for translating the music from the Luanda periphery into conventional language. Together we started to release and remix some kuduro numbers to play at the monthly residency at the Clube Mercado, which was frequented mostly by a clientele who had never set foot in a specifically African club. Maybe that explained the lack of prejudices when we offered them our music. It was insane. Everything was new, fresh and raw. Songs like 'Yah!' and 'Sem Makas' were local bangers, known only to people attending those events.

'Yah!' was our first single and it was given vocals by Petty, a fifteen-year-old firecracker of a girl just arrived from Luanda. The cult around the Buraka project began with that number, in that little basement with a capacity of a hundred and fifty people, who every week packed the Clube Mercado to hear that new sound, which mixed kuduro with other sounds from the peripheries of Rio de Janeiro, Johannesburg and London. The 'yah' of the chorus pulses like a slogan, a four-and-a-half-minute-long incitement to collective insurrection wrapped up in an 808 beat and a catchy, minimal bassline, leaving space for Petty to spit her rhymes, as if her voice were a percussion instrument too. The music lit the fuse that would make the 'opinion-formers' – who dictated trends and shaped the taste of consumers of dance music – surrender to the sounds of kuduro. The video, which cost us fifty euro to produce, quickly hit a million views, contributing still more to kuduro's being firmly embedded in the vocabulary of global electronic music.

To me, 'Yah!' is the only one of our early songs that really reflects the rawness of those nights at the Clube Mercado, where, spontaneously and chaotically, MCs and dancers would invade the stage to join us in celebrating the birth of a movement. The space was closed on the orders of the police, due to some kind of licence problems. But the closing of Mercado didn't prevent the virus from contaminating the city, which forced us, faced with so many requests, to take to the streets with Buraka Som Sistema. We chose the name in tribute to Buraca, which in those days was one of the eleven parishes of Amadora, Portugal's fourth most populous urban area, where Branko and Riot had grown up. Portugal's largest African city.

I took advantage of this moment to give Dr Eugénio a first pressing of the *From Buraka to the World* EP, the first collection of songs, which served as an introduction to the BSS sound. The first run of seven hundred copies had sold out in three weeks. I also gave him the seven-inch 'Yah!', a genuine relic because we pressed only one hundred units for that release.

After my little speech, I explained that being present in the Angolan market would be a dream. Dr Eugénio smiled again, looked at the records on the table, touched them, as though reading them with his fingers, but his eyes were clearly far away from that luxury suite. Finally he said:

'How much does it cost?'

For a few moments I thought he was referring to our records and I hesitated, but I told him we were open to offers. He looked at me again and, this time, he even gave a bit of a laugh.

'How much does the label cost, how much?'

That question took me totally by surprise. 'I've come to discuss the possibility of licensing our records for Angola, no more than that,' I replied. I turned to Kalunga one more time but he, equally surprised, merely shrugged. Dr Eugénio Neto insisted I should give him a price, and I, trying to escape the subject, said I would have to discuss any answer to that question with my partners. And he insisted again, this time handing me a piece of paper and a pen. 'Write down a number.' I refused his request and he passed me a telephone.

'So call your partners and ask them how much your company's worth, and I'll pay double.'

After dealing with an A&R rejection, I'd never considered the possibility of signing an artist's contract again, let alone selling the label. And now, when we were finally seeing the results of our progress – would we be willing to trash everything for a bit of small change? In any case, I needed to consult my partners and share with them Dr Eugénio Neto's offer to buy our company. I asked again if he wouldn't be interested in investing as a partner in our project.

The answer I got from him confirmed that we were on the right path. He said a project like ours would spoil, or in his words, 'misrepresent', the genesis of kuduro, and he leaned towards me, saying: 'Kuduro is ghetto, it's Angolan and it mustn't leave Angola. What you all are doing will destroy that magic.'

I listened in silence and when it was my turn to speak, said in an unwavering voice: 'Sorry you think that way. I'm afraid the company isn't for sale.' I got up and touched Kalunga on the shoulder. He gave a nod. No more words were needed. I held my hand out to Dr Eugénio and he took it. Before turning towards the door, I took another look at the Edward VII park. I contemplated asking if they knew it used to be called 'Freedom Park'. But I kept quiet.

When I was in the elevator, I couldn't help but wonder whether one day we might get Znobia, Sebem, Os Lambas and all the other talented kuduro artists in Angola joining the line-up of the festivals like Lovebox, Sónar or Coachella. Changing people's perceptions of what African music is.

Having some other Angolan kuduro artists on the road at the same time as Buraka Som Sistema would have been great. It might have helped me feel less exotic, like that time we were in London promoting our *Black Diamond* album release in the UK, and I ended up at a Mayfair hotel party. It was one of those private London events where everyone had Victoria's Secret bodies, Pantene hair and symmetrical faces. I felt like I was in a commercial for something. They were all smiles, eyes and teeth, and no one had a problem with showing theirs to their neighbour. I felt like a Londoner too, and threw myself into the middle of the chaos. I fell into the good graces of a model, who seemed to be from Eastern Europe. Things were going well. She wanted to know what kind of music I made, and though I wanted to tell her it was kuduro, I knew I'd end up losing myself in explanations. So I answered: ghetto dance music. It's just what came out. She gave a long sigh, she had no idea what kind of music this was, but it was one of those sighs that invites us to change the subject if we have any wish to remain engaged in that little tête-à-tête. So that's what I did. I changed the subject, we laughed at each other's jokes, we danced and sang without any embarrassment to some of the pop hits of the time, and when we got tired, we went off to one of the bedrooms where we were enthusiastically welcomed by a couple of her friends, an Asian woman and a black woman, both also models, who led us by the hand, across the suite to the inside bedroom, where another two beauties were waiting for us, sitting with their endless legs crossed on the edge of the bed. Between these two was a young guy, likewise delightful, who was very meticulously drawing lines of cocaine on top of a glass table with a credit card. This guy looked like a surfer, blond, broad-shouldered, and above these shoulders a neck that looked like it had been sculpted by Michelangelo's chisel. I felt like I was in a Guy Ritchie film.

One of the models sitting on the bed got up, asked what we wanted to drink and disappeared behind a door. I couldn't identify her nationality, she might have been Puerto Rican, by her long black hair, her tanned skin and that sway of somebody who can always hear music inside them when they walk, a merengue perhaps. Her place was taken by Nefertiti, and no sooner had we sat down on the sofa than the Latin goddess was back, holding out two glasses of gin. I accepted one and, before they offered me the straw that was circulating from hand to hand, I whispered in the ear of the model I'd come with that 'I don't do drugs'. She turned her photogenic face towards me, and with no expression at all, with all the placidity of a Buddhist monk, looked deep into my eyes for a few seconds, as if reading my soul. Then she turned back to the others and ignored me so efficiently that, if I had been a little drunker, I might have begun to doubt my own existence. Just to be sure, I pinched myself and, since I did still have a little bit of shame left, I had no option but to quit the room and leave that party behind.

From time to time, I still think about that model – although not so much for the physical attributes she possessed. Everything about her made sense, even the least of those attributes. Her breasts, for example, two small bumps that would have fitted exactly into my hands; or her ass, which didn't scream for attention, but also didn't avoid inviting us to look at it whenever she went by or turned her back – I was caught in flagrante of this particular delicto several times. What to do? Though personally, I suffer from the ailment in the line from Vinícius de Moraes: 'Buttocks are incredibly important. But the clavicular dip, that's the real problem. A woman without those is like a river without bridges' – and hers were literally two missing arches from the Pont d'Avignon. The *supraclavicular fossa*, the scientific name for that little indentation between the neck and the clavicle, is the most beautiful and sensuous sight on the female body. But like I was saying, it wasn't her physical attributes that kept returning to my mind, it was something much more mundane, it was that phrase 'ghetto dance music' that I'd used to explain what kind of music I made. I should have just said kuduro.

I've never been completely convinced by the nomenclature that gets used to explain the music we make to the world. The term 'bass music' is in fashion nowadays, and I'll admit to having mixed feelings about it, but I can recognise that, absent anything better, the term does serve its purpose. And I'll admit, it is much better than 'ghetto dance music', or 'world ghetto music', as I've also heard it called. We needed a name – who doesn't? If people like Dr Eugénio Neto would come on board, maybe it would be possible to challenge the idea that dance music is a game whose rules could only be defined in New York–London–Berlin. We could even attempt to rebrand our culture using the same Western PR companies pushing all the cool artists globally.

XVI

When my band visited Paris as part of our current tour, I was approached by an American journalist who declined to interview the other members of our group; he only wanted to talk to the Angolan. I let him have what he wanted. While he was curious – a characteristic that is becoming increasingly rare nowadays among media professionals, particularly those specialising in culture – this gentleman was fixated on one specific period in our history: the early years that followed 11 November 1975. Within the first few questions, I understood that to him, Angola's fate was still being dictated by the winds of the Cold War. He talked about Russia as if the Soviet bloc still existed. He saw Fidel Castro surfing the wave of socialist internationalism, still commanding his more than fifteen thousand soldiers from Havana against the imperialist alliance between the South African apartheid regime and Ronald Reagan's America. During the interview, he consulted his notes and came out with a reference to the battle of Cuito Cuanavale and to the Tripartite Accord (between Angola, Cuba and South Africa), signed by the ministers of foreign relations and foreign trade, Afonso Van-Dunem, Isidoro Malmierca Peoli and Roelof Frederik 'Pik' Botha, in New York, and I could see that things were about to fall apart. I had to raise my voice a little and remind him that I'd been invited to speak about music. He acknowledged his mistake and closed his notepad, rather upset at having been thwarted in his dream of interviewing an Angolan citizen. I don't know if the penny actually dropped for him, but we never returned to the subject and he ended up asking me a series of insipid questions about the origins of kuduro, which were met with pretty uninspired answers on my part.

However, I do need to acknowledge that this journalist, unlike the majority of his colleagues on the other side of the Atlantic with whom I have spoken, did at least know that Angola was a piece of ground in southern Africa, washed by the southern Atlantic ocean, between Namibia and the Democratic Republic of Congo. This hardly merits a standing ovation, but frankly, faced with so much ignorance about the African continent, anyone who knows where Angola is and who isn't surprised to learn that Portuguese is the official language, who knows something about our independence or our civil war, is already a journalist with superior expertise to those whom we, at least, had been encountering.

Maybe the American journalist was right. If we are to talk about kuduro, we should begin with the legacy of the civil war and the consequences of the Cold War. Maybe that's just what kuduro is, an unexploded bomb, a land-mine left forgotten on a secondary road. And all it took was for someone to tread on it – Tony Amado – to blow open a door that would transform the country.

I didn't understand what the guy was getting at with his questions about the MPLA, the KGB, the CIA and UNITA. At the time, I wanted to talk about music and not get caught up in those subjects. We were taught from early on to sing Waldemar Bastos's 'Velha Chica', made to repeat the line 'Yo kid you don' talk politics' like a prayer – it was the anthem that marked our generation. Embracing neutrality or defiance; against the policies of comrade President José Eduardo dos Santos or in favour; being in line with the message of an MC Sacerdote or dressing in the colours of the national flag the way the kudurista Dog Murras did; constantly engaging with questions of nationalism, awareness-raising campaigns and get-out-the-vote drives.

For my generation, there was a feeling of disenchantment. The pillars that had held up our parents' dreams had tumbled to the ground. Some of them disappeared without leaving so much as an echo; others fell like ruins of a distant yesteryear that could still be spotted in between the lines of the nostalgic outbursts and speeches from those who had watched Angola turn independent. 'Don't you dare retrieve the utopias that managed to hold out,' they say to us, annoyed, when we ask them about the moment when the dream became a nightmare. 'Don't you dare restore them, they're not from your time, you don't understand them, and you won't know how to give them the shine they deserve so they'll get seen by everyone.

You're lacking in calluses,' they say, 'you're lacking in life. Those dreams are the monuments of an empire that never was. Let us grow old.'

Dreams are always troubling. Political dreams, then, are incredibly dangerous, especially when we forget them, since the possibility always exists that they might return like a spectre to steal away our peace. Their most notable characteristic is the fact of their being collective dreams. Even if they might be born from the mind of a single individual, idealistic dreams are as contagious as chickenpox and quickly end up being other people's dreams; they cross borders and generations, able to mutate, for better or worse, depending on the ending they're given. These dreams, ideas that are not new, are in the same places as they were put by those Angolans who gave them life when they were kids, rebels and revolutionaries.

XVII

As soon as the officers walked into the room, I knew I would not be released that afternoon. 'You're going to appear before a judge on Monday,' the Viking said. 'We'll be transferring you to the detention centre at—'

'You're sending me to prison?!' I interrupted him, incredulous. The reply reached me by means of a harsh chorus.

'It's the judge who'll decide.' I felt the floor disappear from under my feet and my knees give way. All that came out of my mouth was a weary: 'I'm a musician.'

The judoka and the Viking, intrigued, exchanged a

glance. They knew my confession wasn't addressed to them, it was a sigh of defeat, and before I was able to focus on the situation again, the Viking had taken me by the arm and growled a 'We're going.' I saw a twinkle of satisfaction in the judoka's eyes, and I waited for her to let me have more of that delightful prodding of hers, but instead, she took my arm and said flatly: 'You're an illegal musician. You wanted to see Norway, did you? Well, welcome!'

Hope, before it dies, is a complicated thing to manage, and even after all that, I did believe for a few moments that the chief inspector was going to stop them. Everyone was going to re-examine and reconsider my case, restoring my freedom and the chance to reach Oslo before 7 p.m., the time scheduled for me to get up onto the stage, to work. But, of course, nobody deigned even to witness my final walk.

To them, I am no more than an illegal immigrant, undocumented and guilty for daring to stay in Europe. I wanted to turn to the officers and tell them that my artistic identity took shape within the borders of their continent. I'm a musician, a would-be writer and then, of course, also an immigrant.

It even occurred to me, as a last roll of the dice, that I might call our ambassador to Norway, Dr Domingos Culolo. Perhaps he would be moved by my story. I could even tell him that, just like him, my grandfather also worked at the Benguela railway, reminding him of the times he lived in Huambo and recalling my family. And since he was a member of the International Association of Penal Law and former Attorney General before being named ambassador to the Kingdom of Sweden, the Nordic countries and the Baltic States of Estonia and Lithuania, perhaps he'd be able to help me. But deep down, I knew no one would be coming to meet me.

XVIII

The first instance of a kudurista behind bars that came to my notice was when Bruno M, then still going by the name Scocia, ended up in the Luanda Central Prison. Bruno was a rapper and a member of the Alameda Squad, a crew who shook the Luanda streets in the early 2000s. He was arrested at nineteen, and this, to him 'was a necessary evil'. During the time he spent incarcerated, Bruno tried to make the best of the situation, and, under the influence of some kuduristas with whom he was sharing his cell, he started to write rhymes that fell into the cadence of kuduro. His partners in captivity were the first to recognise his talent.

Once free, Bruno didn't forget the praise he'd received from his companions behind bars, already guessing that, where kuduro was concerned, there was no more demanding audience than those who live on the edges of society. But the path to a new type of music had not totally persuaded William Bruno Diogo do Amaral, this being his legal name. He first tried production, going on to instrumentals and the recording of other would-be kuduristas, before launching into it in his own right.

Although he did offer some of his rhymes to various MCs, many turned them down, preferring to have Bruno just working his magic with the computers to make everything sound good. In fact, this was when he earned the nickname Bruno Mágico, which would be adapted to his artist's name of Bruno M, as we know him today.

Recording 'Já Respeita Né' changed everything. Despite all the resistance and the usual hostility towards anything new, there were soon a number of kuduristas rhyming in the style of the Alameda Squad MC, making him believe that, through kuduro, he might be able to change his own life and the lives of the legion of young people who saw him as the messiah of a new kuduro. Tracks like 'I Am' and '1 Para 2' became anthems, and 2005 marked the start of the age of lyricism in the genre invented by Tony Amado.

With a handful of songs circulating underground, Bruno M became a hot commodity. Offers of contracts with labels rained down on his head. The video of '1 Para 2', made by Hochi Fu, showed Avenida dos Combatentes transformed into a Ruff Ryders's Bronx, and lit the fuse for the movement that had begun in the Combatentes neighbourhood and quickly spread from Cunene to Lisbon's Sintra Line. There wasn't a lover of kuduro who didn't know that, after the war cry 'Dos Combatentes, última linha, Seres Produções' had sounded, anything that MC spat would be the bomb. For Bruno M, kuduro was the channel for expressing himself freely. He took on the mission to show society that Angolan youth weren't exactly what old folks claimed: the young weren't that lost.

The album that cemented Bruno M's name in the pantheon of Angola's best kuduristas, *Batida Única*, was released on 3 February 2008 by Dr Eugénio Neto's LS

Productions label. And he has been my travelling companion ever since, his songs waking so many memories in me – from that morning back in 2007 at the Ritz Hotel in Lisbon, when they offered me money to leave kuduro alone, to the moment I met Bruno M himself in person, in the historic Combatentes neighbourhood, now Comandante Valódia, as this place was rechristened in 1975.

As I walked to Bruno's music studio in a domestic backyard on Comandante Valódia avenue, I planned to start the conversation by telling him how much I loved the song 'Valódia' by Santocas. A few weeks before arriving in Luanda, I was on tour in Spain. As soon I stepped into Sala Arena in Madrid, I heard Moreno Veloso playing it during his soundcheck. I was surprised and asked how come a Brazilian knew that song, and he replied with that serenity that seems unique to Bahians: 'My dad sang it to me when I was a kid.' But I didn't start the conversation with Bruno M by telling him about Caetano Veloso's son singing Angolan revolutionary songs. We got caught up in nerding out about music software and the latest plugins for beat-making.

Since it was the composer of 'Já Respeita Né' who I'd been listening to when the Viking and the judoka arrested me, I don't think it would be unreasonable to ask, what would Bruno M do if he were being taken into custody? Might he perhaps admit responsibility, confessing the moment the two officers came in and laid hands on him that kuduro – that's what it is – makes us do unimaginable things, but it's far from being a crime? And might he, intending to plead innocence and asking not to be judged on appearances, treat them to one of our more forgiving sayings – 'mindele ejia kukina wé'? Translating the line from Kimbundu, you would get 'whites can dance too'. But I like to think that our ancestors, imbued with the noblest of Catholic values, meant by this dictum that we ought not to judge one another. We all have something of value to share with the world.

XIX

As I came out of the station, I found two police officers waiting for me: tall, blonde women, both of them with their hair up. Neither ugly nor beautiful at first glance. On their scrubbed faces they wore a dutiful neutrality, but at second glance I did spot some particular attributes – their cheekbones slightly rosy, their eyebrows trimmed to taste. One of them had a little dent in her authoritarian chin, which rested on the slender neck of a Varangian warrior. The other had an upper lip that showed off a rounded Cupid's bow. Both of them blue-eyed. The kind of beauty that is revealed when they leave their uniforms and their working day.

The one with the dimple in her chin came towards us and received me from the Viking's hands. I felt like a child, a naughty schoolboy being led to the principal's office. Unlike the Viking, however, the new officer didn't want to depart from police protocol for a minute and in no time at all had my hands cuffed behind my back. I felt the cold of the steel on my wrists, and a shiver ran up my spine when I heard the crushing sound of them clicking shut. It was the truest sound of humiliation I had ever heard.

'You have the right to remain silent, anything you say can and will be used against you in a court of law,' the officer said to me, her voice like someone in a movie.

'Is this really necessary?' I asked rhetorically.

'Any and every individual in the back seat of this car must be cuffed,' one of the officers explained, adding a 'whether guilty or innocent,' which at the time, allowing as it did the possibility of my hypothetical innocence, somehow left me with a little hope.

XX

Blaming kuduro for my imprisonment is not fair. I am here because I wanted to come, I set off on this trip of my own volition, first by bus, from Sete Rios (Lisbon) to the gare routière Gallieni (Paris), one thousand seven hundred and forty-six kilometres covered in twenty-six hours, via Spain. Then another thirteen and a half hours by train, from Paris's Gare du Nord to Københavns Hovedbanegård in Copenhagen, Denmark. Of all the territories I crossed, I only had my documents checked once, in Germany, somewhere between Cologne and Hamburg. A man, late fifties, had swept through the carriage asking for our tickets. Those who looked foreign he asked for some kind of ID document. As the only black man in the carriage, I was no exception. I showed him my residency card and, unsurprisingly, the conductor wrinkled his nose, trying to understand the information it gave in Portuguese. I hurried to explain what it was. He turned the card over a couple more times and asked for my passport.

The practised lie: 'I've got it in my suitcase,' and I pointed at the trolley bag I had on the shelf above our heads. He looked at it, hesitated, looked at the card again and then handed it back to me. I took a deep breath and thought I was in the clear for good – nothing else could happen on that journey. I was so close to Scandinavia, so close to the stage that I could already feel the lights, the sound exploding from the speakers and the crowd shouting, 'Buraka, Buraka, Buraka.'

After forty-eight hours on the road, I finally reached Gothenburg, my body weary but my soul greatly relieved. I would fulfil my promise to attend the Way Out West festival, and this time, the lack of a passport had in no way diminished me. Before stepping onto the stage, I celebrated with a silent 'Fuuuuck, I made it!', followed by the ritual we usually share, staring into each other's eyes, hands open for a high five that closes for a fist bump. Then a shot of vodka reinforced with a special speech, along with the rousing 'We're gonna smash this whole shit up!'

Passport problems were more of a drain on the band than the endless journeys, the sleepless nights or any bad reviews we might occasionally get from music journalists. Our kryptonite was visas being refused, the timeframe of the SEF – the Portuguese Immigration and Borders Service – for the renewing of residency permits and, of course, passports. While most of the bands who were our direct competition would simply move lock, stock and barrel to London or New York to make the leap into the spotlight, we wouldn't be permitted even to pop over there for a few days. As long as we had foreign citizens in the band, nobody would allow themselves the luxury of dreaming so big. We would do our songs and step as far as we were allowed 'by law' to grow within this fertile ocean-front backyard they call Portugal.

We were well aware that our league was the league of the periphery. We weren't going to be allowed to take the same route as the others to get to the US and the UK. We continued to be kings only of our own village, however much, back in Portugal, local promoters like Luís Montez might put us on the same stage as the biggest stars in pop music; however much in some cases ours might have been the better shows.

At the time, I did consider contacting the Portuguese government, making the most of the fact of our having a socialist government, more sensitive to the question of immigrants and foreigners. I would talk to the prime minister, and if that wasn't possible, to the minister of the Interior, António Costa, the son of a Goan father and a Portuguese mother, a man of dark complexion – someone who would know what being a foreigner was really all about. When Costa left the government, he was replaced by Rui Pereira, a jurist who specialised in criminal law, who I assumed would be less tolerant of foreigners in irregular circumstances, so I gave up on pursuing the Interior brief, turning instead towards Culture. The new minister there, José António Pinto Ribeiro, a humanist lawyer, born in Mozambique – and to whom I'd once been introduced by Nuno Artur Silva – seemed the right person to approach, but I didn't have the nerve. I went on kicking the subject down the road until we happened to run into each other in Luanda. He was on an official visit, and I was back in the motherland to apply for a new passport, since travelling with the band made me run out of pages for visas and stamps every six months. To this day, I don't know where my daring came from. Desperation, I suspect.

João Pignatelli, from the Camões Institute in Luanda, understanding my urgency, let me have an invitation to the reception that was being held in the minister's honour at the Portuguese ambassador's residency, in Miramar. I showed up at the appointed time, in suit and tie, with all the seriousness that the matter required. I still wasn't able to blend into the landscape. I was very obviously a wild-card, a *rara avis* wandering the lawn of that small mansion, surrounded by high-ranking figures from the Angolan state, the United Nations and NGOs, by ambassadors and cultural attachés from a series of diplomatic missions, all delighting in the canapés and champagne and laughing about banalities that committed no one and offended no one, and to which I contributed my own agreeable smile.

I was there on a different kind of mission: I had not come for small talk and wanted no distractions. I had come to ask the minister for Portuguese citizenship. If the footballers Deco and Pepe could be naturalised and start to represent the national team in world championships, well, as far as cultural matters were concerned, Buraka Som Sistema was also playing in world championships, and we deserved citizenship too.

The minister recognised me and hugged me warmly. I didn't waste a minute. I knew it was a matter of moments before much more important people than me, and probably with much thornier subjects to discuss than mine, would steal his attention away. After a couple of casual jokes, I told him I was having trouble getting my Portuguese nationality, and 'I need help.' Ribeiro looked me straight in the eye, smiled and handed me his card, with no apparent formality, and said, 'Call me, I'll be waiting to hear from you.' We smiled, as if we both understood the symbolism of that request. If I had approached him in Lisbon, I'm sure it wouldn't have carried the same weight, but talking about Portuguese nationality in Luanda, in Miramar – the embassy neighbourhood, the neighbourhood where all the diplomats and the country's elite lay their heads, where even the president of the Republic has a house – seemed to carry a different weight. Even if the minister sensed only part of the symbolism of expressing such an idea on that soil, things went deeper for me. I could feel the spirits from the Alto das Cruzes cemetery echoing within me.

When I got back to Lisbon, I found that all the boldness that had led me to approach the Portuguese minister of Culture had stayed behind in Luanda. As the weeks passed, my doubts increased. Maybe I didn't really want to be naturalised Portuguese all that much anyway. Maybe I hadn't the courage to call and repeat my request. Maybe it was pride, my mwangolé complacency making itself heard. I didn't want to be owing favours to a politician, I thought, though I was not altogether persuaded by this argument. Whatever the reason, I gave up on being Portuguese.

When the pages of my passport were once again filled up with visas and stamps, and the date for my return to

Luanda to renew my documents loomed up on the horizon, the idea of going back to focusing on my 'Portuguese nationality' plans started to keep me awake at night once again. As I was not eager to call the minister, I did several times consider talking instead to Luís Montez, the son of old Montez and one of the first promoters to invite Buraka to a large-scale festival in Portugal, who was also the son-in-law of Cavaco Silva, ex-prime minister and ex-president.

Who better than Montez Jr to be moved by my plight; this man, the son of the promotor of the first semba nights, a character from yesteryear, revered by many from the old guard of Angolan music, including Dr Eugénio Neto. Whenever I met him, he made a point of reminding me that we were compatriots, he always talked to me about his Angolan origins. And he really was, because only another Angolan can recognise the love for that dust, that second skin that changes the light falling over the palm trees, over the fresh laundry, over the roadside grocer's, over the cars stuck in the city's traffic.

The first time I heard Luís talking about this feeling was on TV, on RTP2 with its unhurried conversations, on Ana Sousa Dias's programme *On the Other Hand*. The second time was in Alentejo, on the Zambujeira do Mar estate, in a conversation that lasted just a few brief minutes, where he described his visit to the Chiuaua disco in Luanda. Enough for the person standing before me, at that moment, to stop being Mr Luís Montez from the radio stations and the festivals produced by his Música do Coração, which had so helped to shape my taste and made me realise from which side I'd like to see concerts happening – from the stage – and become Luís Montez, one of us, who beneath the sweltering Alentejo sun, thinks of Ilha de Luanda and feels homesick.

It was the enthusiasm with which he talked about the Chiuaua, about kuduro, and about how great Os Lambas were on stage that charmed me. If I hadn't known what he was talking about, I'm sure I wouldn't have allowed myself to be infected by his words. But I'd drunk from the same water as all Luandans, and I believed in that new Angola that Montez was talking about. I was acquainted with it myself.

And who better to understand my misfortune than the son-in-law of Cavaco Silva, the man who, unconsciously and unusually, invented kizomba, the mother of kuduro, grandmother of tarraxinha? Sofia from Rio de Mouro and I teased each other about Cavaco Silva's role in making kizomba the most remarkable cultural force ever to come out of the Lusophone world. It was our inside joke every time I visited her neighbourhood. I would ask her if she could predict that eradicating the slums and shanty towns and relocating its residents in social dwellings like the one she lived in would spark the musical revolution we started to witness taking shape. She hated giving Cavaco Silva's conservative government any credit. She would point a finger out of her window and reply that it was European Union money that had allowed all this to happen. Aside from who should get the credit for the kizomba boom, we did agree that the clash of cultures from the different social and ethnic groups forced to coexist wasn't peaceful to begin with. Even today, from time to time, there would be skirmishes between neighbours, prompted by ancient animosities and old habits that were impossible to shake. We Africans, for example, enjoy listening to music at a yelling pitch, and I know that, as a result, having us as neighbours is not always easy. But there's nothing like proximity, and dialogue, for the resolving of differences. And it was Sofia's generation that was the first to take this step, beginning by inviting the neighbours for a weekend bowl of hearty cachupa or to share a dish of muamba. This happened at work too, since a large proportion of the employees at the big shopping malls like Colombo all came from similar communities and areas. It was just a matter of time until kizomba would bring them together.

XXI

We parked alongside a *prunus padus* in bloom. In Nordic countries, they call that tree Hegg's cherry, a deciduous with scented white blossom and a bitter dark fruit. In the Middle Ages, the bark was believed to have spiritual properties, warding off the plague. In Portugal, it's known as azereiro-of-the-damned.

The prison guard was round in face and belly, and no sooner had he seen me arrive, escorted by the two blonde officers, than he straightened up like a sugar-cane stalk. Once a few words in Norwegian had been exchanged, they opened my suitcase and spread my belongings on top of the counter. An iPod, a pair of headphones, a computer, a cellphone, two books – a copy of Paulo Leminski's *Distraídos venceremos*, a gift from my Brazilian friend

Rodrigo Amarante, and a copy of *Nós, os do Makulusu*
by José Luandino Vieira, stolen from my grandfather's
library – shoes, underwear, a couple of T-shirts and
a change of trousers. Once each of the items had been
logged, my handcuffs were removed and, my wrist still
throbbing, I signed the inventory. The cane stalk took a
long look at my signature, studying it, as if seeking to
determine in that nervous scribble whether I really was
guilty or innocent. Anything might help. He held my
phone out to me and said I had the right to a single call.
'But speak in English!' he warned me.

The first person I thought of was Teresa, generous
and ever-optimistic Tê, my lawyer. I imagined her in her
contemporary dance class, an activity that occupied her
Saturday afternoons, allowing an escape from the court
cases. The news would catch her on the back foot and
there wasn't much she could have done to help from
Lisbon anyway. Then I considered Phil, my manager,
and Belinda, my agent, but both lived in London and,
like Teresa, however concerned and well-intentioned
they might have been, neither one of them would be
able to get me out of this jam before the start of next
week, and everything suggested that I would already be
convicted by then, in a hub for illegal immigrants waiting
to be repatriated. The sugar-cane stalk was starting to
get impatient, and I took the phone from him. I thought
about my father. Not because I felt he could be of any use
to me, but because it seemed that, in anybody else's story,
a father would be the first person on a son's emergency
list. But I needed somebody nearby, and who was close to

me, someone from the band: I needed Branko – only he would understand the seriousness of the situation, acting first and asking questions later.

XXII

Branko has been my real partner since the very start. Not because we began this journey together exactly, but because we were both ready to reach places where nobody around us was in the mood to go. We both had something to prove, not to the world necessarily, but to ourselves. He is, and always has been, the most clear-minded in the group – even when we were all wandering a bit adrift, learning to make music. His obsession with the unknown, with what has not yet been explored, combined with an encyclopedic musical memory, were critical at the moment of determining what we would be able to do with what we were creating.

I was always moved by the relationship my friends have with their parents, and I know that part of my admiration for Branko comes from his relationship with his father. While mine had never seen me on stage, Branko's father got emotional just listening to the songs we created in his son's bedroom. Senhor Jorge Barbosa never once asked us to turn the music down. At our very first concerts, there he was, clapping and whistling like a teen groupie, proud of the fact that passing on his taste for the sound systems he'd installed in the living room had been worth it, and that every weekend he'd made a point of dusting his son's speakers. With the volume turned up to eleven, he played records like Pink Floyd's *Wish You Were Here*. He was a man with many friends, who took his son to Madrid when the boy decided to quit college and go to the Spanish capital to study sound engineering.

I don't know where my father is. Last I heard, via my mother as usual, he was in England, taking some speciality or other in medicine. I didn't want to prolong that conversation, since I could almost have sworn that once, turning into Carnaby Street, I had seen him, a man perhaps in his sixties, somewhat shorter than me, and whose gait, the curvature of his shoulders and the colour of his skin, reminded me of my father, or of the image I have of him, from the last time I saw him. A stranger should never remind a son of his father.

I always imagined that such a day, with a chance meeting, would come. We would look at each other, and maybe we'd each hold out a hand, with the coolness of a job interview, or the understated joy of closing a deal we've wanted for a long time, and which might save us, but which we don't want the other to notice.

Or maybe we'd hug. We would agree to meet the following day, we'd cancel all our engagements and catch up on our conversation some place nice.

It was always a long wait. I had been able to think about almost every possible scenario over the years in which we hadn't seen each other. Twelve, last time I counted. I'd like to see him again, and see if he had white hair, which I would inherit some years later.

The man I saw on the street had black hair. I thought about calling out a 'Dad' that wasn't usually in my vocabulary, but I was afraid that the only thing about him I know well – his voice – would be that of a stranger. All I kept from my childhood was my father's voice, from his phone calls.

I followed that man for a while, hoping that at some point he might turn around and recognise me as his son. He didn't turn, not at any point.

I have asked myself many times whether I could be a good father. Because for that, don't you need to have been a son first?

XXIII

'Yo!' Branko answered at once. In normal circumstances I would have answered in kind. We'd been greeting each other in this economical way for years. But the situation was serious and I had the eyes of the two blonde officers and the sugar-cane stalk fixed on me.

'João, I'm gonna speak English. I'm in prison, you guys have got to get me out of here,' I said. There was no room for long explanations. Once I had ended the call, the phone went back to the hands of the jailer, who also asked me for my glasses. Prison regs, he explained. They must have been afraid I would transform the frame into a screwdriver, and like MacGyver, manage to get the cell door open and bust the hell out of there. Or even worse, they were probably scared that, in despair, I might use one of the lenses to kill myself, by piercing an artery.

The cane stalk asked the two officers to lead me down to one of the cells at the end of the corridor. They led me by the arm, it was procedure and anyway, I no longer had any strength left. I wanted to lie down, shut my eyes and only wake up when it was time to see the judge.

When they tossed me into the cell, I looked at them again, and without my glasses, my eyesight reduced to a few inches' distance, they seemed less like police to me, less like inquisitors. In another cell just like mine, two metres by two of aluminium and stinking of urine, another prisoner was snoring like an electric saw. I lay down on the mattress, a hard surface about a foot off the ground, and felt myself the alonest man in the world.

I remembered Sofia from Rio de Mouro and her proposal of marriage, made years earlier on a dance floor, where I had kissed her hands in thanks, and asked if maybe we could just kizomba.

PART II

PORTUGAL

22 SEPTEMBER 2012

Ay ay ay,
Look at the song of the people,
The people of the land,
Who dance without knowing why.

—Paulo Flores and Eduardo Paim,
'Processos da Banda'

I

Quito Ribeiro, the movie editor who put his arms round my waist in my parents' living room, asked: 'Who invented kizomba?' OK, so the question wasn't actually directed to me. Still, since somebody else had dodged answering it and what with me being the only dance teacher at our weekly gathering of family and friends, they pushed the poor lad into my arms so I could tell him and, also – oh just 'by the way' – show him how to dance it. Poor thing. I looked over his shoulder to see Mário Patrocínio, who'd brought him over, standing by the window alongside my neighbours, Samira, Gilson and Vemba, giggling at his awkwardness. But something else caught my attention. Outside, the neighbourhood was still bright – no sign of autumn approaching. A sultry sun descending behind the Serra de Sintra tinted the clouds with shimmered orange, casting saffron and gold reflections onto building facades, trees and the cable stone in the pavement. On the opposite wall of our living room, a Mondrian persimmon square rests over the Serra da Leba picture my folks hung on the wall when we moved in. I was four years old and I don't have memories of that moment, but I always felt the picture was like a second window, especially at the end of the afternoon. Once they entered our apartment, all our Angolan friends immediately said we were at the border between Sintra and Huíla, which filled my parents with pride. The light touched my dance partner's clove-and-cinnamon skin and made him glow as if the sun desired him more than anyone else in the room. He had a long, handsome face, a scruffy beard hiding his chin. Whenever his hooded brown eyes caught mine, I had to look away.

So how did I get to know kizomba myself? While all my friends were being told old folktales for their bedtime stories, Paizinho, my stepfather, preferred to talk to me about his musical heroes, from Bonga to Belita Palma, Cesária Évora to Eduardo Paim. He'd start with that gruff, solemn voice of an old-school radio announcer, waving his hands with a childish excitement that contrasted with the white hair of his perennially well-trimmed beard.

'Eduardo Paim disembarked in Lisbon at the end of the 1980s, bringing old semba songs with him, the embryo that came into contact with the African diaspora and made kizomba.'

He always liked illustrating those musical stories with dance steps too. So I guess it was inevitable I'd end up with a taste for African music. I'd heard of Eduardo Paim before I heard of Rapunzel. I don't know much about Snow White, but I could tell you that before Eduardo Paim, nobody had ever dared mix Angolan semba with zouk. What 1993 meant for kizomba is always right there on the tip of my tongue. Tropical Band released *Só Pensa Naquilo*, Ruca Van-Dunem dropped *SK . . . Ainda*, Moniz de Almeida gave us the great *Tio Zé* and Tabanka Djaz released two back-to-back classics, *Tabanka* and *Indimigo*. But of all the albums released that year, Paulo Flores's *Brincadeira Tem Hora* is my favourite. That album has bangers like 'Cabelos da Moda' and 'Amores de Hoje', and a heartfelt paean to the kizomba's co-inventors with the song 'Tributo a Cabo Verde'. If there hadn't been this complicity between the two communities, partners in poetry and in revelry, who could have taught Paulo Flores to sing in Creole?

'Follow me, don't be scared. If you trip, just stop, and we'll start over. It's all gonna be fine,' I whispered into Quito Ribeiro's ear, and his hands started shaking. Adorable. I think it's pretty charming when men can show they're afraid. 'First step,' I murmured. 'The gentleman always starts by moving left, OK? We're gonna do the basic step, the foundational one, from two- to eight-four time' – and off we went onto the floor, harmoniously synchronised, moving left to right and back again, 1-2 step, 3-4 step, 5-6 step, 7 and 8 and . . . again.

My thoughts were instantly filled with the steps I taught my students in the beginners' group on alternate days, but I tried to push that image away and focus on the question that brought us together. 'Who invented kizomba?' Actually the guy wasn't coming out of this too badly. I told him that the secret of kizomba is that it's an earth dance. No need to pick up your feet all that much. 'Feel the floor,' I said again whenever I caught one of his feet outside the intended pattern. This thin, metre-eighty guy had fallen into my arms so suddenly I hadn't even had the time to ask myself how he picked up the swing of kizomba so fast, but being Brazilian explained a lot. Their experience with couples' dances like forró and lambada gives them an advantage over other groups. Not even the Argentinians with their tango get it. Apart from them, maybe only the Cubans with their merengue and salsa. Quito Ribeiro's only really glaring mistake was his tendency to raise his hip just a touch at every turn.

It felt good going back to my dance-teacher mode. I missed my dance classes. For the last couple of weeks, working on my final thesis forced me to stay home and, even though we did have our Sunday gatherings, people came for the food, not to get dance classes from me. But here I was, saying to Quito Ribeiro that, unlike bachata, we didn't raise our hip in kizomba. He smiled and immediately corrected himself. I wanted to congratulate him for being such a fast learner, but I held my tongue and rested my head on his shoulder – longing for my dance classes, to go out clubbing and dance with a stranger.

My neighbours Gilson and Samira joined us on the dance floor. By the time their bodies had met, the music had switched to a song in Cabo Verdean Creole, and suddenly the rest of the crowd who had gathered by the window were no longer interested in us dancing; the debate had moved to which nation should claim kizomba. The Angolans presented their arguments first, saying that since the name of the genre in Kimbundu means 'party', there's no way it could have been invented by any other group than themselves. But the Cape Verdeans in the room threw their arms in the air – the name might be Angolan, but, they grumbled, that doesn't diminish Cabo Verde's contributions. Born in Mindelo and raised in Rio de Mouro, Samira weighed in from the dance floor.

'This music is influenced by zouk from the French Antilles, which *also* means "party", right?'

The crowd nodded in agreement, and when she had

finished the vírgula and transitioned to the basic two-step, she continued:

'Maybe the artists who created it decided that kizomba was the best word because of its meaning.'

Paizinho told me that when he arrived in the city, Angolans and Cape Verdeans wandered around Lisbon together, from club to club. From the Aiué to the Kandando, the Kussunguila to the Quo Vadis. The choices were abundant. They had Ondeando, B.Leza, Enclave and Lontra, the first African disco to be labelled mainstream. To show me how awesome Lisbon was back when they were party animals, my parents loved bragging that in August 1993, Prince picked Lontra for a private after-party, following his show at the Alvalade Stadium.

I repositioned Quito Ribeiro's hand, moving it onto my lumbar region. Sweat on my back. My thighs gently touched his, not imposing myself but suggesting how he should proceed. Usually, first-timers would stop before the end of the song; not Quito Ribeiro. He didn't seem to care about the change of roles. It looked like he was leading almost imperceptibly to anybody watching us, but he was actually copying what my thighs told him to do.

Truth was, he didn't dance badly at all. He moved ceremoniously, on the beat, but without neglecting the gracefulness and the joy you need to have while dancing. As if he was coming back to someplace familiar and as if it wasn't his first time dancing kizomba. It didn't have anything to do with our sharing an ocean or a language. I felt it was something else, and not just the music; perhaps it was the vulnerable way he'd let himself go. I was intrigued.

'Sorry, did I do something wrong?' he asked and I looked up.

'No,' I said, grinning. 'You're doing just fine.'

'Your eyes are saying the opposite.'

'I thought our feet were doing the talking,' I said.

He then stopped and steered my body to the side, his eyes locked in, biting his lower lip so as not to lose focus. Then, when our bodies joined again, our faces were a hand's breadth apart.

'How did I do?' he asked.

And just like that, what had been puzzling me became clear. Quito Ribeiro's soft and nasal tone, with his stretch of the vowels in diphthongs, made him belong, effortlessly, to the place I called home. And wow, I really didn't want that song to end. All I desired at that moment was to rest my head on his shoulder and decipher in detail that woody and citrus scent on his neck.

'So, you won't tell me?' he insisted, creating a pair of dimples on his cheeks as he showed me his perfect teeth.

'You're a fast learner,' I said, though I'd meant to say something different. I sighed when the song was over.

II

I wouldn't have known how to defend myself from Samira's jokes if I danced three songs in a row with Quito Ribeiro, so we let go, and for a moment, we didn't know what to do with our hands. We just stood in front of each other, waiting to see who would flinch first. I did.

'How about a beer?' I asked. I went to the fridge in

the kitchen, feeling Samira's eyes burning the back of my head.

When I came back into the room, I found Quito Ribeiro browsing through my mother's art installation of family portraits, her proudest possessions. I held the drink out to him, he took it and thanked me by clinking the necks of our bottles.

'I have so many questions,' he said, turning back to the photos and picking up one of the frames.

'I was three years old.'

'You look happy.' He pointed to a photograph of me dancing kizomba.

'That was a happy day, my partner and I won first prize.'

'Your parents always go with you to your dance competitions?' he asked, picking up another picture of me at a dance workshop.

'They used to at first, yeah, but then, like most parents, they started worrying about my studies.'

'I can imagine that, with your mother being a teacher,' he said, and I nodded.

'Now, I only travel to kizomba dance conferences when college allows.'

'What are you studying?' he asked.

'Anthropology, I'm doing my MA,' I said, and he looked at me askance. 'What?'

'I didn't expect that.'

'Really? Say more.' I put my index finger on my chin.

'It's nothing like that. I just thought you would be doing something dance-related.'

'You sound like my colleagues at Lisbon Nova Uni.'

Quito returned the picture to the table and sighed.

'I thought you were going to say I sounded like your parents.' He laughed.

'I like anthropology, and I even saw myself following in my mom's footsteps and becoming a primary or secondary schoolteacher.'

'You still can, no?' he asked.

'Well, with kizomba classes in as high demand as they are now, I think my career path is decided,' I said.

Quito Ribeiro continued to browse through a succession of my family's old photographs. He stopped at an image of a happy baby-faced Paizinho, seated on a motorcycle, wearing bell-bottomed jeans with a T-shirt a size too small. His dark skin was glowing and his hair was perfectly rounded, mirroring the crown of the mulemba tree in the background. Next was a photo of my mom on the beach, a slender teen with blonde hair tied into a ponytail; shoulders sunburned and a diamond-shaped face, with deep-set blue eyes facing up to the lens with a defiant look.

'You look exactly like your mother,' he said and then glanced back at a picture of me, two weeks old in my grandmother's arms, followed by another of my parents and me at an amusement park in Lisbon, and several others where we were dancing. I picked one up and showed it to him.

'That's my favourite,' I said.

In the picture, Paizinho is holding my hand while I spin around him. In his free hand, he has a silk handkerchief. Both of us are smiling, with sweat pouring from our foreheads.

'My mother took this one.' I smiled, and he smiled back.

'From the look on both of your faces, I can't say who is prouder,' Quito Ribeiro said.

'Probably me.' I laughed.

When that picture was taken, I was just happy to dance with him and my mother, but with time, I started to realise how lucky I was to have him. We don't share the same genes, him and me – his skin the colour of 95 per cent cocoa chocolate; mine, pale ivory. His hair is fuzzy, and mine is just like my mom's, straight and long. My mom told me that back when she lived in Huambo, her hair was curly, but the winter in Lisbon, with 80 per cent humidity, took all her identity away. Her complaints were often suffused with self-deprecating humour, but in truth, she never managed to adjust to the reality of the returnee after she and my grandparents were forced to leave the country in '75. Paizinho and I couldn't be more different, yet we breathe and feel music exactly the same way. He's not a professional dancer but taught me everything I know about this dance. First with his bed-time stories and seeing him dancing with my mom, and later, when I was maybe five or six (my parents said it was earlier), I'd give him my hands and stand on his shoes, letting myself be carried by the rhythmic steps of my first kizombas. Eduardo Paim and Paulo Flores became members of the family. Actually, it was them who brought my parents together. Uncle Paulo and Uncle Paim started to be ever-present, days and nights, in moments of joy and sadness, witnessing everything as I grew up. But my first memories of kizomba were even earlier, from my mom.

Maybe they're her memories, but I know I still have a picture of my mom, recently divorced and suffocating with homesickness for the country of her birth. She'd leave me at my grandma's every weekend and dive head first into the African nightlife in São Bento. My grandma wasn't best pleased with her daughter's bohemian lifestyle, and somehow their quarrels about it are woven in with my first memories of kizomba. Before I'd heard one single musical note I saw my mom all dolled up, arguing with my grandma about music. The whole house shook when they bumped heads. My grandmother would ask: 'Well, if you're so keen on blacks, why don't you just go back to Angola?', and my mom always replied: 'Yeah, I should have stayed!' Everything at a yell. 'If your husband and you had treated those blacks with a bit more dignity, I wouldn't have had to run away to this shithole country of yours,' my mom concluded. I think it was only when she met Paizinho that she came to terms with living in Portugal. Every now and then, whenever something annoyed her in the school where she taught, or when the winter was unbearable, she'd turn to him and say she was fed up, adding, 'That's it, I'm going back to my country, I'm done with this place, you can keep it.'

Quito picked up a picture of Paizinho wearing a heavy coat in the middle of the snow in front of an apartment building.

'That's his student dorm in East Berlin,' I said.

'What year is this?' Quito asked.

'I'm not sure, but I think it's early '80s,' I said and turned around to look for Paizinho in the room.

'Never mind, I'm just curious. I didn't think Lisbon experienced such hard winters.'

'He went to the GDR on a scholarship, but after the fall of the Berlin Wall, instead of going back to Angola, he moved to Portugal, where he met my mom.'

'Escape from Berlin.' Quito Ribeiro returned the picture to the gallery.

'It's more escape from MPLA, the government.'

'Is he a political exile?'

'A self-imposed exile. He thinks he'd get arrested if he set foot in Angola again. Since his scholarship was from the army.'

'And he feels like he's a deserter.'

'My mom always tells him the government has bigger problems to worry about than an Angolan student who has gone missing behind the Iron Curtain.'

Quito Ribeiro laughed.

'He says that he'll go back when the country's destiny stops being in the hands of José Eduardo dos Santos,' I said.

'From what Mário Patrocínio told me, things won't be changing there all that soon,' he said.

'I already told him to get over it. I'd love to discover Angola with my parents, but it's obvious I'm either going on my own or not at all. Maybe kizomba will take me there before they do.'

I heard the first chords of the Cape Verdean singer Mika Mendes's song, and I started humming the tune. Quito Ribeiro held his arm out, and as I stepped towards him, I saw Samira out of the corner of my eye, ostentatiously counting on her fingers. I smiled and put my arms on his shoulders, and when the lyrics about a beating heart filled the room, I twisted gently around him. Nothing too scandalous, I mean, we were still practically strangers, and it was still my parents' house. Maybe I should invite him to get out of there.

Our eyes had smiled silently at his awkwardness as he tried not to lose his grip on the rhythm. Maybe he too was trying to understand all this, waiting for the party to end before saying something. He must have read the signs. I'm sure a Bahian can read what a body's telling them. My hand on the back of his neck, my face on his chest. He must have noticed from the beating of my heart that I was about to make a move.

Mário Patrocínio was smiling at Quito. I didn't dare look back, nor did I dare ask him what was happening. When I did the comma-step and our bodies switched direction, I saw that he was staring at his own feet, trying his best not to trip, going with the flow of the song, avoiding any movement outside of what was expected from a dance apprentice: control and patience.

'Maybe you should change your flight to Rio and stay in Lisbon another week,' Mário said to Quito Ribeiro.

Oh yes, I thought. Do stay.

I wanted to say it out loud to him, but the words were heavy on my tongue. I couldn't quite pick the right tone. I wanted to whisper in his ear. But as I was getting ready to summon up the courage and starting to count to three internally, Mário Patrocínio, the dude who pushed him into my arms in the first place, pre-empted me with the classic kizomba-party trick. 'Hey, Quito Ribeiro, would you just hold this beer for me?'

He turned and we were separated. My next-door neighbour, a woman in her sixties, jumped in front of him, all smiles.

'Do you want to finish the song with me?' she asked.

Quito Ribeiro's eyes went back and forth between the woman and the beer in his hand until Vemba showed up.

'Let me help you with that,' he said, taking the bottle.

'This is my first day dancing kizomba,' said Quito Ribeiro.

'Don't worry, I'm just starting to learn,' said my neighbour.

And off they went, trying their best not to step on each other's toes. Our eyes didn't meet again for five songs. Maybe I imagined it, but I felt we were avoiding each other on purpose. Maybe trying to make sense of what was happening.

III

'Look at you, Mr Movie Director,' I said to Mário Patrocínio.

'Should I take this as a compliment?' he asked.

Since we met in college, Mário Patrocínio and I liked to make fun of each other. I'd never been able to take him seriously. I couldn't tell you why. Our group from the Nova Uni used to drag him off to the African nights, and I never imagined those outings of ours would feed his choice of profession. Of all of us, he was the one with the fewest African reference points. Most of the group was made up of Angolans and Cape Verdeans. He and I were the only ones born in Lisbon. Even though they no longer hold Angolan citizenship, my parents are proud Africans who act like they never left. Mário's family was Portuguese through and through.

'I still can't believe you managed to visit Angola before me,' I said.

'Crazy, isn't it?' He grinned.

'Do you remember how you described kuduro the first time you experienced it?' I laughed.

'How could I forget?'

'You were interpreting it wrongly.'

'I just described it like I saw it. In the middle of the dance floor people made a circle, and two dancers in the centre were twisting their bodies, competing.'

'You said they were battling it out for the title of best kudurista of the night.' I chuckled.

'And you couldn't wait to correct me.'

'No one was there defending a title of any sort, it was just a party night, and everyone got involved. You heard how the spectators were cheering the dancers.'

'You win, girl. I already got it.'

It's the music that's always the big winner at a kuduro party. Wild, raw, fierce, the only force with the power to make everybody present levitate a few centimetres off the floor.

Those parties were indeed the start of the adventure that led Mário Patrocínio to take his camera and dip his head into the musical movements coming out of places on the fringes of the big urban centres like Rio de Janeiro and Luanda.

'OK, Mr Movie Director, I see Luanda did at least make you a better dancer,' I said, and he bowed and turned to Samira, Gilson and Quito Ribeiro.

'Did you hear what our dance anthropologist just said to me?'

They all turned to Mário Patrocínio.

'That I'm a great dancer.'

Samira laughed.

'When Sofia starts giving compliments, she wants you to do her a favour,' Samira said.

'Come on, I was being honest,' I said.

Mário Patrocínio shrugged.

'How did you two meet?' Samira pointed to Mário Patrocínio and Quito Ribeiro, who gestured to the movie director, inviting him to take the lead.

'I got invited to work on the production of a video clip for a baile funk MC at the German Complex in Rio de Janeiro's Northern Zone.'

'We didn't meet at the German Complex, to be clear,' said Quito Ribeiro.

'Sorry, I'm giving you the long version, but I can always reduce it to just one sentence,' said Mário Patrocínio.

'The calulu isn't ready yet. I think we can have the long version,' said Gilson.

'I went there for the video but stayed three years, observing and filming the lives of regular citizens and drug dealers. The struggle for survival of the three hundred thousand people who make their home in those favelas,' said Mário Patrocínio.

'Why's it called the German Complex?' asked Vemba.

'The hill was named after Leonard Kaczmarkiewicz, a Polish immigrant who owned the lands that became the favela.'

'Shouldn't it be called the Polish Complex, then?' insisted Vemba.

'You know how it is. The guy looked German and people didn't bother to enquire into the details and get his nationality right.'

'It's like how they look at black people, it doesn't matter if some of us were born in Europe, they still call us all immigrants,' said Samira.

Everyone nodded.

'So what happened then?' Gilson turned to Mário Patrocínio.

'After three years, my brother – who was there with me – he and I came back to Portugal with a hard disk holding a terabyte of images, and not a cent in our pockets,' said Mário Patrocínio.

'And then Quito Ribeiro showed up with a bag full of cash and saved the day,' I said.

'I wish.' Quito Ribeiro laughed.

'We scraped money together and made a documentary with those images from the German Complex,' Mário Patrocínio continued.

'And we met at a Rio de Janeiro film festival,' said Quito Ribeiro.

'At the documentary's premiere in Brazil,' said Mário Patrocínio.

'The *award-winning* documentary, Mr Movie Director,' I said.

'Yeah, and then we won the human rights award at the Artivist Film Festival in LA,' said Mário Patrocínio.

'Mário approached me and invited me to edit the movie he was producing about kuduro, and here I am,' said Quito Ribeiro.

'Thank you, bro,' said Mário Patrocínio.

'Before working on this movie, everything I heard about Angola was from friends that went there to work in advertising,' said Quito Ribeiro.

'Angola is the new Dubai,' said Samira.

'So I hear. They told me it's more like Brazil, but in Africa, outside of that privileged bubble, it's every man for himself for anybody.'

'Angola is not for amateurs, that's what Paizinho likes to say,' I responded.

'I get all the hardship and stuff, but that whole "but in Africa" thing bothers me,' said Quito Ribeiro.

'Explain?' asked Vemba.

'That phrase, coming from people who basically became advertising execs overnight, reinforced the idea that the sun only rises for a few lucky ones, and all the terrible poverty was basically unfixable.'

The room fell silent.

'I want to believe it's fixable,' I said, turning to Quito Ribeiro.

'Me too,' he said.

'Congratulations on the film, guys. Can't wait to see it,' said Gilson, raising his beer, and we all did the same.

IV

'So, if someone asks me and I answer that Lisbon is considered the mecca of kizomba, even though it isn't its birthplace, I wouldn't be saying anything crazy, right?' asked Quito Ribeiro.

'Not at all. This was where the dance steps got codified, and that's what opened the door to its mass consumption,' I said.

'This could make a good documentary,' Quito said, smiling.

'You should convince Mário.'

'I think you should be the one doing it.'

'Kalaf said that to me once.'

'Who?'

'A friend of mine, I don't think you know him.'

Quito Ribeiro had edited a movie about kuduro. I was sure he would've heard of Kalaf and his band Buraka Som Sistema, but I didn't want to give Samira any more ammunition. She was already squinting at me from the other side of the room. If she had caught me talking about my husband-on-paper to the man I was flirting with, she would have lost it. She still doesn't believe our marriage was just to help him get his documents in order. But honestly, nothing ever happened between Kalaf and me.

'He's right. You should listen to your friend,' said Quito Ribeiro.

'Nah, there are a few films on kizomba already.'

'But your perspective is what would make the difference.'

'Would you edit it?'

'Sure. And you can start from the beginning.'

'When I started to dance or when I decided to do a thesis about it?'

'Both.' He laughed, and I couldn't resist laughing too.

'You're a menace: I barely have space to breathe with the Masters already, and now you're charming me with ideas that will incinerate what's left of my social life.'

'I'm just curious. For example, how and when did Lisbon become the hotspot for this dance?'

'I would say things started to change with the Africadançar Festival in 2007.'

'A dance festival?'

'Yes, organised by an event producer and choreographer called Paulo Magalhães. I was nineteen, and for the first time, I felt a space had been created where Angolans and Cape Verdeans could devote themselves to creating teaching techniques and guidelines common to anybody who wanted to learn or teach people kizomba.'

'You see, that's a great opening for the film. You've got to do it.'

'A thesis is not enough.' I shrugged.

'I wonder how many people will read that compared to watching a movie.'

'You say that like documentaries have a huge audience.' I chuckled.

'Fair enough, but that's something you could involve your parents in too.'

Then suddenly, it all became clear.

'My friends, I outdid myself this time. The calulu is

going to be divine,' announced Paizinho, and the whole room erupted into a cheerful burst of claps, hurrahs and whistlings.

'I don't know if I can make a film about kizomba, but I'm sure I can tell a story about how that man convinced me that kizomba is one of the best dance styles in the world,' I said, turning back to Quito Ribeiro.

'Who convinced who?' asked Paizinho, approaching us.

'You – I was just telling Quito how kizomba became part of my life,' I said.

'I didn't know it existed before coming to Lisbon, unfortunately,' said Quito Ribeiro.

'All of us who love it believe that kizomba should be as celebrated as salsa, cha-cha-cha and tango,' I said.

Quito Ribeiro nodded.

'And unlike the tango, whose African roots have been erased, in kizomba, those roots are the foundation that gives the dance its strength. It's only a matter of time until the world embraces it,' said Paizinho.

'The yard, just like in samba, is the cornerstone,' I said to Quito Ribeiro.

'Yes, and it's not just samba – Candomblé also has the yard as the place of worship,' added Quito.

'In my country, it's the ground zero, the most important place for Angolans to socialise. That's where you get conversations, food, drinks, storytelling, reminiscences and all kinds of performances. It's the "laboratory" for countless cultural forms that endure through time and keep social bonds together,' said Paizinho.

'That's exactly the same within the Afro-Brazilian community,' said Quito Ribeiro.

Paizinho picked up his thread: 'It's also a place for family, a place of cultural resistance against the colonial presence, and where dances and genres of music got sketched out, like "sugar", which then led to kuduro, and semba, which, over time, led to kizomba. Angolans like dancing to anything. They don't limit themselves. They like interpreting a rhythm in their own way, which is usually kind of theatrical, fusing together steps from different dances and rhythms.'

Eduardo Paim's 'Esse Madié' came out of the speakers. Paizinho turned and called for my mother. She smiled, passed the platter of salty snacks she was carrying to Samira and met him in the middle of the living room. Paizinho held her in the crook of his arm. My mother placed her left hand on his right shoulder, touched his face softly with her right hand before he took it with his left hand, kissed her palm gently and then, with their fingers intertwined and just like the Angolan dance master João Cometa, he glided across the living-room floor marking out steps from yesteryear. Rotating and swaying to the rhythm, as if at that moment only the two of them existed in the world. I learned a lot at the Angolan Mestre Petchu and the Cape Verdean Zé Barbosa dance workshops, but I've got to applaud my first teacher.

'I don't think the film should open with Africadançar,' I said.

Quito Ribeiro frowned.

'I have to convince Paizinho to visit Angola,' I said.

'You two arriving in Luanda. That would make a great opening to a film.'

'Would you come with me?' I smiled.

'That's an invitation?'

V

Kizomba's like a sponge. Being a relatively new dance, it isn't closed off to influences from other music genres. It's not unusual to see dancers doing a moonwalk or a ndombolo step in the middle of the floor. Nothing in the dance is pure. The same goes for the music.

'When I told my stepdad I wanted to be a kizomba teacher, he made sure I knew the fundamentals,' I said to Quito Ribeiro, sitting next to me.

'They were hard to learn?' he asked.

'I didn't have a choice. Otherwise, he would have repeated them a thousand times until I memorised them.'

'Maybe he didn't want you to look bad.'

'I just wanted to dance, but he gave me a list of recommendations that included always worshipping Kassav, the iconic music band from the French Antilles, and quizzing me if I could name the main genres that were the basis of zouk.'

Quito Ribeiro dimpled his cheeks with a smile as I continued, 'Cadence-lypso, gwoka and compas direct.'

'Never heard of any of them.'

'Before the genre got its current name, it was called passada,' I said, copying Paizinho's hand gesture and tone of voice. Quito Ribeiro burst out laughing.

I got up and stopped the music. The room groaned their disappointment in unison, and before they could boo me away from the iPod, I put on Jocelyne Béroard's 'Mi Tchè-Mwen'. I couldn't resist melting my parents' nostalgic hearts with the Kassav vocalist's solo hit. They embraced and danced as they always did, eyes closed, with their foreheads touching and moving at half-tempo as if their ears were catching hidden melodies that the rest of us couldn't hear. They moved so slowly, as if that zouk song were a Nat King Cole ballad and they had to feel every second of it. They did that with all the zouk songs of that era, from Jean-Michel Rotin's 'Lè ou Lov" to Annick and Jean-Claude's 'Sentimental'.

Quito Ribeiro stood up and joined me.

'This is a masterclass,' he whispered.

'That's how I learned, sitting here, turning the cassettes around when they came to an end and watching how they slowly draw these same steps over and over again until all the guests had left and it would be just the three of us in the room. Then we would dance and sing for another hour or two until one of us remembered that the next day was Monday and we had to call it a night.'

Quito Ribeiro was staring at the footwork of all the couples in the middle of the living room.

'You asked me who invented kizomba,' I said.

Quito Ribeiro turned to me for the answer, and I pointed to my parents again.

'This is it. A family party, music playing and people dancing. That's what created the genre, so I credit the people who gave life to it, since they started to dance the rumbas, merengues and modern Colombian cumbias – and allowed themselves to be inspired by it.'

'And mixing it with their own local music,' he said.

'Get it?'

'Same story in Bahia. It's impossible to point out who invented axé music, for example. It's just African culture manifesting itself.'

'Yes,' I nodded, 'it's culture.'

I scrolled down my zouk playlist, played another track from the Antilles, and no sooner did the first synthesiser notes of Frédéric Caracas and Eric Brouta's 'Chèché Mwen' ring out than my father kissed my mother's hand and turned to me, holding out his arm. The whole room stopped to watch us dance, all except my mom, who, being old school, doesn't hold with the idea of staying on the outside just clapping.

'Fine for you to dance badly, but you've all got to get involved,' she said, pulling the guests out one by one, dancing half a dozen bars with a few of them, before moving on to pair up next with whomever was nearest. And she was away, calling more people into the middle of the room, always following the rhythm, the music, always keeping in tempo. Despite being white, she's got a natural rhythm. Everything about my mom sways like an African woman. It's not hard to answer when people ask me where my sense of rhythm comes from. I inherited it from her. And, of course, despite not being his biological daughter, having been brought up by an Angolan father made all the difference.

When the song came to an end, while the room was still

clapping, my mom took charge of the iPod and put on her Brazilian music playlist. Chico Buarque's voice filled the room. I went over to Quito, who was avidly watching all the activity.

'Do you mind?' I asked him.

'Why would I mind?' His dimples smiled at me yet again.

'My mom loves Brazilian music,' I said.

'I haven't listened to Chico in years,' he said.

My mother was one of those Chico Buarque stans who sighed deeply and praised his blue eyes, a wildcat's eyes, one of those big jungle cats, eyes that are glaucous and lit up, that's how Tom Jobim described the blue eyes of the composer of 'Pedaço de Mim' – the song my mom claimed was the greatest song about loss, since nothing else had ever managed to describe the pain of that feeling quite like that tune. And what's more, she thought nobody sang about women as well as Chico did. But the song we were listening to wasn't about a woman. 'Fado Tropical' was a composition he wrote with the Luso-Mozambican film-maker Ruy Guerra.

And it really was like a fado, despite being tropical. I sat down on the floor to listen in silence, and Quito copied my movement, going a little further. He lay down on his back, eyes fixed on the ceiling light. As I watched him lying there, totally engrossed in the song, I wondered if hearing Chico sing made him homesick.

'Do you believe Brazil is condemned to remain "a vast Portugal" forever, like the song says?' I asked.

He looked over at me and smiled.

'With all due respect to Chico and Ruy,' said Quito Ribeiro, 'the country's at a point of no return – just being Brazil is all we have left.'

VI

Chico Buarque was singing the lines 'sardines, cassava / on a smooth tile', when Senhor Ludomir Rosa Semedo, our Cape Verdean neighbour from across the hall, came into the living room and right away started dancing lundu movements to the sound of that 'tropical' fado. In his white suit and hat, he looked like a character from Chico's own *Ópera do Malandro*. He danced a few bars before collapsing wearily into the chair next to us, panting and fanning himself with his panama hat.

'I'm sorry, I didn't see you there. Is this chair free?' he asked.

'It's all yours,' said Quito.

Senhor Ludomir Rosa Semedo kept on fanning himself and then, sensing that the sweat on his face wasn't drying, he removed the colourful handkerchief adorning his lapel and wiped it across his forehead. When he saw my mother, he raised his arms.

'Neighbour! Please come to the aid of your old friend from the Barlavento Islands,' he said.

'What's troubling you, my dear?' asked my mother as she approached him.

'I need to get my breath back, my body can't take this.'

'Blood-pressure pills or a nice cold bottle of Sagres?' asked my mom, laughing.

'A Sagres, my dear neighbour, if you'd be so kind.'

Having made his request, he put his hat back on, and now he wanted to know about Quito Ribeiro.

'And you, my friend, you are Brazilian from where exactly?'

'Salvador da Bahia,' said Quito Ribeiro.

'Ah, Bahia, the first station block of Brazil . . .' He sighed deeply, his eyes on the window, staring out at some point beyond the building opposite, beyond the Serra das Minas, far beyond the parish boundary.

'You've been in Bahia yourself, then, senhor?' asked Quito, bringing him back into the room, though hesitating to interrupt his reflections.

'Never – I wish . . .' he replied.

From that long sigh and the distant gaze, I could have sworn I was in the company of someone who'd been there and who had suddenly been overwhelmed by a nostalgic longing for the intense smell of a plate of hot vatapá. When he stood up again, I thought he was about to start singing Caymmi . . . But he didn't.

'Ludomir Rosa Semedo, at your service,' he said, offering his hand. Quito copied his movement, likewise getting to his feet and holding my neighbour's hand.

'Quito Ribeiro, my dear Cape Verdean friend, a great pleasure.'

The old man collapsed back into his chair and Quito Ribeiro returned to the floor. When my mom handed Senhor Ludomir Rosa Semedo the beer he smiled, raised the bottle as if in a toast and downed half of it in one go. Contented, he clicked his tongue and pulled out the handkerchief once again to wipe his moustache.

'Quito! Quito . . . Ribeiro!' repeated Senhor Ludomir Rosa Semedo, musing. 'San Francisco de Quito?' he said. 'How does a Bahian come to be christened with the name of the capital of Ecuador?'

Quito shrugged and said, amused: 'I guess the same way a Cape Verdean comes to be christened with a Slavic name?'

Senhor Ludomir Rosa Semedo laughed and brought the bottle back to his lips, sipping what was left of the beer. Then he put down the bottle and started to explain the origins of his name. Since I knew the story already, I got up as soon as he started talking about how his father was a fan of classical music; Polish composers particularly. I knew the whole thing by heart.

Senhor Semedo's father had begun his journey led by the obvious hand of Frédéric François Chopin, but he quickly ventured into less familiar seas and discovered Ignacy Jan Paderewski's opera *Manru* and his *Violin Sonata, Op. 13*, which led him in turn to Grażyna Bacewicz's Caprices. It was his mother, admitted Senhor Ludomir Rosa Semedo, who'd been mostly responsible. Semedo's father had been ready to call him Estanislau, in tribute to Stanisław Moniuszko, father of the Polish National Opera, but his son had been born on 1 January 1953, New Year's Day, and the day the composer Ludomir Różycki died. Semedo's father didn't want to let the day go by unmarked and registered his son with the name of the composer of *Pan Twardowski*, the first large-scale Polish ballet to be performed abroad. He only didn't go with the Pole's surname too because the child's mother, who loathed classical music and only liked koladeras, mornas and fados, fought for him to be spared, hence the agreement at which they arrived: Różycki became Rosa (which according to her was a secret tribute to the fado of that name, the one from *Nos tempos em que eu cantava* performed by the great Alfred Marceneiro). When I came back, bringing beers for everyone, I noticed that Senhor Ludomir Rosa Semedo had taken his hat off again, which he brought to his chest and then, suddenly, chin raised, started to sing fado.

'My mother used to say I had quite a knack for fado,' admitted Senhor Ludomir Rosa Semedo, putting on his hat again and sitting back down. 'But it was dancing that really called to me. If fado hadn't lost its dancing side, I might have become a fadista.'

'And classical music?' Quito asked.

'What about it, my dear Bahian?' he replied, grabbing the beer from my hands.

'If your father was such a fan, I imagine he'd have sat you down in front of a piano the first chance he got.'

'He did try, but it never worked out. My first love was the guitar – actually, it was women, but it was the guitar that got me to the women – but like I said, dancing felt more of a calling. When I was a young man, nobody was dancing waltzes. Now, koladeras . . .'

'Koladeras?'

Senhor Rosa Semedo gave him a complicit look.

'Oh yes, the koladera – the soundtrack to sin, popularised by Bana and Ildo Lobo.'

I took Senhor Ludomir's cue and put on Bana's 'Best Koladeras of All Time'.

'The rhythm is alive, thrilling, so your body allows itself to be carried away with no effort,' said Ludomir Rosa Semedo.

And he was right. All around us, at that moment, no foot or neck was still.

'Senhor Ludomir, I wonder if you could tell us when koladera became popular,' asked Samira.

'Some time between the 1920s and 1950s.' Ludomir Rosa Semedo brought his hat to his chest and raised his forearm as if picking fruit from an imaginary tree. 'It showed up unannounced, like all good things in life.'

Laughter erupted in the room, but it didn't bother him.

'It started to be heard at the old dances, played by "wood-and-strings" groups, which is what they used to call the trio of guitar, cavaquinho and violin,' he said and turned, slightly raising his empty beer bottle as he did so towards Vemba, who disappeared behind the living-room door.

'People didn't want to listen solely to the melancholic sound of the morna. So those who were most daring and impatient would ask the musicians to change the time signature, from quadruple-time to double-time, and encouraged the dancing and the partying until well into the small hours.'

Vemba came back holding a few beers, which he passed over to the people who raised their hands.

'Koladera, for dancing nice and close, squeezed real tight.' Senhor Ludomir Rosa Semedo smiled, like a naughty kid, and took a sip of his beer. 'There are lots of theories about the origin of our koladeras, in our Cape Verdean Creole. They say it started out as a dance for women, accompanied by clapping, and soon men joined in too, so it became a dance for couples.'

'Hey, Unk' Jon! Yo' mek it bicom koladera!' said another neighbour, also from São Vicente, who was listening in on our conversation. Ludomir Rosa Semedo's eyes shone as he remembered his island birthplace, the city of Mindelo of his childhood.

'Koladera was born out of a need to break through the boredom,' he sighed, before giving an unexpected laugh that attracted the attention of everyone in the room. He got up and began to sing and dance with a light swagger that floated like a feather carried on the São Vicente sea breeze. '"My beloved youth", which Bana is singing, was written by the great B.Leza, the composer who didn't just revolutionise mornas but also taught his compatriots from 1950s Mindelo to believe in the power of romance.'

'Senhor Ludomir, we might be young, but we do know about our composers,' said Gilson.

'Oh, I don't doubt that, but back then, people used to approach B.Leza and ask him to write a morna for their beloved. At the time, serenades actually worked and oaths of eternal love were easier to believe when accompanied by an irresistible melody,' said Ludomir Rosa Semedo. '"A real koladera is one that's hiding a morna inside it," the composer used to say. But it was the morna that travelled first, leaving behind the koladera, its cheekier cousin, trapped on São Vicente.'

He walked back to sit next to Quito Ribeiro.

'Not that koladera cared. After all, there was plenty on
the island to entertain her. From out of that water – or
rather, from out of that powder – koladera was made.'

Ludomir Rosa Semedo touched Quito Ribeiro's shoulder. 'Actually it's no accident that B.Leza stumbled across
South America's rhythms and chords. The semitones Brazil gave the world found fertile ground in B.Leza Xavier
da Cruz's guitar, out of which they sprouted into treasures
like "Luiza" or "Lua Nha Testemunha",' said Ludomir
Rosa Semedo, who then looked at me and nodded. I took
the iPod and picked a song for him.

'"Ribeira de Paul"!' he shouted when he heard the first
chords, then he shut his eyes and whistled the melody
with the sort of satisfied expression you normally see on
the face of somebody savouring an Italian ice cream after
a day on the beach. He only opened them again when the
song came to an end. And in a gesture that was as old as
the song we'd just heard, he raised his hat in thanks.

'Who are your favourite composers from Cape Verde?'

Senhor Ludomir Rosa Semedo smiled and turned to
Quito, who didn't wait for an answer.

'I'd like to take advantage of the last hours I have in
Lisbon and learn as much about Africa as I can,' explained
Quito.

'But there's nothing better than going there and experiencing it for yourself,' said Ludomir Rosa Semedo.

Quito Ribeiro took a moment to collect his thoughts.

'I definitely should. Especially when you read about
that thing with the tectonic plates,' he said.

'Tectonic what?' asked Gilson.

Quito turned to him.

'Apparently, the distance between South America and Africa is increasing by three centimetres every year,' said Quito Ribeiro, smiling.

'My favourite is the poet and musician Manuel Jesus Lopes, or Manuel d'Novas, the nickname he picked up when working on board the *Novas Alegrias*, a ship that connected Cape Verde with Senegal,' Ludomir cut in.

Quito Ribeiro pulled his phone out and Senhor Ludomir Rosa Semedo paused with a smile lingering on his lips. His gaze was lost somewhere beyond the window, maybe trying to find more composers' names, possibly searching for the memories of a lost Creole passion from the Mindelo of his youth. Quito waited patiently, with his fingers poised.

'Manuel d'Novas was one of the first Cape Verdean composers to bring humour into the genre.' Ludomir Rosa Semedo turned to him.

'And since you're going to the trouble, start with the album *Partida* from Voz de Cabo Verde, which came out in 1968, where among other pearls from our songbook, you'll find a version of "Nem Eu" by your own Bahian compatriot Dorival Caymmi.'

Senhor Ludomir Rosa Semedo was all smiles. Proud to be showing the musical affinities between São Vicente and Salvador da Bahia.

'Are you a musician yourself?' asked Quito Ribeiro.

'No, I'm an accountant, and a painter in my spare time.'

Quito returned the phone to his pocket, stood up and grabbed two beers from the table, handing one to Senhor Ludomir.

'Actually, when I'm painting, that's the only time I can listen to classical music. I listen to the Polish composers my father loved so much and that he handed down to me. When I was a child, I'd hear them coming from my father's record player. Then when he died I couldn't get rid of the thing, even though it no longer worked,' he said, taking a sip of his drink. 'My ex-wife couldn't stand classical music and I wasn't prepared to let go of my inheritance.' He laughed.

'You left your wife because she didn't like your Polish composers?' asked Quito Ribeiro with his eyes wide.

'No, I left her because I fell in love with another woman – and that second marriage, well, yes, that one did end because of my Poles,' concluded Rosa Semedo.

'How so?' Quito Ribeiro pressed him.

I was still a teenager, but I remember Ludomir Rosa Semedo lamenting the situation to my parents at our kitchen table. His second marriage followed hot on the heels of the first one ending. The couple met at the Cape Verdean Association, a mini cultural centre that occupies the eighth floor of a faded building on Rua Duque de Palmela, just yards from the Marquês de Pombal roundabout. It was there, in the Association's restaurant, where every day a hungry battalion of bankers, journalists and business execs from the neighbourhood crowded in to enjoy the cachupa, tuna steak and chicken curry – dishes prepared by Zita, a Creole woman from the island of Sal – that Ludomir met his second wife. Tuesday and Thursday lunches are the most popular, and they're the days you'll find the most Cape Verdeans in the hall. A lot of them don't even come for the food, they just show up to appease their nostalgia for mornas and koladeras with a few dance steps and a couple of glasses of wine.

'It was a Tuesday in winter,' said Rosa Semedo to Quito Ribeiro.

'I asked her to dance, stealing her off a gentleman in a necktie. She swore the man was only a work colleague, but I suspected he was more than that – he wouldn't let go of her! I had to deploy the old wine-glass trick.'

Quito, not wanting to interrupt Rosa Semedo's story, turned to me and winked.

'The man in the tie, disorientated and finding himself with a full glass of wine in his hand, watched me lead his companion off to dance to the rhythm of Bana's "Guenta Canela". He was just left standing there looking foolish, but at least he had the wine to wash down his shame,' said Senhor Ludomir, laughing.

'But the Poles?' Quito Ribeiro noticed that Ludomir was already diverting his gaze to the window.

'The Poles came into this story because of how they inspired my painting. When my father died, I went back to my canvases, I even suspect I might have started painting again just to listen to the records I'd inherited from him. Finally, I decided to rent a studio away from home, because whenever I picked up a brush I always used to end up painting women. But that wasn't the cause of the divorce. My problem started when I realised – or my wife realised – that all those women were really one woman, and that she had an awful lot of my ex in her. When I painted my wife's portrait and she noticed that the face looked more like my ex-wife's than her own, she invited me to go live in the studio full time,' said Rosa Semedo.

'Is it true, I wonder, what they say about how we always fall in love with the same sort of person?' Quito Ribeiro asked.

Ludomir Rosa Semedo shrugged, paused, took off his hat and caressed the brim with his delicate fingers.

'They're both fascinating women, with symmetrical faces and infectious laughs. Educated in prestigious schools, and confident. They moved so graciously that I would often slow my pace, without them noticing, of course, just to watch them walk. Both of them, women of an unparalleled radiance. They're different women, the two of them, but also one and the same, accompanied by movements of perfect harmony. They tarnish white walls with the bright colours they always wear. An explosion of shades and tones that would make you stop looking at their bodies and smiles and stand there fascinated by the festival of colour on the wall. They're totally different, but whenever I painted them, I'd mix them up,' the painter-accountant said.

'And did you have children, Senhor Ludomir?' asked Quito.

'No, we would have had time, but we had no desire to,' he replied. It was impossible to read in between those lines, or in the wrinkles of his expression, any thread of sadness. But he didn't seem altogether comfortable with the subject, and suddenly he beat his chest with the energy of a young soldier about to set out to war.

'If I ever fall in love again, let it be on a winter's day,

preferably in a cold and colourless place, somewhere simple and devoid of any objects that might compel me to look anywhere but at one single point,' said Ludomir Rosa Semedo as he got up, turned round and headed for the kitchen, stopping to take a couple of lundu steps with our wannabe dancer from next door.

'Hey, Sofia, put on some Amália,' shouted Rosa Semedo, 'I'm going to show you all how you dance fado.' I did as he asked, and when the voice of Vinicius de Moraes, co-writer of the 'Girl from Ipanema', filled the room, telling us how bold it was to have created a fado for Amália, I heard my mom calling me. Quito stayed where he was on the floor; I could feel his eyes following me to the kitchen door. When I came back into the living room, two beers in hand, Quito got up and asked if we could go to a fado house. I agreed.

'But first the calulu,' I said.

VII

The whole neighbourhood must have got a whiff of the stew – the Angolan staple that gave Paizinho the reputation of food master throughout the entire Linha de Sintra – because in no time at all the kitchen was packed.

'A gastronomical rhyme in tribute to our international guest. Angolan calulu and Bahian caruru are distant cousins,' said Paizinho when he saw Quito coming into the kitchen.

'What an honour, Seu António,' said Quito, using his Brazilian form of respect.

'Oh, not at all,' he replied with a smile. 'And when I introduced myself I did say I was called António de Sousa but that you could address me as Paizinho. Please don't make me feel like an old man.'

Quito blushed, avoiding eye contact with Paizinho.

'In Angola, when we have the same name as our father, instead of being called "junior", we are called "little dad" – Paizinho,' said Vemba.

'Got it,' murmured Quito, soaking up every piece of information and every gesture that brought him closer to the people around him.

The kitchen was already bursting at the seams and before I knew it, Quito was next to the stove, holding the paddle for beating funge. My father claimed that oar-shaped piece of wood had fed several generations of his family.

'It's the most widely used correctional tool in Angola,' he joked.

I went over to tell my dad he oughtn't to be making the guests work. But when I was just about to rescue him, Quito insisted he wanted to stay, that he wanted to learn. My father found the whole scene highly entertaining.

'You really could have asked him to help chop vegetables, or something else simple like that, Dad. Straight into beating the funge!' I said, amused at Paizinho's behaviour.

'It's all done, child, it was only the funge left,' he replied.

Mário Patrocínio came into the kitchen, followed by Kalaf and Gilson.

'Mário, you're just back from Angola, aren't you?' I

asked, looking over at the funge that was still left to beat.

'I am, but nobody taught me how to do it,' Mário laughed, then gestured at the others who had followed him into the kitchen, suggesting they might be up to the task.

Kalaf, my husband-on-paper – dressed as he had been on our wedding day, in a black suit and white shirt with a collar and a thin tie, like those members of the Nation of Islam, the disciples of Malcolm X – took a step forward, straightened his thick-framed glasses and, just as he was about to take off his jacket . . .

'Oh, for God's sake, I can't have such a distinguished guest beating funge in my kitchen.' Paizinho stopped him and looked at Vemba, who jumped to the stove. My father always takes advantage of moments like these to regale us with tales from his homeland, and since he'd gotten himself an audience of people connected with the arts he felt more inspired.

'I learned this calulu recipe from my aunts at their restaurant,' said Paizinho.

'Tia Filomena and Tia São,' said Vemba, laughing.

'My dear Vemba, an old story can always be new on the day you tell it.'

The kitchen erupted into laughter.

'So as I was saying, those ladies weren't actual aunts but it's one of those African things, close friends becoming relatives. Tia Filomena was my grandmother's goddaughter, and Tia São, her best friend, became an aunt by marriage. Neither one of them ever left Benguela, I don't think they even had a passport, but whenever we sat down at their table we were carried off on a gastronomical journey to every corner of the globe. In the geography lessons of tastes, we were able to learn the locations of the Alentejo of açorda, the Hungary of goulash, the Salvador da Bahia of vatapá.'

Vemba brought the paddle back to the pan, and before the water reached boiling point he started adding handfuls of manioc flour. Turning the paddle in a circular motion, he dissolved the flour till it had transformed into a smooth paste. In one continuous movement, he took the pan off the stove and put it onto the floor, between his legs. My father quickly handed him two pieces of cloth to protect his legs from the heat. And then, like an Olympic rower heading up the River Tagus, Vemba began a frantic assault, with quick and precise movements, eliminating any clumps of flour that hadn't already disintegrated. When I saw the sweat forming on his forehead, I looked at Quito, who nodded, understanding at last why I'd wanted to spare him. The physical demands of beating funge are kind of like resistance sports, and like a rowing race it requires muscular strength from its athletes as well as an ability to withstand fatigue.

'Imagine those mamas in Africa who've got to beat funge every day,' said Paizinho to Quito Ribeiro.

'Respect,' Quito smiled.

'I'm able to travel to Benguela now. Sometimes I ask myself how and why I've put up with thirty winters in Europe and stayed away from my country so long,' said Paizinho, opening the calulu pan. He wasn't really the type to give in to homesickness. For an Angolan, he can even live pretty well without funge, which is the Angolans' gastronomical emblem. It was me and my mom who asked him to cook something typically Angolan at least once a week.

'It's like opening a photo album. The smells bring me faces, places and conversations I thought I'd lost,' he said, while the wooden spoon paid a visit to the inside of the pot, very careful not to let the fish break apart.

'Calulu is a dish for cooking slowly,' he added, looking at me.

I know there'll come a day when I'll have to take on the production of the Sunday lunches. And I'm ready, I think. From watching him so much, I know a lot of his recipes by heart. Even his little tricks, like how for calulu you don't need to add water to make the sauce, it'll come from the ingredients themselves, you've just got to lower the intensity of the flame and wait. After thirty minutes, the okra goes in the pan. Once the vegetables are cooked and the fish is just right, you dissolve a soup spoon of manioc flour in water to thicken the sauce and let it perfect for a few moments longer.

'In the south of Angola, they eat calulu with corn funge – or pirão, that's what the Bailundos call it. Kalaf's from Benguela – he knows,' said Paizinho, and Kalaf nodded, agreeing with his father-in-law-on-paper. My mother handed me three bottles of wine, and I followed her as she carried a tray of wine glasses to the living room.

VIII

'When are you getting your divorce?' My mom poked me, and as always, when she brought up the subject, I couldn't contain my laughter, which made her even more annoyed.

'It's not like I'm going to find a proper husband any time soon, so what's the rush?'

My mom gave me a side-eye and shook her head.

'It won't take long,' I said. 'You'll know when you get your invitation to the party.'

'What party?'

'The divorce.'

'You two didn't do anything when you married, no cake, no rings. Why would you celebrate the divorce?'

'Our marriage was for bureaucracy, but our divorce is for love.'

'So, you do love him?' she grinned.

'Not like that,' I said, frowning. 'Brotherly love. Stop being naughty. He's my friend. I've known him since you and Paizinho used to take me to the Imbondeiro club.'

'He was never a good dancer. I remember you trying to teach him the same way you're trying now with this shy Brazilian.'

'Mom.'

'What?'

'I know what you're doing. Please stop.'

'What did I say?' She smiled.

'Yeah, right. I've got your number.'

Kalaf and I clicked because I didn't have anyone I could geek out about kizomba with, besides my step-father. We always enjoyed the intellectual aspect of the genre. For years we would go to clubs together. He was interested in the music, and me in the dance. This was before he became a rock star with Buraka Som Sistema. He was the first person I told about my plans to get a

PhD in anthropology; we were talking on the phone, and he asked if he could come to Rio de Mouro. I'd never had him visit before. My parents were watching television, so he and I sat at the kitchen table.

'What is this whole freedom thing anyway, Sofia?' Kalaf said to me that night, inconsolable.

'To me, freedom has always been linked to the idea of movement, of exploring the world without restrictions,' I remember him saying, to which I replied, 'I always associated it with having the power to choose.'

'Yes, choosing while still being completely free from any commitments is a luxury only mad people can have. At least, that's what I was taught.'

'It's definitely a privilege,' I said. He fell quiet. I looked at him. His eyes were sad, and shoulders slumped, and he continued.

'Freedom as we know it is an unattainable ideal.'

I knew then he'd come to ask me to marry him, so before he'd even popped the question, I said, 'I do.'

Since I like provoking my parents, whenever I know Kalaf's going to be at our lunches I joke that their son-in-law's coming to visit. My father always grumbles, but deep down, since he's conceited like every Angolan, I know he likes the idea of having a son-in-law who's one of his fellow countrymen, and a famous one to boot. Even if only on paper.

When we entered the living room, Samira came over and helped my mother empty the tray of wine glasses.

'Your mom said you were planning to spend the weekend doing research at uni,' said Samira.

'Yes,' I said, 'I'm glad she convinced me to give myself a break.'

'This girl has always loved to read, ever since she was a child, but now if I don't knock on her bedroom door, I won't see her,' my mom said to Samira.

'Mom,' I feigned irritation, 'you always exaggerate so much!'

'I get her point, Dona Isabel,' said Samira, 'it's not enough to be a good dancer. She actually has to think it through.'

'This dance culture gave me so much. I want to honour it,' I said.

'I know,' said my mom, squeezing my cheeks. 'Just don't forget to eat in the meantime.'

'You're right,' I replied, hugging her. 'It's not like Quissamã is going anywhere.'

'What else is there to know about that place? How nice that you've met someone now who actually lives in Rio de Janeiro,' said my mom.

Samira smiled and winked at her.

'Quissamã's in the north of the state of Rio, Mom,' I said, tickling her ribs. 'That's like asking someone who lives in Lisbon about a town in Porto.'

'OK, my mistake!' she said, trying to avoid my hands. 'I thought it was part of the same city.'

'No,' I grinned, 'it's three hours' drive from Rio.'

'Jesus,' she sighed, 'sometimes I forget how small Portugal actually is.'

Both Samira and I nodded.

'Three hours' drive: that's the distance between Luanda and Kissama National Park,' she said.

'Isn't it amazing that a town in Brazil has a Kimbundu name?'

'What does it mean?' asked Samira.

'Torch,' I said.

'And they do the belly-bump.' My mom's eyes shone with a childlike excitement. 'Just like the massemba dance from Angola,' she added, grabbing Samira's hand.

'Like kola from Cape Verde too. The belly-bump dance is also part of that,' said Samira.

'Yes,' I smiled, 'you took me to see the Kola San Jon street parade at Cova da Moura years ago.'

We should do it again next year,' said Samira.

'I hope I will be done with the writing by then.'

'Just treat it as part of your research,' said Samira, smiling. 'Writing a dissertation on dance cultures and not dancing is almost a sacrilege.'

IX

'What do you reckon, Senhor Paizinho, should I beat it a bit more?' asked Vemba.

Paizinho inspected the elastic grey paste in the pan and gave a thumbs up. Vemba put the pan back onto the stove.

'Being from Luanda and the son of quicongos, I prefer to eat it with bombô funge,' said Paizinho, handing Vemba a beer.

'Cooking is a game of memory and patience. At least, that's what I learned from watching my aunts,' he said to Quito Ribeiro, pointing to the piles of empty plates on the kitchen table.

'When I was little I'd sit in a corner, making myself invisible, with a soda in one hand and a slice of cake in the other, just watching them.'

Paizinho took Quito's plate and served him the funge.

'But not sweets,' I said, smiling at him as I entered the kitchen. 'Here sweets are up to the women of the house, aren't they?'

'I didn't learn to make a single dessert from my aunts. Mind you, Tia São was a first-rate maker of sweets. Her sin, she used to say, was that she couldn't resist sugar. Which is why she was fat.'

My mom came into the kitchen.

'Is that any way to talk about your aunt?' she asked and took the plate out of his hand, a natural gesture that's been repeated for as long as I remember. My father gets carried away in conversation, so you could be standing there for fifteen minutes waiting for him to serve that one plate. But my mom, his constant accomplice in a silent dialogue, is always able to anticipate what he's thinking. He sat back down, took another gulp of his beer and continued.

'Tia Filomena, on the other hand, was a stick insect. However much she ate, and she ate plenty, she never managed to weigh more than fifty kilos. All the other women used to die of envy. At that time, I didn't really know why; she wasn't the most beautiful, or the most sought-after,' Paizinho recalled.

'The men who used to hang around the restaurant only had eyes for Tia São,' added my mother, passing me the plates.

Paizinho continued: 'At her height, a full metre-seventy, with her ample hips and chubby face, all the men's heads turned whenever she walked past, and she humoured them. She'd parade past, laughing at the compliments and filling the yard with all the charm of a young woman who knows full well she's an object of desire.'

I served some calulu onto the plates and passed them to the lads. First was Vemba, who thanked me and pulled a chair up to the kitchen table, and he was soon joined by the other three. My mom went back to the living room to call in the other guests. I sat down next to Quito.

'I don't know if Mário's already done the honours, but Kalaf is part of Buraka Som Sistema, the band that popularised kuduro in parts of the world you could never have imagined,' I said to Quito Ribeiro.

'Yes, Luís Kalaff's namesake,' he replied.

'We've met,' Kalaf added.

'He told you where his name comes from?' I asked Quito Ribeiro, but didn't wait for his reply. 'I don't know why he keeps insisting on that theory about it being a tribute to Luís Kalaff, when *Turandot*'s a much more lyrical explanation.' I turned to Kalaf and he smiled.

'That theory could even be true, but my parents never confirmed it, and besides, I'm convinced that Luís Kalaff's merengues were a whole lot more popular in Angola than Giacomo Puccini's opera. And so—'

'And who's to say your parents chose to follow what was popular when they came to baptise you?' I said and my husband-on-paper shrugged. Quito came to his defence.

'In Salvador, Luís Kalaff and And-His-Happy-Dominicans along with artists like Carlinhos Brown and Luiz Caldas, the father of axé music, they were all hugely influential,' he said.

'The plot of *Turandot* is part of a collection of fairy tales from the ancient Persian empire, called *The Thousand and One Days*, or *Les Mille* in the French version, published under the name of François Pétis de la Croix,' said Ludomir Rosa Semedo, coming into the kitchen. His impeccable French accent drew laughter from everybody. He paid them no attention, and instead just pressed on with *Turandot*.

'Not to be confused with *One Thousand and One Nights*,' he said, very seriously. He was already well used to the playfulness and banter on this side of the corridor.

'Puccini died without having finished the play. He hadn't concluded the third act and he'd left sketches for how he wanted the love triangle between Prince Calaf, Princess Turandot and Liù the slave-girl to end. Arturo Toscanini, who conducted the premiere in 1926, so hated Franco Alfano's ending that, at the end of Liù's death scene, he turned to the audience and said: "Ladies and gentlemen, this is where Giacomo Puccini stopped."'

'Oh, Senhor Ludomir, so now we know the slave-girl dies in the end,' Vemba sighed, disappointed.

'That should be no obstacle to your going to see it, just like knowing in advance that Romeo and Juliet are going to die should not prevent your seeing that play,' said Ludomir Rosa Semedo.

'Maybe he didn't know that either,' joked Gilson.

Ludomir Rosa Semedo shook his head.

'In 2001, the Italian composer Luciano Berio composed a new ending for *Turandot*,' he said.

Vemba perked up again, turning to Ludomir Rosa Semedo, and raising his hand, asked, 'So did the slave-girl Liù survive?'

'No, poor thing, she still dies, to protect Prince Calaf,' said Ludomir Rosa Semedo.

Everyone turned to look at Kalaf.

'Look, this whole soap opera's nothing to do with me!' he protested.

'Hey, you know that Kalaf visited us at our studio,' said Mário Patrocínio.

'So you saw the final cut of the movie – is it good?' I asked Kalaf.

'Come on, Sofia,' vented Mário Patrocínio, rolling his eyes. While Kalaf was still searching for words, Paizinho stepped in.

'Who made this movie?' he asked.

'Mário and his brother Pedro Patrocínio,' I answered quickly.

'Congrats, Mário,' said Paizinho, raising his bottle of beer.

'And it was produced by Coréon Dú,' I added, followed by a pause of several seconds in which everyone at the table exchanged glances. Suddenly, everybody's faces were filled with those 'I know but I'd rather not know' expressions, as if they'd seen the results of my medical tests and wanted to spare me something devastating. At that point in the game, whatever people said about

Coréon Dú, it was not going to change a thing. The film had been made.

'What is it about Coréon Dú? Is it just that he's the son of the Angolan president?' asked Quito Ribeiro, finding such a protracted pause in an otherwise very animated conversation kind of strange.

Kalaf shrugged, and it was obvious he was choosing his words with care. I didn't blame him. Of all the people there, he was probably the one who had to be the most diplomatic. He didn't talk about the movie, though he must have had something to say on the subject, given his own experience as part of such a successful kuduro group. Since nobody else was stepping forward, I turned to Quito Ribeiro.

'Coréon Dú isn't the son of just any old president,' I said, and just as Quito was about to reply, Kalaf cut him off.

'There's either nothing or everything wrong with Coréon Dú. Depends whether you turn a blind eye to the circumstances surrounding him.'

We all looked at Kalaf, not bothering to hide our expectant expressions and our hope that he might develop the thought further. Artists have this tendency to sit on the fence, taking a Swiss position when it comes to giving an opinion on another artist's work. Perhaps Mário Patrocínio, just like Kalaf, was choosing his words with care.

'This guy's the son of a man who's been in power more than thirty years,' said Samira.

'We're always hearing about projects connected to the family, and some of them do have the merit of being good ideas,' I said, 'but it's hard to get the word *nepotism* out of your head, if not worse.'

'We Angolans, who are so good at argument, are very poor at reasoning and stubborn when it comes to changing our minds,' Kalaf shrugged.

Vemba nodded his agreement, and Kalaf continued, 'Unfortunately, since 1975, we were never taught to live with change. Those on top never invited us, the people, to give our opinions in favour of or against any little thing at all.'

My father looked at me as if secretly grateful. This was the kind of gathering he likes. Actually, every Angolan I know loves it when, in the middle of the kizomba, the funge and the beer, the conversation turns inevitably to politics.

'The fear of another civil war is real,' said Vemba. 'People will always choose what they know over real change.'

'We're condemned to grumbling, sunk in the irritation of our impotent annoyance. Waiting for dawn to break, for some light to be shed. If the line of succession doesn't have somebody with the surname dos Santos, then who's it to be?' asked Kalaf.

The kitchen went quiet. The only sounds were the fridge and a distant song coming from the living room, barely perceptible. It was Ruy Mingas playing.

'There's no one in the world more alone than an unchallenged leader,' said Paizinho, breaking the silence.

I leaned over Quito Ribeiro.

'Paizinho has a particular grudge against the president,' I whispered, but he heard me and shook his head.

'It's not that I hate him, it's just disappointment, pure and simple,' he said and I nodded.

'Ah, I believed in that man, kid, but in time I realised that the only people loyal to men like José Eduardo dos Santos are their enemies. Friends are fallible, enemies aren't.'

'An enemy's not likely to betray your trust, and if they do they'd be betraying their own nature,' said Quito Ribeiro, smiling.

'Do you all know the fable of the frog and the scorpion?' asked Paizinho, getting up and moving towards the fridge.

'It's one of my favourites,' he said, handing round the beers. When nobody answered, he took a gulp of his beer, clicked his tongue, and began the way most stories begin.

'Once upon a time there was a scorpion who asked a frog to help him get across a river, as he couldn't swim. The frog refused, as she was afraid of the notorious venom in the scorpion's stinger. But the scorpion argued, "You needn't be afraid, Mrs Frog . . . If I attack you, both of us will drown, and I don't want to die." And the frog was convinced.' Everyone at the table had their eyes on my father, who was talking with his whole body. 'The scorpion got up onto the frog's back, and as she was swimming, he watched the movement of her muscles. And about halfway across, the scorpion wounded her with his stinger. As she began to feel the pain from the venom, about to surrender to death, the frog asked the scorpion: "Why did you do that, you crazy animal? Now we're both going to die!" And the scorpion answered

her: "I'm sorry, I couldn't help it . . . It's my nature."'
Everyone in the kitchen, disappointed, sighed in unison.

X

In the living room the wine was starting to take effect
and everyone was nice and lively. My mother was in
one corner talking to the neighbour who wanted to be
a dancer. Or rather, instructing her. Whenever my mom
gets her hands on a fresh pair of ears she can't resist going
into teacher mode. She worked more than fifteen years at
the high school in Amadora, the region with the largest
African population.

'This country's African history is very, very badly told.
In the sixteenth century, Africans represented 10 per cent of
the population of Lisbon and the Algarve,' she was saying.

To see her at a first plain glance you wouldn't think she
loved African culture so intensely, seeming just another
fifty-something blonde – not a dumb bimbo but also not
the type you'd find in a library scouring great tomes in
search of dusty royal charters from the Portuguese mon-
archy. Quito Ribeiro, who up until that point had not
caught many people's attention, moved discreetly towards
my mom to hear what she was saying. But as soon as my
neighbours registered his presence in the room, he became
the target of their assault. They wanted to know how he
was finding Lisbon, what monuments he'd visited and
which beach he thought the loveliest.

'Unfortunately, I haven't been to any of the beaches,'
he said.

'Haven't you visited the Tamariz Beach in Estoril? That's practically like going to Rio and not visiting Copacabana!' exclaimed Senhor Ludomir. My other neighbour, who had taken to Quito since he was the only one who didn't avoid dancing with her, came out in his defence and knocked back Rosa Semedo's comment.

'Oh, leave the boy alone; maybe he doesn't even like the beach, poor thing!' But Senhor Ludomir Rosa Semedo wasn't satisfied.

'But why ever not?! Don't tell me you're one of those blacks who can't swim?' he said, pointing at a group of young people sitting on the sofa, Vemba among them. Quito replied that he hadn't had time yet, but Senhor Ludomir Rosa Semedo didn't hear him.

'As you all know, we blacks aren't much given to aquatic activities. If we like the beach, it's more for the company than for leaping into the water,' he said, eager to share his theory. Vemba took advantage of the pause in his speech to defend himself.

'This whole thing about blacks not being able to swim is actually a total myth,' he said.

'Personally, I think of myself as a pretty mediocre swimmer and my own visits to the beach have always been like surgical strikes. I can bear an hour, but more than that starts being quite an ordeal,' said Paizinho as he took a seat on the old brown leather Chesterfield, his favourite armchair right across from where my mother was.

'And I can confirm that – I can count the number of times we've been to the beach together on my fingers,' said my mom, laughing.

'I don't know exactly where my aversion to the sea began, maybe the same time I started getting interested in girls, around the age of thirteen,' said Paizinho, making all the eyes in the room turn to my mother, followed by whistles and laughter. My father, amused, just shrugged and blew her a kiss.

'You needn't worry about the past, my little coconut sweetie,' said Paizinho.

'My heart is all yours,' she replied in her best movie-star voice. The whistling increased, and she blew a kiss back.

'As I was trying to say, before I got interrupted by this shameless pair here, I'm certain our alienation from the sea is hereditary. It's a manifestation of our genetic memory,' said Ludomir Rosa Semedo.

'Ludomir, you can't ignore the fact that over five hundred years of slave trading left after-effects, profound traumas embedded deep in our subconscious, which manifests when we wet our ankles in a large expanse of water,' said Paizinho.

The room burst into a great collective laughter, and Paizinho, attempting to nip it in the bud, soldiered on.

'I'm being serious! And the same thing applies our relationship to authority figures. When we're standing in front of a police officer we get all tame, and I'm talking from my own experience. No word of a lie, my wife here can vouch for that. When my car gets stopped by police, I'm all "Oh yes, boss," "Whatever you say, officer," even if deep down I'm always wondering why it is I'm kissing that policeman's ass.'

The room dissolved into laughter again.

'Whereas my wife, on the other hand, pity the poor police officer who dares to stop her! She abuses them in a way that's made me fear for our lives. Am I not telling the truth?' he asked, turning to Kalaf, standing by the window behind the armchair.

'My experience with the police has left me traumatised. But I agree that it can be challenging to think and speak eloquently in front of police officers,' said Kalaf, laughing.

The room was then divided into islands, discussing what it means to be black in Europe. Except for my mom, the whites, who were scattered among the various clusters, listened but kept quiet.

'With all the physical abilities that've been bestowed upon us, it's surprisingly rare that you see black people venturing into an Olympic swimming pool,' said Paizinho.

'Of course, some people point to socio-economic factors to explain why there aren't many. You can make your own footballs with socks and plastic bags and play on any old bit of wasteland. Swimming needs water,' said my mom.

'Lots of water, and we all know what a luxury that is for black communities in Africa. Another reason, maybe the only really relevant one, is knowing how little money an Olympic swimmer makes if he's not a total medal-hogger like Michael Phelps,' said Paizinho.

Samira left the group where Quito Ribeiro, Kalaf and Mário Patrocínio were debating pan-Africanism and circled back to the Paizinho group where the 'would-be dancer' neighbour smiled at her.

'What about those toned bodies the swimmers used to

show off? They were a hit with the girls, weren't they?'
she said.

'Oh, but it's only really during the Olympics,' said Samira,
'because in everyday life, in the real world, *Caras* magazine
is never going to run stories about the gold medallist from
Beijing with gossip like: "divorced from actress so-and-
so who laid waste to his heart and his wallet, swimming
breaststroke out of the marriage with half his fortune and
with his lover, a promising young woman, a record-holder
in the hundred-metre butterfly".' Paizinho turned to them.

'Swimming doesn't bring you money, that's what a
lot of African parents are thinking about when they're
contemplating signing their child up for some sporting
activity or other. If it's a matter of keeping the kids busy
after school, they might as well at least be doing a sport
that offers a "way out" and that might guarantee them a
scholarship,' he said and Samira nodded.

'Running, that's something we can do on any stretch
of open ground. Whereas swimming, in most cases that'd
mean the parents having to leave their neighbourhood,'
she said.

'I think if there was more infrastructure we would find
it easy to push back against that idea that blacks are afraid
of swimming,' said Paizinho.

'We'd also have more like Edvaldo Valério, the
Afro-Brazilian swimming champion,' said Quito Ribeiro,
joining them.

'He won a bronze in the relay at the Sydney games.
I remember seeing your Bahian compatriot doing his
heat,' replied Paizinho, who'd always been a fan of the

Olympics. And since he has friends like Senhor Ludomir Rosa Semedo who like arguing with him, he'd been keeping a close watch on aquatic contests in which black athletes were competing, in order to defend his theory about black people's hereditary relationship to the sea.

'In Sydney, in the hundred-metres freestyle, there was another black swimmer who really stood out, Eric Moussambani, from Equatorial Guinea – not for winning a medal or for setting a new Olympic record, but for having finished the preliminary heat unopposed. Eric Moussambani's story moved the whole sporting world,' said Paizinho. 'When two swimmers were disqualified for false starts, Moussambani, also known as "Eric the Eel", was left alone in the pool, and having had only six months' training as a swimmer, and never having competed in an Olympic pool before, swam the distance in a laughable time and ended the heat practically with no lungs left. Everyone identified with his Olympic adventure.'

'It's the taking part that counts, is that not the Olympic spirit?' asked Vemba.

'Swimming badly is at the top of stereotypes generally associated with black people,' said Paizinho.

'Immediately followed by "never respecting schedules",' added Ludomir Rosa Semedo.

'While I enjoy speculating about the genetic memory of the descendants of Africans scattered across the world, I do believe that if necessary we should do an Eric Moussambani and dive in head first. If not for the medal, then at least so we have a good story to tell,' said Paizinho. In the meantime, the Ruy Mingas record had come to an end. I asked my father what he felt like hearing.

'Something by our other sportsman,' he replied. From the stack of vinyl heaped up beside the record player, I pulled out two Bonga albums and held them up for him to choose. 'They're both very good . . . Let's listen to *Angola 72*. My Bahian friend,' said my father to Quito Ribeiro, 'this is the semba from my homeland.'

My stepfather turns into a different person whenever he stumbles onto any bit of Angolan musical history, whether on 33-inch or 45-inch, however scratched or mouldy. He can't help himself. I've seen him haggling like a market stallholder in Marrakesh. He begs, he calls on Our Lady of Fátima, he even throws in some emotional blackmail, invoking our ancestors so that he might be granted the right to be the faithful guardian of that particular record. I never saw my father lost for words until the day we went to see Waldemar Bastos playing. It actually scared me, I thought he might be having a coronary. Deep breaths. This man, who so likes surrendering to the pleasures of substantial conversation, when standing in front of one of his heroes of Angolan music . . . total silence. My mom always says that after all the time the two of them have spent at the flea market chasing after records, he's assured of the status of unofficial Semba Ambassador, a missionary wandering through this free world, spreading the doctrine, the gospel according to Liceu Vieira Dias.

'Now, my esteemed Bahian brother, there's no way I'm letting you leave this house without taking a little selection away with you, a retrospective of classics from Bonga to Yuri da Cunha, via Sofia Rosa, Elias Diá Kimuezo, old-school and new stuff,' said Paizinho. True to the tradition that whenever somebody shows an interest in Angolan music, he offers them a home-made mix CD with a special selection of music from his country.

'I would be honoured,' said Quito Ribeiro, who turned to me, grinning from ear to ear.

'Back in the day, whenever anyone seemed interested in this music, he'd lend them his records, and some were never returned, breaking his heart into pieces, and I hated seeing him sad,' I muttered.

'I can imagine, and I won't abuse his generosity. I promise,' he said, and I smiled.

'One time a young singer came over to the house, who told him she wanted to record an album of sembas. And so what happened? He lent her some of his rarities, and she still hasn't returned them.'

'That's criminal.'

'Yes, and since then, I have started policing him,' I said, frowning at my stepfather.

'I regret it to this day. I know I committed the very worst sin against the vinyl collector's ten commandments. But I was moved by her enthusiasm,' Paizinho replied, his eyes sad.

'You were flirting with that young lady, and she took advantage of you,' said my mom, laughing at Paizinho.

'Nothing of the sort! I still get nightmares. It's like I lent the Gutenberg Bible to an atheist. I'm sure Jesus would have approved of such a charitable act, but a part of me is still tortured by never seeing those relics again,' he said.

'And the album the young lady recorded, did it end up being any good?' asked Quito Ribeiro.

I turned to Quito.

'She didn't release anything. Can you believe it?' I said.

'I suggest we leave Paizinho's pain alone. I still want to know what our distinguished Bahian thinks of this city!' Senhor Ludomir Rosa Semedo reminded everybody.

Quito was quiet for a moment and then, looking at me, finally declared: 'I feel very close to what I really am here, maybe closer to that than I've been since I was ten years old. This city has a rhythm that's just its own, it's easy to feel at home here. I could live in this place.'

Everybody raised their glasses and bottles in a toast. I kept my eyes fixed on Quito, and his found mine in turn. For a moment, I thought he would come over to me and ask if I could translate into words what my eyes were saying to him. I watched him failing to know what to do with his hands, since the bottle he was holding was empty. He tried to engage in conversation with someone, but his eyes found mine again, though he didn't dare to hold my gaze for long. He opted to look down at the floor, and then I noticed how he bit his lower lip, moving his teeth from left to right, caressing it as if trying to calm the urge to taste my tongue. I felt something start at my fingertips, go through me, up the back of my neck, which could have made me slow-dance all night with him, regardless of the genre or tempo of the song being played. It was desire. I looked at that lower lip he was biting and wanted to suck it free, I wanted to taste his tongue, wanted him to look at me one more time so I could invite him to follow me. But he didn't.

He chose instead to join Kalaf. They both had kuduro as a common interest, and I guessed they went back to talking about Mário Patrocínio's movie as they were whispering something they didn't want anyone to hear. I gave up and went back to the middle of the room, where the semba was lively. A circle opened up, and as soon as Senhor Ludomir Rosa Semedo saw me, he opened his arms inviting me to join him in Carlos Burity's 'Uabite Boba'. As soon as the track ended, thinking I was going to keep dancing with Senhor Ludomir Rosa Semedo, I was surprised by Quito who repeated the old glass trick, only this time the victim was Ludomir himself, who offered no resistance.

'Oh, this Bahian learns fast, oh yes!' said Ludomir Rosa Semedo as he stepped aside to make way for Quito Ribeiro.

And once again I found myself entwined in Quito's arms.

'Was it you who chose this song?' And he didn't answer me, instead making a *hummm, hummm* sound that was almost musical. 'And how did you get to Nelson Freitas's "Saia Branca"?' I insisted.

'Easy, senhorita. I consulted the locals and this track was suggested because of a line sung in Creole which I don't dare to repeat for fear of getting it wrong,' he said.

'N'cre perguntab pa dança / Ma coragem n'ca traze ma mi,' I said to him, smiling.

'It's my farewell dance,' added Quito Ribeiro.

'Where are you going so soon?'

'I go back to Rio tomorrow,' he said.

I didn't answer. That dance didn't feel like a farewell to me. If we could read what our bodies were telling us, I'd say we weren't ready for a goodbye just yet. How could we say farewell without a proper kiss? Why hadn't we kissed already? Our faces kept coming closer and closer, and our mouths were on the verge of touching, on the cusp of kissing. What was holding us back? Did he think I found this amusing? The anticipation of it. His body against mine, our mouths burning with words we feared misplacing. I wanted to make him blush and lose his composure. Before we kissed, I wanted him to know that his scent was inviting me to bite his earlobe softly, and while doing it, I wanted to hear him moan because that would make his mouth an even more desirable destination.

'Let's go hear some fado!' I said.

Quito stopped, looked at me very seriously, with Nelson Freitas still singing out of the speakers . . .

'. . . say where you from
and where you goin'
for me to be beside you.'

'Could there be any better way for you to say goodbye to Lisbon?'

XI

When Quito Ribeiro and I arrived in Chiado, the sun had already set behind the buildings around Luís de Camões square. It was nearly dark and over the terracotta roofs the sky had turned a deep blue. The place was busy, all the tables at Benard and A Brasileira were full, and even the Fernando Pessoa statue had company, with a couple occupying the seat beside the author of *The Book of Disquiet*.

I had brought him there without thinking. This couldn't be somewhere Quito Ribeiro didn't already know, as it was the most visited hill in the city. You can't be a tourist in Lisbon without coming through Chiado at least half a dozen times. If not for Bairro Alto right next door, then for the Fnac store in the Chiado shopping centre; if not for the theatre, then for an espresso at Brasileira, a distant, pale memory of the ones they used to serve. But hey! – how can you resist if they say that it was precisely inside a coffee cup that Chiado was invented?

I don't remember the last time I stepped inside Brasileira. The place hadn't changed a bit. The waiters still forced us to fight for their attention. I wondered if that was the case when men were wearing suits and ties at this counter, just like Fernando Pessoa. Those were the men who plotted cultural revolutions here. Nowadays, when I cross the Chiado square, I wonder who might step up and start a new cultural revolution like Pessoa and his generation did at the beginning of the twentieth century. The men and women who could do it no longer sit in cafés. Instead they occupy the squares dancing or playing music for the visitors sitting at the terraces, who savour their galão with gusto and are delighted to be experiencing the real Lisbon.

Standing at the counter of Brasileira, I stretched out my arm, calling out to the waiter whose gaze was fixed on the opposite side of the room.

'Hey, boss! If you wouldn't mind . . .' called Quito Ribeiro and the waiter acknowledged him with a nod.

'I learned to do that during our lunch breaks at Mário Patrocínio's studio.'

'Senhor Ludomir did say you were a fast learner.' I laughed.

'I'm going to start using it back home whenever a waiter ignores me.'

'I'm sure you guys have a similar way of getting their attention.'

'Yes, but it's the way you do it.'

'Is that so?' I raised my eyebrow.

'Don't laugh.' He giggled. 'Best to do it assertively, but not too loud, because you don't want to be aggressive, and not too quiet, so you don't come across as too timid. The secret's being firm while also showing reverence for the person serving us. It always worked,' he said, waiting for my reply, but since I did in fact already know all the tricks, I kept quiet.

'Depending on our level of familiarity or degree of regularity at the place in question, we can add variations, kind of like "Hey, boss, don't forget about us," or appealing to the guy's Christian kindness, calling out to him, "Boss, for the love of God . . ."' he said with a proud smile.

'And if you're still getting ignored after all that, best just to seek out some other establishment,' I said, noticing that the waiter was about to attend to another customer who had come in after us. I held up my hand.

'Excuse me,' I said, and the waiter quickly appeared.

'I'm sorry,' he said with a broad grin.

'Sometimes just a louder version of the classic "Excuse me" will do,' I whispered to Quito Ribeiro.

The waiter was a compatriot of Quito's, a north-easterner, who while he was gathering up the crockery left by the previous customer was simultaneously wiping down the counter.

'Two bottles of Pedras Salgadas water,' said Quito, receiving a confirmatory nod from the waiter, who raced off without even noticing the German family next to us, one of whom had an arm up.

'What have you got waiting for you when you touch down in Rio?' I asked.

'A blank page and a pencil on top of a desk. I've been avoiding them for some time,' he said, after a long pause.

'Out of fear?' I pressed him, and he took even longer to respond.

'Four men go into a fancy restaurant in Lisbon, without a reservation, but the employee just asks them to wait at the bar till there's a table ready for them. They agree. The drinks they've been served aren't even half-finished when the waiter reappears, interrupts the lively conversation they're enjoying and leads them to their table. One of the best in the restaurant.' Quito paused, perhaps to retrieve a detail of the story. But I didn't wait for him to resume the thread.

'Are you going to write a movie?'

He smiled and picked up the story again.

'I was one of the four men.'

'So it's a documentary?' I insisted.

'I don't yet know what it's going to be. I have to start

writing first.' And he turned his eyes back to the collection of bottles displayed behind the counter, as if looking at the dozens of labels for an opening line.

'The situation could be totally banal and have no cinematographic merit at all – except it wasn't, not for me, because those four of us, we were all black. The only black people in that restaurant and nobody so much as glanced at us. And we were talking and laughing pretty loud too.' Quito looked me in the eye. 'In the city where I live, a situation like that, four relatively young black men in an expensive restaurant, laughing, eating and drinking, would be very rare if not impossible.'

I tried to reconstruct the picture in my head, knowing that nothing I said could get close to what Quito had just shared. I just listened.

'Maybe I'll never even get round to shooting it, but I wanted to do something, because the experience of a black man in a European capital like Lisbon, though it does have some crossover and some similarities, is so different from our experience in Brazil. And apart from the music, which travels really fast, the thoughts of black people never make it across the Atlantic.'

As I had nothing to add, I examined the labels of the bottles arranged in front of us.

'And you?' asked Quito.

I turned to find his dimples greeting me again.

'What awaits you when you wake up tomorrow morning?'

'Same as last week – college and dance classes and rehearsals for the Bratislava Kizomba Festival.'

'Bratislava, eh? Kizomba's going far!'

'Every day I get an invitation to some new festival or some gathering of kizomba-lovers.' I smiled. 'This year alone I've already visited Ljubljana, Prague, Minsk, Zurich, and after Bratislava I go on to Budapest, Warsaw and Stuttgart. Then Miami's next. It'll be my first time in America,' I said, as Quito Ribeiro listened to me with his lips on the verge of a smile.

'And when's Brazil going to be included in your world tour?' he asked.

I shrugged, but then, not wanting him to think I was avoiding the country because of him, I rushed to come up with something to suggest the contrary.

'I'd love to visit Rio in Carnival,' I said.

'Oh, you'd really enjoy it, I'm sure. Everybody's got to watch the samba school parades at least once in their life. But the real beauty of Carnival you find on the streets, far from the Sambadrome, in Rio's regular neighbourhoods. Improvised Carnival groups parading down the streets, and that, yeah, that really is an impressive sight!' he said, smiling widely.

'I've heard about those street parties, they last the whole Carnival month, right?'

'Yeah, and someone who dances as well as you would love it.'

I answered his compliment with a smile.

'Do you join the Carnival festivities?' I asked.

'In Rio, only for the first couple of years of living there.'

'That's too bad.'

'That's life, and nowadays, I prefer Carnival in Bahia.

Whenever you visit Brazil, if you get the chance, go to the Bahia Carnival too, and also now the Olinda one. You won't regret it, I promise you.'

I couldn't help laughing at this suggestion of so many different Carnival events.

'I'm not sure I've got the energy for all that. Let's start slow, one at a time, OK?'

'I got a question, something I'm curious about,' he said. I brought my elbow to the counter and rested my chin on my hand. 'How did kizomba end up in Eastern Europe?'

'You said it yourself: music travels fast. There's no way you can pin it down, besides which, there's this character by the name of Mestre Petchu, he's like this Yoda of kizomba,' I said.

Quito laughed but it was totally true. I went on: 'Most of the teachers—'

'Or Jedi,' Quito interrupted me.

'Yeah, or that . . . most of the ones who're teaching kizomba around the world learned from Mestre Petchu, here in Lisbon. And you're standing in front of one of his disciples.'

'So you're telling me I've had the honour of being introduced to the wonderful world of kizomba by the actual Obi-Wan Kizomba and nobody told me?'

I brushed some imaginary dust off my shoulders.

'All these *Star Wars* references are totally lost on me – I'm just plain Sofia. Or as my college friends call me, Sofia the Kizombeira.'

Quito couldn't contain himself when he heard my nickname. He did try not to laugh, but couldn't help it.

'It's what happens when you've got a name as common as mine,' I said.

Quito Ribeiro nodded.

'There are three Sofias in my class alone. Gothic Sofia, Sofia Auntie – the biggest society airhead in the class – and me, the kizomba one. All because one day somebody discovered a video of me dancing in front of a crowd of students at a kizomba workshop. They posted it on Facebook and I've had the nickname ever since. It doesn't bother me at all.'

'It's a cool nickname,' he said.

'When they start flooding me with annoying questions, I tell them kizomba's doing just fine, thank you. You thank people for their interest and continue on your way, unfazed, along the path of glory and popular acclaim.'

Quito stretched out his thin, bony fingers, took hold of his glass and raised it.

'A path without the interference or influence of the defenders of good taste.' I raised my water and clinked his glass.

'To bad taste,' he said.

'Cheesy people have hearts that beat inside them too.'

Quito took a gulp, but I saw the question forming in the line right in the middle of his forehead.

'*Tacky* people have hearts that beat in them too,' I rephrased my line. And he nodded his agreement. 'Anybody who's even slightly attentive to the ways of the people, of the disdained and the mocked, knows that what's kitsch or tacky today will be in fashion tomorrow,' I said.

'In Brazil we say "brega" for tacky.'

'And of course the opposite happens too. There's nothing I enjoy more than seeing clothing brands that for decades were synonymous with preppy-boys from Cascais, like Lacoste or Ralph Lauren, being adopted by my neighbours the rudeboys from the Sintra Line. The whole combo, sweatpants with the ends stuffed into their socks, Lacoste polo shirts and Air Max trainers, became the uniform of the rudeboy par excellence,' I said.

'You really think kizomba's tacky?' he asked.

'I do, but lots of other things are tacky too. Love, for example. When you verbalise it, there's no way you can stop it sounding kitsch, which is just a cooler way of saying tacky.'

Quito Ribeiro laughed.

In love, sounding tacky is a given, running away from that would be like betraying nature. What would happen to songs if every songwriter was scared of sounding tacky? He asked me to imagine Cartola tossing 'Roses Don't Speak' into the trash, for example, or Vinicius and Tom deciding not to write 'Girl from Ipanema' after all. 'It would do us good to be a bit more tacky,' he said.

We both looked at one another, astonished by its obviousness.

'We all need a bit more love, we need people to sing to us, to lull us to sleep, to cheer us up. There's nothing like a song to soothe us like a balm, to restore hope. Nothing like a song to draw us out of the dark, to raise us up off the ground, to shake off the dust,' he said.

'Nothing like a love song for teaching us to say sorry, to listen, to correct, to forgive,' I said.

'We need more love, though in Brazil, we'd probably say, "We need more love, *porra!*" for extra emphasis.'

'And in Portugal, a "We need more love, *caralho!*" might be punchier,' I replied.

Quito Ribeiro turned away, and went back to looking for words on the shelf of bottles behind the counter.

'Yeah, that'd get across the urgency of needing a mother-and-child type of love, a broad type of love, a foundational type of love, a guiding-star type of love that frees us from our sins, from blindness, from the absurd. A type of love that dries our tears and licks our wounds but doesn't hide our scars because they're every bit as useful to us as books ever were,' he said.

'Let's go hear some fado!' I said, and an enthusiastic Quito Ribeiro threw his arms in the air.

'*Oba*, let's go!'

XII

We were almost at Bairro Alto, where there are a lot of nice-for-the-tourists fado houses. But I wanted Quito to experience the real thing. So I decided to change tack, going down Rua Garrett to take him to Alfama. But it was still early. Not wanting us to be the only two people rattling around in the whole fado house, I decided to kill a bit of time, walking up to the Largo de São Cristovão to visit the studio of some musician friends. A place of creation that was christened The Sacristy because, according to the people who founded the space, concert halls are the temples, the places of worship, while The Sacristy's the place for meditation and prayer. Drawing parallels between religious cults and music proved not to be that hard, if I'm honest. To me, this similarity becomes even more obvious in nightclubs. It's no accident that Faithless's 'God Is a DJ' had the reach it did. Music is religion.

The Sacristy studio was hidden in a quiet street behind the church that gave the neighbourhood its name, São Cristovão. A proper little neighbourhood on the hill that looks out onto the São Jorge castle. We approached the door, a big iron plate that still showed some traces of a grey-blue that just went on resisting the implacable assault of rust. If you weren't intimately familiar with the guitar chords escaping through the cracks you wouldn't guess some of the great promises of new Portuguese music were behind that door. Maybe you'd think there was a workshop for retreading tyres or some other employment headed for extinction hidden behind it. It was nine at night and the street was already in its pyjamas and ready for bed. Inside some of those buildings, which the 1755 earthquake had spared from destruction, you would find, probably sitting in front of their TVs, people who are Lisboetas to the bone.

Inside the studio, behind the glass, Toty Sa'Med was bent over his guitar, contorting his fingers in search of an impossible chord. As we approached, Fred, the sound engineer, a man as young as the singer, turned towards me. Did I want my presence to be announced?

'Let him play,' I smiled, and, since I had Fred's attention, I gestured to turn up the volume on the speakers, to let the Angolan semba fill that Sacristy. A place where some of the most important names in the Portuguese musical landscape come to seek refuge and perfect their songs. I've read their names painted on the various instrument cases scattered around the space. Sara Tavares, Ana Moura, the Legendary Tigerman, Linda Martini. I wanted to let the semba take over the space, settle in, touch the bougainvillea sitting sadly in its vase, lounge across that old burgundy velvet couch or on one of the Turkish rugs. I wanted to let the voice of that Luandan lad carrying those sembas over from the old days – sembas my father used to sing me to sleep with in my crib – settle in and seduce Quito Ribeiro.

The sound engineer, noticing me humming along to the lines we were hearing, turned back to me again. He wanted to know what language it was and if it was an original song.

'The language is Quimbundo, and the song's "Belina",' I said and turned to Quito Ribeiro, adding in a whisper, 'it's one of the classics from the late Artur Nunes.'

There are some songs I've related to long before I could have really known them. The songs of my life started to become a part of me well before I realised that's what they would be. They were always present, in record form, waiting for me finally to wake up to life and carry them with me to the ends of the earth. Forever. I felt Quito Ribeiro knew what that was like because I could feel the same love for music in him.

'Which record would you save from a fire?'

He scratched his head, gave me a long *hmmm* as an answer and looked into my eyes. Without blinking, with my chest brimming with pride, I declared, 'Mine is *Monangambé and Other Angolan Songs* by Ruy Mingas.'

Toty Sa'Med waved hello from behind the glass and

gestured to the sound engineer that he was ready to record. I've always been fascinated by the space where music happens. Kalaf used to invite me to rooms like that. Some smelled of leather sofas, and others stank of cigarettes, each with its own magic nourished by the people who occupied them – the musicians. I saw some who prefer to start the act of creation first thing in the morning, others at nightfall. Some need a pizza before anything, and others have got to start by burning some incense.

'Once, I met a singer who could only record while dressed in white from head to toe,' I said to Quito.

'White, among other things, repels negative energy and heightens the vibrations; it stimulates memory,' he replied.

XIII

Quito Ribeiro snapped a photo with his mobile phone as we walked through Alfama, the neighbourhood whose very name is synonymous with fado. Despite the narrowness of the streets, the street lamps, with their orange-tinted light, were not strong enough to dissipate all the shadows covering the sidewalk. The wind made that September night chillier than I'd expected, and we'd both come out wearing only T-shirts. I tucked mine inside my jeans. Quito Ribeiro had his flapping over his skinny torso like the garments hanging from clotheslines on the facades of the buildings that he was scrutinising.

'They look like flags,' he said, snapping another photo. 'This part of Lisbon feels like a truer Lisbon,' he added, getting ready to take another picture. 'Sorry for the cliché.'

I smiled when I saw him taking a shot of a building covered with tiles.

'I guess you guys must be tired of hearing tourists saying that,' he said, hiding the phone in his jeans.

'Do you want me to take your picture?' I offered, and he smiled.

'Let's take one together?' he asked. 'That would make me feel less of a tourist.'

'Sure,' I said.

I moved closer to him, and we stood under a street lamp. I put my arm on his waist, and he draped his over my shoulders. Before the click, we jostled towards the light to get a better picture. I could see his goosebumps. I wanted to apologise for the weather, rub his arms, and then we could face the cold together, walking the rest of the way with arms around each other, but instead, I joined him, making goofy grimaces at the camera lens and laughing out loud when he showed me the pictures. We looked like a couple who'd just got a spray tan. When we arrived at Parreirinha de Alfama, a fado house located at Beco do Espírito Santo, all the tables were occupied, so we took the only two available chairs, at the table of a French couple. We laughed every time we looked at each other, recalling our orange faces, until the French couple frowned at us, saying, 'Quiet now, they're going to sing fado.'

XIV

That voice – it hypnotised us. A woman with her hand outstretched, eyes shut, as if the audience didn't even exist.

Like she was possessed, and the black shawl covering her shoulders was heavy as lead and was a sign of the deepest mourning. The fadista's voice reached us with a tremble, on the verge of cracking, such was the pain that coloured her song, this musical lament of misfortune.

'This house is Dona Argentina Santos's,' I whispered in Quito Ribeiro's ear, as I pointed discreetly at the little old lady sitting beside the bar. 'She started out as a cook in this restaurant and she's been running it herself since the 1950s. She's eighty-eight now.'

The Frenchman with whom we shared the table brought his finger to his lips, reminding me again of the golden rule in fado houses: while somebody is singing, silence reigns. A tradition that dates from the time when fado still lived in the mouths of sailors, prostitutes and rogues. Since the police didn't have much tolerance for that sort of trouble, the nights always ended in a brawl, so when the noisiest establishments started to get threatened with closure, they began to ask for silence during the musical numbers so as not to wake the neighbours who might call the officers of the law. The audience, maybe because they didn't want to have to drink without musical entertainment, got into the habit of policing themselves. It's a habit that persists to this day. I smiled my acknowledgement and, apologising, waited for the fadista to finish.

'You know when Mr Ludomir danced it in our living room?' I asked Quito a few minutes later, and he nodded. 'He was actually dancing lundum, the genre that preceded fado. And we have to thank Brazil for that.' His eyes widened. 'When Dom João VI and the Portuguese court returned from Brazil in 1821, they brought this music.'

'You're telling me fado was invented in my country?'

I nodded.

'And lundum drew inspiration from the drumming of the Bantu slaves brought over from Angola.'

'It's hard to imagine this music with African drums,' he whispered. 'I'm just being honest.'

'Sometimes, I wonder how fado would be perceived if it had kept lundum alive. The dance was very sexual, with lots of belly-bumps, swaying of hips mixed with Iberian dances and finger clicking.'

'Almost like an ancient kizomba,' he observed.

'Right, and just like kizomba, the lower classes living in poor riverfront neighbourhoods like Alfama were the ones who made it cool.'

'And when did all the sexiness disappear, leaving only the tears?'

'Well, not everyone who studies fado goes along with this theory. To some people, connecting the origins of fado to Brazil and the culture clash between the enslaved Bantu people and the Portuguese aristocracy living in exile in Rio de Janeiro is total blasphemy.'

Quito Ribeiro smiled and gestured a brain explosion with his hands.

'My dream . . .' Noticing that I paused to look at the French couple again, Quito Ribeiro leaned even closer so I could continue whispering in his ear. 'The thesis I'm writing looks at the points of connection between the massemba – the dance associated with the Angolan semba (the father of kizomba) – and lundum that is still alive in Brazil in a place called Quissamã, but I can tell you more when we leave this place.'

Quito Ribeiro glanced at the French couple, who were looking increasingly annoyed.

'Ah, I'd like to read that thesis,' he said.

'Well, I still have a long way to go.' I smiled at him.

'Shall we —' Quito was about to invite me to do something when the second fadista came onto the stage. A middle-aged man, in a suit and tie, guitar under his arm, looking like a nice little old granddad, a João Gilberto type. His Lisbon accent held a voice that was mature but didn't seem to fit with his age. If you closed your eyes you'd guess the fadista before us had only about thirty years of life in his throat.

I leaned over to Quito and asked, in a whisper, 'What were you about to say?' '*Sssssssshhhhhhhhhhhhhhh*,' went the French couple next to us, with a threatening look, fed up of our little secrets. The two of us laughed, apologising, and Quito gestured, with a smile and a slight shake of his head, that what he had to say wasn't all that important.

And that's when everything suddenly looked very clear to me and I brought the red wine to my lips. Quito leaned over towards me again and whispered an invitation: 'I think your fado is great and I'd really like to be the one to take you to Quissamã.'

I smiled awkwardly and took another sip of wine, looking away towards Dona Argentina, the diva of the more heartfelt type of fado, who was sitting quietly in her little corner. In her silence, she gave life to the objects scattered around the walls of the room. The low ceilings, the altar to Our Lady of Fátima, the bust of Amália Rodrigues, the grapes, the vine leaves and the jugs of wine, a small extension of the galleries of the Fado Museum just yards from where we sat.

And when my eyes met Quito's again, he was still in the same position, looking at me. With a mixture of curiosity and a drop of fear. Who knows, maybe it wasn't fear, maybe the fear was mine and I was trying to find some excuse not to admit I *liked* the way he looked at me. And since *fado* also means *fate*, could this Bahia boy, with a smile on his face, be determining the start of mine? This question formed only in my thoughts, but it seemed to have reached Quito Ribeiro somehow too, and he gave me his hand. We surrendered, at last, to the silence.

XV

The French couple got up and walked off, leaving us alone at the table, holding hands, and Quito ventured a 'Sofia . . .' I was nervous and did what I always do when I don't know what to do: I started jabbering away ten-to-the-dozen. And I was ready to do just that, to pour out a century of fado history all at once just to calm the butterflies in my stomach, when he looked directly at me as if reading what was going on in my soul.

'You know, fado actually went through an aristocratic phase . . .' I said, but he didn't listen.

'What would've happened if we'd met in my first week over here?' he asked and I chose to respond with a question: 'Would we be here now?' He must have found this funny because he quickly adopted the same strategy: 'Would we have danced?' It was obvious we didn't have answers to any of these questions. 'I don't know what Lisbon has in store for us, but whatever it is, this meeting of ours was already worth it,' he said, with his eyes, with his lips, with that accent of his that curled around our language like a sea forming a wave before it breaks on the beach. I don't know the sea in Bahia, but I imagine it's got to be beautiful and musical, given the number of songs Dorival Caymmi devoted to it.

I nodded, agreeing but not knowing what else to say. I raised my glass again and remembered: when I'm nervous, either I talk too much or I can calm myself down by dancing. He was looking at me as though waiting for me to return his gaze. I put down my glass, and when I didn't feel I could postpone it any longer, I turned to face him and said: 'Either we ask for another jug of wine or we go find someplace to dance.'

'Let's dance.'

XVI

The question that first brought us together hadn't stopped echoing within him. Who invented kizomba? He still wanted to know. I resisted the impulse to answer like a would-be anthropologist and, before inviting him to take the long way round, it occurred to me: what if I answered that kizomba *hadn't* been invented? How close would we be to the truth then? Yes, that's it, my sweet Bahian, kizomba just happened in the hands and feet of those people who danced it for the first time. At the moment when the magic occurred, they weren't thinking about how they were inventing anything at all. They were just dancing.

Outside the Fado Museum we stood waiting for a taxi, once again in silence. 'There are other options,' I said after a while. Quito laughed and looked at me.

'We could walk another few metres and go to Lux, a house and techno club. We'll probably find Mário Patrocí-nio there, or Kalaf, maybe even both – they love that club. We could also look for other places. But for that, we'd have to head over towards São Bento.' Quito was thoughtful for a few moments. I don't think meeting up with Mário and Kalaf was quite what he had in mind.

'São Bento,' he replied, preventing us from lapsing back into silence. 'Thank you for showing me your city,' he added.

'No need to thank me. In exchange you'll just have to show me Rio when I go there,' I said.

'I'll be offended if you don't look me up,' he said. 'I'll take you to all the classics. You know that in the two weeks I've been here I haven't had time to see the museums, monuments, parks, the iconic neighbourhoods. I haven't visited Madragoa or Pastéis de Belém.'

I stopped him in the middle of the street. 'Quito Ribeiro, are you telling me you haven't tasted pastéis de nata?'

He laughed. 'Only in a café in Baixa. But I've been told I need to try those ancestral ones, which have got some special recipe, right?'

'Well, one more reason right there for you to come

back.' And then, without waiting for his reply, I asked him, 'What else could bring you back here?'

'You,' he answered at once.

I smiled and considered telling him to stay longer, not to leave tomorrow. But during a flirtation, what comes out of my mouth is rarely what I'm actually thinking, so I just said, innocently: 'Me? But Quito Ribeiro, I'm a married woman!' And we both burst out laughing.

We were outside number 73 Poço dos Negros.

'This was where my parents met,' I told him with a smile, my eyes fixed on the building's facade. For me, those four floors are like a monument raised to my parents' love.

'Oh, and after telling me that semba is this thing or that thing and about how kizomba's on a course to conquer the world, now you're going to tell me about your parents' love, are you? Well, let's see if you can still manage the same certainty and level of detail there, little Miss Anthropologist,' Quito teased me.

'It all began in the small hours of a December morning. Neither one of them, both living the bohemian life, can remember where they were coming from that night, whether it was from Noites Longas, from Zé da Guiné and Hernâni Miguel, or from the Almada Carvalhais palace, the first B.Leza, after it was Baile . . .' I said, trying my best to recount the narrative as eloquently as the historian José Hermano Saraiva would have done.

'I heard the story of Zé da Guiné in Rio,' Quito said.

'Well, I'll bet they didn't tell it to you with all the details I know. But if you already know about them, let's go on.' I turned to face the facade again. 'So anyway, this place was the home of Ti Lina and Dona Alda, two women from São Vicente who changed the way Lisboetas end their nights when they opened their doors to any compatriots who wanted to stop by, serving bowls of cachupa and a few typical Cape Verdean savoury snacks.'

Quito Ribeiro took out his phone and snapped a photo of the building.

'The restaurant was totally illegal but got more popular as the news spread from mouth to mouth and soon became the place where bohemian Lisboetas would start or end their nights,' I said and turned to find him pointing his camera at me. I couldn't help laughing.

'As I was saying, people considered it one of the first African cultural centres. Actually, the São Bento neighbourhood is regarded as the tenth island of the Cape Verde archipelago.'

Quito took a step back to inspect the street and its collection of decadent buildings, and since no cars were passing at that time of the evening, I joined him.

'There are very few tourists, or indeed even Lisboetas, who have any idea that the Largo Dr António de Sousa Macedo,' I said, pointing to the corner where the rails of the no. 28 tram come together, 'that point there, is also known as the Creole triangle.'

He took another picture and I pulled him to follow me down the street.

'That's the city I'm interested in knowing,' he said.

'Successive waves of African migrants have passed through these steep, crooked alleyways, but you really don't notice it right away. You need to look carefully.'

'It's not in the guidebooks.'

'Only academics are interested in this kind of stuff.' I smiled. 'The first Cape Verdeans, who started arriving in the 1960s, had suitcases filled with dreams of a better life, and once they'd disembarked here, they scattered around the floors of these small buildings, embedding themselves into a popular narrative woven over the centuries . . .'

Quito interrupted, reminding me: 'Sofia, the story of your parents.'

'OK, OK. It's just we're not far from the place that was the starting point for the African presence in this city. I thought it was important to tell you that. Anyway,' I said, sulkily, 'basically my parents met dancing.'

'Oh, go on, tell the story properly now. Plus it starts like ours,' said Quito.

'Sure – sorry. So, early that December morning, coming from someplace or other they can't remember, they ran into one another at Ti Lina and Dona Alda's house. Neither one of them had noticed the other when, all of a sudden, the radio, which usually only played mornas and koladeras, started playing a Paulo Flores song, "Kapuete Kamundanda". They both got to their feet at almost exactly the same moment . . .'

'Aaah – so awesome. And so then they started to dance, right?' Quito said. I looked at him, amused.

'May I finish my story?' And I went on: 'My father was dancing and my mother was singing.' And I started to imitate my mom's dancing, singing what words I knew, closing my eyes, the same way my mom closes hers whenever a song really gets to her. With my eyes still closed and

whistling the melody of what is one of the first songs to
bear the sign of kizomba, and knowing how narrow that
pavement was, I pulled Quito out into the middle of the
road, dancing with him as if we were also in Ti Lina and
Dona Alda's living room.

'When each became aware of the other's presence,
they both asked the same question – "Angola?" – not
expecting an answer. There was no need, only an Angolan
would make such a fuss at finding a compatriot in a Cape
Verdean enclave.'

Quito Ribeiro burst out laughing.

'They threw themselves into each other's arms and
they're still in that same dance today. The end.'

Quito looked back at the facade of the building and
I put my arm through his, inviting him to continue our
walk.

XVII

We entered the first floor of a half-abandoned building
on the corner of Rua Boqueirão Ferreiros and Rua da
Boavista. An improvised bar on the same floor as the
studio-slash-rehearsal-room that the choreographer and
dancer Avelino Chantre lends out to some kizomba DJs
for organising parties – or, as they casually prefer to call
them, 'get-togethers'. A refuge where lots of Lisbon's
new bohemians stop by for one last glass, one final dance
before they consider the night finished. In the living room,
on one side, the girls holding their glasses of Fanta and
Amarula formed little groups round the edge of the dance

floor. Though the atmosphere was much more relaxed than at the African discos, that didn't stop them from wearing their miniskirts, Tchuna Baby shorts and crop tops. Their necks and wrists exuded the Frenchest of perfumes. Their beautifully done hair added to the kaleidoscope of fragrances; so much richness that it would take a Jean-Baptiste Grenouille to decipher and map all its layers of odours. The guys, totally nonchalant, wandered about the space triumphantly, halfway between a recce and pure exhibitionism. Kind of ridiculous, I had to admit. Starched shirts, shoes without socks, capri pants showing their ankles. They always end up near the bar, smiling at the gorgeous employee who never responded to their pick-up lines. They drank beer, and whisky and Cokes.

The women marked the tempo, one-two-one-two, to the rhythm of the music, undulating their waists gently, never taking their eyes off the dance floor where couples danced slowly together, drowning in each other's arms, waiting for a man to be bold enough to approach them with an invitation for a dance. Rouge-lipsticked mouths hummed along with the romantic lines coming out of the speakers. The guys, acting 'too cool for school', as they used to say, kept their eyes on the area on the edge of the dance floor, trying to decipher, in the gloom, which girl they were going to extend an invitation to. They studied their movements as attentively as any officer of the Judicial Police. The moment a song began, the man positioned himself in front of the lady he had in his sights and, without speaking so much as a comma, launched himself into a game of well-rehearsed glances and movements. An economy of gestures, perfected over the course of a whole childhood spent in yard parties, watching the old guys in the salon in their nostalgic semba, and also, of course, taking gulps from the glasses of beer that had been left unattended at their mercy.

I nudged Quito to pay attention and watch how things were about to unfold. The woman in question took a step towards the young man, and he, victorious, walked to the dance floor casting his eyes round him like a glad-iator in the middle of the Colosseum, before settling his gaze on her and spreading his arms. The minutes that followed were of the utmost importance. Each ended up dancing with others throughout that night, but that first dance defined what sort of night they would have. There was something sexual about it, but it was not what you usually see between two lovers before coitus. While they danced, they became one. They were not interested in what was happening around them, they were on their own planet, and they danced like nobody was watching them, as if the room was empty. Those out of the game didn't hide our admiration and a touch of jealousy that it wasn't us in those arms, dancing those steps and loving that music the way only a good dancer can really love a song.

'It looks like when you're in the middle of the room, even if you seem to be only focused on your partner, there's this whole collective choreography everyone seems to follow, a code of movement, right?' Quito asked.

'Yes,' I answered. 'The space available for dancing is tiny, but everyone can guess at the movement of the couple next to them and they design their own moves in the space the other couple has just left – you've got to avoid knocking shoulders at all costs.'

It was such a lovely sight, a crowd of bodies tangled up together, dancing in a rhythmic softness, unfolding into an economy of almost frayed steps. The man, virtually motionless, the woman with her waist glued to her partner, spinning slowly, copying the movements of sex.

Quito Ribeiro looked at me when he noticed the movement of the dancers becoming more explicit.

'So, that's the tarraxinha, Quito Ribeiro,' I laughed, 'kizomba's cheekiest relative.' The dance goes way beyond the limits of eroticism that generally apply to ballroom dances in Africa. Because of its alleged 'semi-pornographic' movements, the tarraxinha was essentially banned to preserve good manners and the decency of 'family girls'. I pulled Quito out onto the dance floor, and without me needing to show him the way, he put his hands in the right place, on the curve of my waist.

'Let's do it,' I said. 'The names of the steps are very instructive.'

'I don't know if I'm ready,' he protested.

'The first step we call washing the clothes,' I whispered as I used my hips to describe the movement of washing clothes by hand in a sink. 'The second, the weathervane.' I spun my waist from left to right. 'The little square, which comes third, is where you draw a square with your hips,' I said, and he sighed. 'And finally, the serpent. That's the most unnerving of all the tarraxinha's movements, based on the sliding of a snake.'

By the time we parted after three tarraxos songs, it felt like the room had doubled in temperature.

'Drinks?' He pointed at the bar.

I nodded and he followed me there.

'How do the men manage it?' he asked while we waited for our drinks.

'I think you're biologically better qualified to answer that question,' I laughed.

'Seriously, Sofia,' he said, 'if those first three steps don't leave the guys with a hard-on, the serpent's *definitely* going to do it!'

'And?' I asked.

He smiled and dodged the question, saved by the bartender who had placed our drinks in front of us.

'Some women take it personally,' I said, taking the glass he handed me. 'It offends them if, after a tarraxinha, their partner doesn't show any signs of satisfaction down in his flies,' I added, laughing, as if by way of warning.

We toasted, took a sip of our drinks and looked over to the dance floor.

'To answer your question,' he said, turning towards me. 'Yeah, I know – men are so fucking predictable.' I laughed even more.

'But hey, I'll tell you a little trick. If a guy doesn't want to have to leave the room with the flag raised, he's just got to recite to himself the names of all the players on every Brazilian football team who's won the World Cup, starting with the 1958 cup, then 1962, 1970 then 1994 with Saint Romário in charge, not forgetting the 2002 one that made us five-time champions.'

'I'm flattered,' I joked.

Quito smiled and let his gaze wander over to the couples dancing in the middle of the room. And I asked myself, what sort of man was this Quito Ribeiro? Perhaps he was wondering about me, too. I knew these were his last hours in Lisbon, but all the same, I wanted to see if he was really as shy as he seemed. Or maybe he was just reserved. Knowing how to manage our social performance is often the key to success in this game of flirting. I knew how crucial it was to be patient and how to deal healthily with nervous anticipation and expectation. On the other hand, a fear of rejection could also look like a lack of courage. Navigating that whole sea of insecurities and indecisions can be emotionally costly. To put it another way, attempting seduction is not a cheap sport.

As he turned his eyes back to mine, the DJ put on one of Fofandó's kuduros. We moved over to the edge of the dance floor, where a circle was forming of people watching and applauding a group of dancers as they unfolded into acrobatics, each more spectacular than the next.

'The last two weeks of my life have been spent totally absorbed by this universe,' Quito Ribeiro said with an ear-to-ear grin. 'A thousand times better seeing it live, I'll admit.'

'I'm glad you were able to experience it before leaving the city.'

'It's like the characters from the movie are right here and like we're in Luanda, and at some point, we will see the kuduristas Nagrelha or Titica, or Príncipe Ouro Negro and Presidente Gasolina will pop up.'

'If those people appeared here, I would lose my mind,' I laughed.

'But why isn't kuduro huge?' he asked, turning to me. 'What's missing?'

I shrugged.

He went on: 'When you search for kuduro on YouTube, the first thing that comes up is "Danza Kuduro", by Don Omar with Lucenzo.'

'And that's gringo kuduro,' I said. 'The only other video that comes close is "Sound of Kuduro" by Buraka Som Sistema.'

'And why is that?' Quito took a sip of his drink, pensively. 'Lack of investment from record companies?'

'That too,' I said, 'but mainly because nobody really gets kuduro, not even the platforms supposed to get it.'

'Same happens with most of the music born in the outskirts of the big Brazilian cities,' he said. 'Poor people's music, black people's music, favela music.'

'Yeah, the problem is not exclusive to kuduro,' I replied.

We both shrugged.

'Hey, do you remember the theme song of that TV soap, *Avenida Brasil*?' I asked.

'Oh, vaguely – why?'

'About a year ago, I met a Brazilian ballroom-dancing promotor at a kizomba workshop in Budapest. He sent me an e-mail the day the soap was premiering, saying he wanted to take kuduro artists to Brazil because the opening song was a kuduro.'

'Seriously? And did you?'

'Course not. I'm just a dance teacher. I don't know anything about promotion or agenting artists,' I said, laughing. 'But the mistake needed correcting. The song was inspired by "Danza Kuduro".'

Quito laughed.

'If the DJ played that song here at this party, people would throw drinks in his face.'

'I'm really sorry TV Globo picked the Lucenzo and not Titica.'

'Wouldn't that be amazing?' I smiled and gestured the headline with my fingers. 'A song by Titica, an Angolan transgender kudurista, opening the prime-time telenovela.'

'That would have been revolutionary in Brazil,' he said.

The DJ switched the music back to kizomba, and the couples rushed back onto the dance floor. Quito Ribeiro and I stood there watching them, savouring our drinks unhurriedly.

'Kizomba is nourishment,' I said, leaning slightly over him. 'But the musical genre that best reflects that frantic, prosperous, colourful, desirable, misunderstood, totally contradictory urgency of the new Angola and its people – that's got to be kuduro.'

XVIII

When we came out onto the street, day was almost breaking. We got into the first taxi that appeared which dropped us at Pastéis de Belém. Since the bakery was still closed, we went to take a look at the Jerónimos Monastery. The sidewalks were practically deserted. If you don't count the occasional cars going up and down the avenue, the only living souls in that corner of the city were the rubbish collectors. We went on walking and crossed the gardens of Praça do Império, heading towards the Navigators monument, before plunging into the level crossing that connects Avenida da Índia to Avenida Brasília. I stopped to look at the eternal Tagus. I couldn't help myself saying: 'The river that brought us Africa.'

We stood there in silence a few moments.

'But wasn't it the Algarve where the first slaves landed?' he asked.

'Well, yeah, in Lagos, but I'm not from the Algarve, I'm a Lisboeta. To me, Africa arrived on this river and emptied onto this bank,' I said.

His eyes scanned the view, starting at the bridge and ending at the Belém Tower.

'Of course it's not the same Lisbon any more, and that's just as well! But the city I commemorate began the moment the Africans disembarked into this Sea of Straw.' We stepped onto the compass rose in front of the imposing Monument of the Discoveries.

'This place marks the start of our Brazilian-Portuguese relationship,' I said.

'Oh, so this is the Restelo beach, where Pedro Álvares Cabral's three caravels set sail?' he asked, eyes fixed on the waters of the Tagus as if searching for traces of that time.

I pointed to the mouth of the river and told him that was the precise point.

'Have you had a good night?' I asked, my voice cracking, showing signs of tiredness.

'God, Sofia, I loved it!' he replied. 'Much more than I
could have imagined.'

'What did you expect?' I asked.

He smiled and offered me his arm, and I put mine
through it like we'd done on the way out of the fado place.
A repeated movement but, like that first time, one that
surprised me with how everything with us just flowed. I
didn't have the nerve to exchange the feeling for words,
but this was how long friendships and great loves begin.
Maybe I wouldn't regret it if I did share some of the
things that were going through my head, starting with
that 'beginning of a long friendship' thought, but when I'd
finally filled my lungs ready to speak, he did the same and
our words, my 'You know . . .' and his 'Today . . .' tumbled
over each other, twice, interspersed with laughter. Until he
suggested I might want to take the lead.

'Very kind of you, Senhor Ribeiro,' I said, offering him
a small bow, a light tip of my head.

'Please,' he said, 'I insist.'

But I felt I'd lost my bearings, so – scared to make the
moment awkward – I rushed to fish out another subject.

'I didn't teach you how to steer your dance partner to
the side, in kizomba, did I?'

'Now we're out of the club, you ask me that?' he
laughed, looking at me in amazement.

He was totally right. Dance has always been my comfort zone.

'We ended up only dancing tarraxinha. We never got the

chance,' I said, taking his hand and putting my other arm around his shoulders.

'We don't have any music,' he said.

'You're just going to have to feel it.' I smiled.

And we started with the basic step. I kept giving him instructions, making it easier for him to follow the movements, but I tried not to turn the moment into a dance lesson.

'One, two, three, four, step forward, five, six, step back, seven, eight. Exit for the lady, one, two, and round, three, four, a step for the lady, five and six,' I mumbled and then pressured his shoulder slightly. 'Exit for the gentleman and seven and eight.' Our knees clashed. He stopped and scratched the back of his head, embarrassed.

'I feel totally lost, Sofia.' I smiled, but he insisted: 'The counting, the numbers, all these geometric steps, they sound like the calculations for launching a rocket into space.'

'I'm sorry.'

'No,' he said, 'can we just try it without numbers?'

He moved towards me but stopped before taking my hand.

'I swear I'll shut up. We've still got a lot to say to each other in silence,' he said, smiling. 'But has it ever occurred to you it might have been the Infante Dom Henrique who's responsible for the invention of kizomba?'

'What?' I cracked up.

'Since it was under him, in Lagos in 1444, they auctioned more than two hundred men, women and children – blacks,' he said.

I pulled myself together.

'Oh, I wouldn't go that far. About ten minutes' walk from here, there's a man asleep who, I would say, created the conditions for kizomba and all its musical ramifications to develop in the amazing way it did,' I said, pointing to the direction of the Belém Palace. 'His name is Aníbal Cavaco Silva.'

'What – your president of the Republic?' He widened his eyes.

'Yeah, him!' I laughed. 'Kalaf and I like to play around with that theory. The fate of kizomba was written on the 5th of November 1985. The day he became prime minister.'

'You even have a date.' Quito Ribeiro laughed.

'His government was responsible for the policies to eliminate the slum housing, and therefore for the re-accommodating of those low-income families, many of African origin, in areas of social housing.'

'I get your point.'

'And in parallel with that, shopping malls started to spring up and multiply, giving work opportunities for many young people from those social housing neighbour-hoods, including me.'

'But what about the music, the zouk from the Antilles and Angolan semba?' he asked.

'I'm not saying that was Cavaco Silva's aim. I'm sure it wasn't. But you can say the same thing about his gov-ernment that you say about Pedro Álvares Cabral: he was headed for India, and he ended up in Brazil. Or even what you say about Christopher Columbus.'

'I will have to get a good night's sleep before I can debate your theory properly.'

'Joking aside, my point is that Cavaco Silva accidentally gave us the missing ingredient to make kizomba the most amazing musical genre by gathering us together in the same space.'

'What ingredient, if I may ask?'

'Us,' I said smiling. 'Kizomba would be bigger than fado.'

'Oh! That I believe without any shadow of a doubt.'

Quito smiled, rubbed his hands and shook off his nerves. He gestured for me to come closer, and I offered no resistance.

'Listen to the music that's inside you,' I said. 'Kizomba isn't about the steps, it's the joy that fills you when you dance.' He took a deep breath and put his arms around me again. He felt lighter. One, two, and out. Our feet slid across the map of the world engraved in the centre of this compass rose. When our bodies came back together, his lips found mine.

'You are the joy that fills me, Sofia. I've known since the moment our eyes first met.'

PART III

NORWAY

9 AUGUST 2008

Like Duke Ellington taught us, so long as something
sounds good and feels good, well, then it is.
And that's all we need.

—Eyvind

I

Mari Gunnhild was standing in the chief inspector's office, watching the planes coming in to land at Rygge airport. From my desk I could see them both in that fishbowl, her with her back to me, him with his eyes on the report we'd just written. In the corner of the window, a Ryanair Boeing 737 touched down, almost as if it had dropped out of nowhere.

She's not young any more, and it's hard to describe her beauty exactly. The curve of her neck is quite attractive, and her eyes are alert and friendly. She never wears make-up. Her fashion choices consist of a pair of bell-bottomed jeans with a tight-fitting T-shirt, to show off her arm muscles, which some people might not think very attractive or feminine but that's not how I see it. Her still-adolescent face rescues all the femininity that her muscular body tries to hide.

The chief inspector was moving his lips, she stepped away from the window, turned towards him and offered a few words. I couldn't hear the conversation, but I could imagine what each one was saying. I've been there myself plenty of times; I know that particular script by heart. The inspector would start by asking if the arrested man had any narcotics on him. She'd answer no. Then he'd ask if he resisted at all. She'd answer no again. Since the individual claims to be an Angolan national, the chief inspector would find that fact strange. When I looked at the expired passport he showed us when we pulled him off the bus, I thought it odd. African immigrants outside of the countries in the Horn of Africa don't show up often in these parts without a valid passport. But there he was, an Angolan national who looked to be about twenty-five or twenty-six. He wore a pair of raw selvedge denim jeans, a grey hoodie, headphones covering one of his ears and had a backpack occupying the vacant seat next to him. At first, he was reticent, speaking in a deep soft voice as if all that politeness would make his story more believable. Then, as he handed over his documents, his eyes shifted. He became more defiant. Having hit the end of the road, his pride was now non-negotiable, despite having been caught breaking the law. I didn't want to assume his innocence right there and then, but that kind of boldness is something we don't encounter every day at the border.

The boss handed her one of the pages from the report. He stretched out his arm to gesture to one of the chairs across the desk from him. She looked at them for a few seconds, and I knew what she was thinking right then. Those are the chairs no officer ever wants to sit in. When the inspector tells you to sit in one of those, you're never leaving that fishbowl with good news. Before sitting down she threw me a hard stare through the window. It's a look that said 'This is going to go to shit – and *you're* the one who should be in this chair.' Mari's a woman of action, the write-ups and admin always got left to me. We had a deal. She'd cover for me when I arrived late. Not that I'm in the habit of arriving late, but from time to time I do like going out to hear music and it's happened that on a couple of mornings I didn't hear my alarm. OK, more than a couple of mornings. So to thank her for all the times she saved my ass, I offered to write all our reports. And to present them too. But since the incident, the inspector's been keeping an eye on me, suspicious of anything I write.

Two winters ago, we arrested a group of illegal immigrants who'd come in from Eritrea. We did exactly what was required of us. If they don't show their documents, we send them to the detention centre – nothing unusual about that. But then the inspector called me into the fishbowl and made me sit in that same chair Mari found herself in. He started out by asking if I knew that the girl travelling with this group was a minor. I said I'd asked and she told me she was sixteen but she might have been lying. She didn't have any documents on her to prove her age. I know exactly what processes I'm supposed to follow, I said. We send on to the centres any applicants for international protection subject to the procedures in the Dublin Regulation, those whose claims for family reunification have been turned down and also those people stopped at the border, to prevent their illegal entry. The inspector got irritated and said he did not need a lesson on our country's immigration law from me. And that's when he stood up, walked over to the window, watched a Norwegian Air Boeing take off and said that the kid from Eritrea had killed herself. She was pregnant, he said. The autopsy report was on his desk. He also said there was going to be an internal investigation. He sent me home that same afternoon. When Mari saw me come out the fishbowl, pick up my jacket and my thermos of coffee, she thought we were about to be sent off on some mission. I didn't say a word.

In the days that followed my conversation with the inspector, I had a dream that would be repeated for weeks on end. I dreamed about the young Eritrean girl. Her song kept coming back to me, the one she sang in the hours she spent locked up in the station. In the same cell where the Angolan guy was now. A sad song, in her language, which seeped into my skin, under my nails and into my scalp. The investigation didn't find anybody culpable. Not the guards, not the assistants at the asylum service, not me. There's no way we could have predicted what would happen. Maybe they should send psychologists to the front line. More sensitive people to do the dirty work of hunting down the illegals trying to get across our borders.

To this day I still hear that girl's voice and her song, that same song. I thought about seeing a psychologist, but I was scared they'd diagnose me with something that would make it impossible for me to do my job. I like being a police officer, I come from a family of police officers. My granddad, my dad, my brother, they all wore the uniform before me. And I do love this shit. Except the coffee. All the rest of it I love. Even writing reports.

II

If you want to understand things, you've got to know how to talk to yourself.

I spent the days that followed the upheavals at the refugee centre in total silence. I shut myself up at home and disconnected the phone. I spent my time looking out the window at an old oak losing its leaves as every thermometer in Oslo plummeted to glacial temperatures. I just sat there enjoying watching the sunlight as it slipped away to play hide-and-seek, seeing the night arrive all of a sudden, every day earlier than the day before. And even when it was raining, the light still didn't deign to leave the stage, staying as long as there were clouds for it to nestle in. I was missing work so much I thought the boredom would drive me mad. When I got sick of the window, I turned on the TV. The same faces, the same news – refugees, refugees . . . Whenever a conflict breaks out on some corner of the planet, within two or three weeks we've got them hopping over our borders. I can tell from the news who's going to be coming. Iraqis, Russians, Congolese, Eritreans.

When they fall into my hands, I do like making things very clear to them, telling them that more than half will be sent back. Still, it's worth their risk if the place they have to go back to isn't an option. I know a lot of them will succumb to the temptation to skip to another country, but don't even try it – I like telling them that. The first thing we're going to do is take your fingerprints, and that'll allow us to follow your tracks and know when you request asylum in some other European country. And they'll lie in their interviews, saying oh, it's their first time applying. They always lie. Asylum seekers don't get it, that they're only allowed to ask once. Our system's all interconnected. True, it doesn't always work brilliantly, but when it does work, they get sent back to the country where they requested asylum for the first time. And when this happens, they lose any right to stay and are immediately repatriated. What these asylum seekers also don't normally know is that, even when they are granted asylum, they can still be sent home at any moment, once the situation in their country of origin has got back to normal, like what happened to those refugees who were victims of the war in Kosovo.

I've had it up to here with those tie-wearing commentators endlessly spouting their tedious statistics. Always the same old nauseating refrain. A total of 1,300 refugees were accepted for 'settlement' in Norway in 2007. And whose fault is that? Ours! Us, the police, it's because *we* let them through. Some moderate affirmative action for immigrants who apply for posts in public administration is going to be trialled in a two-year pilot project, starting this year. This means that if the candidates have the same or similar qualifications, an immigrant candidate should take priority. And whose fault is that? The police who let them in, of course. Last year, a total of 223 immigrant candidates got selected for municipal posts. Of these, 140 originated from Asia, Africa and Latin America. A total of 825.7 million Norwegian kroner will be allocated to the programme for support and integration of immigrants and their families. And those soft, delicate fingers, so nicely tidied up by Asian manicurists, get pointed at whom? At the police. Every society, however civilised or prosperous, houses all kinds of folks and all kinds of dogmas. There are saints and assholes, the heretics and the devout, there's honour and corruption, compassion and cynicism. All kinds of personalities, including the guy who all first-worlders refuse to admit exists: the literate racist. An

inconvenient figure who hides behind the skirts of tradition whenever they need some argument to justify their
idiocy. They want more restrictions, tougher laws and a
heavier hand enforcing them.

The news was tiring. After hopping through the chan-
nels twice or more, I would wander back to the window,
only to find everything just where I'd left it. After a week
of this, and when I finally ran out of subjects for keeping
up a healthy tête-à-tête with myself, I went out.

I took the car and drove round the city with no
particular destination in mind. I found myself, to my
own surprise, outside my parents' place. I knew they
weren't home. At that time of year they liked to go dip
their feet in the warm sea that bathes the beaches of Palma
de Mallorca. But since I keep their keys on me, I got out
of the car and went to pay a visit to my old bedroom. It
was empty, Mum had long ago cleared the room to use it
for her Pilates classes. I went to the garage and found my
bedroom in half a dozen cardboard boxes. I opened the
nearest one, full of books from the time I was studying for
the detectives' exam. I started rifling through the pages of
one of them, looking for an answer to why I'd given up
pursuing that dream. I closed the book. I knew the answer
deep down, and besides, I hadn't come here to revisit old
frustrations. I opened a second box and there were my old
CDs. My hip-hop collection, Pete Rock & CL Smooth's
The Main Ingredient, *Lyricist Lounge, Volume One*, all
my A Tribe Called Quest albums, my copy of *Reasonable
Doubt*. All of them there, just as they'd been when I left
home, or rather, when I slammed the door after yelling

at my father I didn't want to be like him. That I didn't need to be a detective to be a good policeman like him and my brother after him. I was tired of being told what I had to be. I'd already graduated from the academy, he should be satisfied. At that point I thought I would never wear a uniform. Youthful rebellion? No doubt. My mum even asked me what she should do with my things when she told me about her plans to reassign my room. I told her to burn them. When I think about that, I don't know whether to laugh or cry.

The first year away from home I spent travelling; I went backpacking in Asia. To Thailand first, where I lived for six months shirtless in shorts and flip-flops. Then I met a group of Australians, graduating students in search of one last adventure before the inevitability of having to become adults, and trailed after them across Malaysia. We visited Laos and Vietnam. When they got tired and returned home, I followed their example and came back to Oslo, but not to my parents' place. I ended up first on my brother's sofa, then at a girlfriend's house. Since she was working as a bartender she got me a job doing security at the club where she worked. The relationship didn't last. We lived like vampires, sleeping all day and working at night. It wasn't long before we got sick of each other. I learned my lesson: don't work with people you're sleeping with. I went back to my brother's sofa and one day I woke up and they were right there, the papers to enrol for immigration police. It didn't take me long. After a coffee and two laps around the park, a routine I'd tried to adopt to detox from my months of nocturnal living, I signed the papers and put them in the post. And soon I got called into that fishbowl and sat my ass down in that very same chair to listen to the inspector's stories about his own days as a rookie at the academy, in the final year of my father's career. Apparently my dad had been some kind of mentor to him and now he insisted on taking me in and returning the favour. I couldn't stop thinking, 'I never asked for this crap,' but I did need to straighten my life out. Maybe it's true what they say, the apple doesn't fall far from the tree. And of course I said nothing to the inspector.

One week later, I was on the street with a handgun and a badge around my neck. And in my head, 'D'evils', with Jay-Z telling me that just surviving is not an option. What he wants is to live life to the full.

III

My first day on the job was a Saturday, in March 1998. It was still practically dark as we drove down to Holmlia, one of Oslo's immigrant neighbourhoods. My chief of patrol said weekends were best for catching them off guard, and we didn't need to worry about their lawyers 'cause they only worked Monday to Friday. We wouldn't get one of them calling us at the station requesting their release pursuant to this or that UN resolution. And the small hours of the morning are best because we can catch them when they're still asleep. We fan out across the neighbourhood and start knocking on doors. Two violent knocks, followed by the announcement 'Immigration police.' We wait a moment. If we don't hear a word, we kick the door down and drag

them out of bed. We cuff anyone we catch in an illegal
situation and throw them in the car. On that first day we
caught thirty of them, mostly Iraqis and Turks. The action
sent my adrenaline skyrocketing. I never thought it could
feel so good. I felt useful, maybe for the first time ever. I
couldn't keep the feeling to myself and shared it with the
chief of patrol as we made our way back to the station.
He just smiled, and didn't say a word the whole drive. He
was assessing my behaviour. I know this because when the
inspector called me the following week, he made reference
to my efforts on the ground and repeated what I'd said to
the chief of patrol. I found that weird at first, your typical
Norwegian doesn't go in for a lot of idle chit-chat. Over
the centuries, in the gruelling winter months, Norwegians
have developed the habit of passing each other in the street
without exchanging so much as a glance. This can come
across as rude to non-Norwegians, but in reality it's just
our practical good sense making itself heard. When the
thermometers drop below zero, all tolerance for small
talk disappears. What really is inconvenient and rude is
when we're forced to shake hands with thermal gloves
on and restrict our conversation to a nod of the head,
since the smile we give someone greeting us is going be
hidden behind a woollen scarf anyway. In this way, all
King Harald V's subjects agreed between them that the
best way of handling the situation would be to limit all
unnecessary greetings until after the thaw.

While other peoples have the habit of greeting one
another effusively whenever they meet on the street, our
interaction is limited to a 'Hey, great seeing you last night

– thanks!' Short, simple and to the point. Norwegians are people of few words that carry a lot of meaning. It was almost four weeks before I had what you could call any kind of dialogue with my chief of patrol, and the subject, as you'd expect, was work-related. It happened when we were headed back after one of our weekend patrols. He was sitting up straight, tapping his foot and looking at us as if we had all failed the mission. Clearly, something was bothering him. I avoided making eye contact. He finally said, with a sigh, that around 40 per cent of those immigrants we picked up would have been given asylum or residency permission on humanitarian grounds, which troubled him since, of all the crimes committed in Norway for which prints are taken, 10 per cent were committed by asylum seekers. He wasn't necessarily talking to me or any other agent in that car. Still, I cleared my throat and said, 'They only represent 0.3 per cent of the population.' Everyone turned to me, wide-eyed, and I could have shut up at that moment, but no, I didn't know where I was going with that, but I got carried away. 'And of the 1,039 people who got criminal records in January, 113 were asylum seekers,' I said. The chief squinted at me, making me immediately regret having opened my mouth. 'I read it in the newspaper,' I said, smiling to avoid further questioning. I wasn't ready to reveal that I'd been reading reports on immigration as part of my research for a crime novel. There's one thing worse than being considered a nuisance, and that's being labelled a crime novelist while working on the force. I wasn't that dumb, so I allowed the chief to school me all the way to the station, and he did so with pleasure, and every time he pulled out a statistic, he would call me Mr Stats.

'So, Mr Stats, do you know that we will double the number of asylum seekers from last year?' he said, and I nodded. 'Mr Stats, of the roughly three thousand we deport, do you know how many leave voluntarily?' And I shook my head. 'Less than 2 per cent,' he said.

Like the Angolan guy we caught today, more than 95 per cent of the immigrants don't have proper documents with them when they appear before the police, and as the chief pointed out, the numbers are growing at a scary speed. Some of our superiors are confident that getting into the Eurodac database and accessing the fingerprints of all asylum seekers who enter the Schengen area will help us solve the problem. Some of the people were showing up with their fingers damaged. They use abrasive chemicals to destroy their prints, but little do they know that we don't fall for that: police procedure is to lock them all up until the wounds are healed, which takes around five or six weeks. Politicians are nervous. If we want their country of origin to accept their return, the Norwegian authorities have got to be able to produce the correct identity of the person destined for repatriation. If they refuse to cooperate, that's almost impossible to get. Besides, even if their real identity does get established, it has to be confirmed in the country of origin, which is often really hard and always takes ages. The orders we have are to keep an eye on them. The crimes the immigrant community gets involved in aren't just drug-related. The number of sexual offences is on the rise too. The Dublin

Regulation says we should only take prints of those over fourteen, but I know some forces want to change that and push to start even earlier.

IV

The first time I really had to deal with death in my family was in 2006, when my paternal granddad passed away. I was getting ready to start my shift when I got a call from my brother. In his usual way he didn't start with any words of greeting but went straight to the matter: 'Granddad died.' That's just like him. Only this time, his voice was slower, more hesitant. Those two little words seemed much longer, he delivered them in such a dragged-out way. My granddad lived alone; my grandma died when I was seven, and I do have a vague memory of her funeral. My granddad, true to how he always was, didn't shed a single tear, as my mum said to her sisters-in-law in the kitchen. And they watched his movements, waiting for the moment when he broke down, but he never did. He received people's condolences standing ramrod straight as if he were at a reception for a head of state. I didn't go to the cemetery, my mum said it was no place for a child, maybe worried that my granddad might make a scene at the sight of my grandmother's coffin being lowered into the earth. He didn't. He loved the woman, but he was too well acquainted with death to be affected by it. More than forty years in a career as a police detective had made him like that. It dried up his tears and his capacity to be moved by death. He didn't cry, but nor did he smile again. I hardly ever saw him smiling, laughing, relaxed and happy, the way Mum said he used to when my grandma was alive.

My brother picked me up the day after that call and we travelled to Kristiansund for the funeral. We left Oslo early. Around 6 a.m. we were already on the motorway. My parents had gone as soon as they'd heard the news. My brother, who loves driving, had chosen to leave at that time of the morning because he knew we'd have the road practically to ourselves. He chose *People's Instinctive Travels and the Paths of Rhythm*, an album by A Tribe Called Quest (his favourite band), and we set off towards Atlanterhavsveien. 'You can't go north without crossing the Storseisundbrua Bridge,' he said, repeating out loud what my granddad used to say when we were kids. There's no more beautiful route than that zigzagging road across eight low bridges that almost brush the sea – viaducts and causeways that link the group of reefs and islands between Molde and the west coast of Nordmøre. You can't cross Hustadvika without it sending a shiver up your spine. It's a stretch of ocean known as one of the most dangerous sea passages in the world. When it's stormy, cars are shaken by the violent waves that break on the highway. When we were little, in the school holidays, we'd beg our granddad to take us to see the waves. He also liked feeling the car shaking all over the place from those sheets of water. It was here that he surprised us by his lips breaking into a smile, a slight, shy one but a smile all the same. When we were lucky, on the calmer days we could see whales and seals in those waters. Those memories made my eyes mist up, though the time of day and the previous night without much sleep meant they were hidden behind the dark lenses of my Ray-Bans. I missed my granddad.

'I don't want to leave you driving without any company. I'll stay awake if I possibly can,' I said to my brother, who, in a better mood than on the previous day's call, told me not to worry, he had Q-Tip, Ali Shaheed and Phife Dawg for company.

My grandfather's body was already in its oak coffin, dressed in his old uniform. His eyes closed, hands clasped together. My father's hand lay on top of them, in the silence. I couldn't see any movement from him, not even his body pulsing as it breathed in and out. I looked at those hands again. How like mine they looked, those long bony fingers and narrow wrists, sticking out of his shirt cuffs! My father, wearing funeral black, his shoulders hunched, face pale as marble, stood next to him; his eyes, still dry, had their pupils dilated, like two blue buoys adrift on a sclera of reddened waters. If tears flowed down his face, they would have come out as salty as the waters of Lake Natron in Tanzania. It occurred to me I'd never seen my father cry. The strangest thing was that those red eyes weren't even the proof he'd cried, they could easily have been the result of one or more sleepless nights. It was hard to see him looking so fragile, much older than I remembered. I saw myself in his face, and his face in that of the lifeless body of his father, my granddad. Never had I felt so close to those two men as I did in that moment.

He was standing in silence. When we approached, he turned and hugged my brother for a few seconds. Then he turned to me. His forehead was creased, his eyebrows raised like two arms of a bridge opening to let a boat pass through. The wrinkles and the paleness made the melancholy that had overtaken his face even graver. We didn't exchange a word. We hugged for a long minute, maybe more, until my mum came into the room without our noticing. My face was buried in my father's shoulder, a place I hadn't been in so long. So long actually that I couldn't remember the last time we'd hugged like that.

I heard my mother's voice before anything else, then I felt her hand on my shoulder. 'They're together now,' she said, joining my brother, whose face was covered in tears, even though he wasn't making any crying sound. She asked me if I wanted to say a few words in the church and I said yes. She'd always praised my gift with words, and my father and brother preferred it to be me who went up into the pulpit at Kirkelandet Church. They always thought me the most eloquent in the family. The whole city would be turning out for my grandfather, who had served the city of Kristiansund devotedly, first as a police inspector and then, after retirement, through his involvement in the city's various cultural activities. He never missed an outing to the opera. Curiously, when my grandmother was alive, he always found some excuse not to have to go. My grandma used to say, 'We must keep up the tradition. It's the oldest opera company in the country.'

After the priest had read a few passages from the Bible and the choir chanted one of the hymns, I went up into the pulpit. I took a piece of paper from my pocket with a few notes I'd quickly jotted down. I tapped the microphone gently, cleared my throat, and looked out over the crowd that filled the house of God, which Odd Østbye had designed in 1964 – one of the most daring buildings in our architecture, breaking totally with what we know about traditional churches, a true poem in concrete inspired by 'quartz in roses', a metaphor suggesting the idea of a church sparkling amid the flowers. Nine hundred people, all of them in total silence. People who knew my granddad better than I did. Former colleagues, friends, neighbours, relatives, and those who didn't know him but whose lives must have been affected by him somehow. Otherwise why would they have dressed in black and left their houses to come sit in a church?

'For those of you who knew my grandfather Sigurd,' I began, 'my apologies, what I have to say isn't really for you. I want to talk to those who never had the opportunity to get to know him well, and who were sorry his smile was buried with my grandmother. I want you to know he smiled when he was with my brother and me, when we begged him to take us to see the sea on the Atlantic road.' Those scribbled notes were no use to me at all. At first, my tongue weighed heavy, but after sharing one of my grandfather's favourite jokes and managing to drag out a laugh from my listeners, everything flowed.

Back at the house they served wine. I went for coffee. If I drank alcohol, there was a serious risk I'd pass out in the middle of the living room. My father pulled me into a corner and thanked me. It was the first time we'd talked alone since I'd left home after I finished the academy. It was the first time we acknowledged that we missed each other, and that what had been said no longer mattered. I hadn't forgotten what my dad had said but we made our peace and it felt great. My mother, who'd really suffered in those years in which we hadn't spoken, was happy to see us smoking the peace pipe together. She had always stubbornly insisted on having us sit at the same table once a month, even if the conversation between me and my dad had never been any more than a 'Pass the salt,' usually with no clear addressee.

The taste of the coffee on my tongue awoke a desire for a cigarette, a habit I'd long been trying to quit, but which, because of my mostly sleepless nights, was proving harder than I'd imagined. My strategy for quitting had been not to smoke during the day, and to keep myself in line I never carried a pack with me when I went out.

I went out into the yard in the hope of spotting somebody with a lit cigarette, the same yard where I'd taken my first clandestine puffs – me and my brother and Ava, the daughter of the couple next door, Lebanese immigrants who'd arrived in the 1960s. A girl who for a good part of those years had been my partner in the first discoveries of childhood. By the fence separating the two backyards there was a group of older men, former colleagues of my grandfather's, now retired, who no longer had any vices, or at least not the kind that reduce your life expectancy. Our names are still written on that fence. Igor, Eyvind and Ava, in that order, according to our ages, above the words 'summer 1986'. And that's where I smelled tobacco. I turned and there she was – Ava, the girl next door.

'I didn't know you'd be here,' I said, startled, 'back in Kristiansund.'

'You haven't changed. When was the last time we saw each other?'

'Fifteen years ago.' We both considered the significance of that number, as if they were some other people's fifteen years, amazed at everything each of us had experienced without sharing anything with the other. How well the years looked on her. She was so beautiful. She'd kept that same slender figure she had as a girl of fifteen, olive skin whose golden complexion I always associated with the sand we found on Mediterranean beaches. I don't know the Lebanese coast, but I don't suppose it's very different from beaches in Greece or southern Italy. Her hair was the same as ever, long and a deep black. The only difference was that now, instead of tying it back in her old pony-tail, she wore it loose over her shoulders. Her eyes, maybe from the black eyeliner and the long lashes that filtered the light, left a lattice of shadows over her eyelids. Those two irises were much more hazel than the ones I'd been visited by in my dreams. How did we get here? How had so much time passed without our even noticing?

I asked for a cigarette and she passed me the one she had in her mouth, shrugging, indicating that it was her last one. I remembered the last time we'd met. It was the year Jay-Z released *Vol. 2 . . . Hard Knock Life*, and that album had become the soundtrack to our summer. Ava had never much liked rap, and I remember we spent whole afternoons trying to evangelise each other, me with the word of Hova and her trying to foist System of a Down onto me. The only reason I put up with them was because they were produced by Rick Rubin. Rock was never my scene.

'And your parents?' I asked, and she told me they'd retired five years ago and decided to move to Beirut. The decision surprised me and I immediately asked why. Ava just looked at me, took the cigarette from my fingers, brought it to her mouth, inhaled and handed it back. I copied the movement and, while I puffed away on that cigarette end, I tried to understand why we hadn't worked out, and, not having moved all that far apart, why we hadn't stayed in touch. Our goodbyes had never been verbal, we had a code. On the last night of the summer holidays, once her parents were asleep, she would turn her bedroom light off and on again three times, and leave the window open. When the coast was clear on my side, I would head over, one step at a time on tiptoes, trying not to make any noise. Then in a single bound I'd leap over to her window and land in her arms. That's how it was until she started dating other guys, something I'll admit I wasn't expecting. During the year there was total radio silence with no promises to wait, and even if there had been, how were two teenagers going to keep up a long-distance relationship? That next summer I kept an eye on her window, in the hope of seeing that light blinking three times. It didn't.

In the two summers in which she started to be a girlfriend to other people, our friendship oscillated like the Kristiansund weather. The same day it could both be thirty degrees and suddenly plummet to ten. We stopped having patience for one another, and in order to avoid the disappointment of seeing her with someone else, I started refusing to go to Kristiansund in the summer altogether. My parents didn't suspect a thing – they blamed typical late-adolescence hormone swings and left me in peace. Maybe if they'd insisted I would have gone, even if reluctantly. Who knows, maybe if I'd actually seen Ava with one of those fools who didn't know anything about anything I might have summoned the courage to grab one of those World War II cannons from the Kvalvik Fort, open the breech, place my heart inside it, aim it at her and fire. And to hell with everything. But it didn't happen. Or not that kind of explosion, at least. What would happen some years later, one summer, before starting college, was that I found myself back in Kristiansund to celebrate my grandfather's eightieth, a surprise party. My grandfather went on hiding his smile, but you could see in his eyes that he was pleased. Not at turning eighty (he made a point of reminding everybody that the last time he'd celebrated a birthday had been the year they diagnosed his wife's cancer – he stopped celebrating because he didn't want to count the years he lived without her). If he'd spotted us arriving, he would have seen us off at gunpoint. But since he had no choice, and this was probably the last time he'd see a lot of these people who'd travelled from far away to attend, he wasn't going to send anyone away without at least wetting their whistle first. It wasn't celebrating exactly, it was more just 'being' – well-being. And how everyone drank that night! The first to quit the backyard were the birthday boy himself and the senior crowd. Then my parents, Ava's parents, followed by the younger crowd including my brother. Only the two of us were left, always the hardiest in the neighbourhood. We had that reputation. When everybody else surrendered to tiredness, the two of us always stayed later to shoot the breeze. And there we were again. In silence. A silence that stretched out to her house, followed us into her bedroom, took off its shoes, sat down on the bed, looked up at the ceiling, settled on our hands as they touched, rested against our lips, which kissed while we took off our clothes, first hers and then mine, with the slowness and the fluidity of a t'ai chi master, all so that nobody might hear.

It was almost daytime before that silence of ours was broken. I wanted to get up, to avoid being surprised by her family. I thought about suggesting we get out of bed and go face the day, which promised to be a lovely one, looking at the light peeking through the slit between the not-quite-closed curtains. But something made me keep quiet. I avoided any sudden movements and just stayed put. I couldn't help feeling kind of pathetic, but I didn't want to seem insensitive, even if there was no guarantee we'd ever experience another dawn like it.

I was there because I wanted to be, it's true. But the constant duel between our masculine selves and whatever feminine we have within us does substantially condition how we deal with concrete facts. The girl likes the boy, and vice versa. The girl declares that what happened that night was a moment of weakness. And the boy sinks into the pillow feeling like he's once again reading the only book he managed to save when he was shipwrecked on a desert island.

There was enough light to allow me to walk round the

room without tripping over anything, gathering up my clothes scattered across the floor. My shirt insisted on still not appearing, but I started dressing myself reasonably calmly. I didn't want to suggest that I was running away, even if my silence might have implied such a thing. I glanced one last time at the place I believed the shirt had landed when we'd undressed. I smiled, pulled my jacket over my bare trunk and left the room, just praying my shirt wouldn't be discovered by her mother who might then ask me to explain something that even I could not understand. And as I leapt over the border fence separating the two houses, while I still had one foot on Lebanese soil, I heard that 'good morning' in my granddad's voice. He'd apparently risen early to clean up the yard, and the way he looked at me was so natural it was as if he'd known from the very first that that was how I was living out my secret romance. He gestured a small hello, I jumped down off the fence and joined him in gathering up the empty bottles spread around the yard.

We would never talk of that episode again. It makes me sorry, I wish I'd shared, for example, what had been going through my head at that moment. My mind, curiously, was not on the humiliation of being caught leaping the fence at that time of the morning, or it being discovered that we were lovers. My mind was on that sea of pillows. Would the one that had served for my comfort have been cherished or tossed away from the bed, like a foul insect, the moment I jumped out of that window without a word?

'You know my granddad saw me that morning?' I said, and handed the cigarette to her.

'Yeah, he told me,' said Ava. She was clearly choosing her words. 'He came to find me the day you said you were going to enlist at the police academy.' I waited, not interrupting her. 'He asked me to go to Oslo to try and convince you not to join the force.' I struggled to understand at first, it was like she was talking about some other person, someone who wasn't my granddad. 'He didn't want you to follow the fate of all the other men of your family; he hoped you might be the first to do something different with your life.'

'He never told me, Ava,' I replied.

'I dunno what he thought you should do instead. I didn't ask him. I hadn't seen you in years,' she said before pausing to inhale and blow the smoke out through her nose.

'I was dealing with my own ghosts, but he said you needed me. More than even you imagined,' she added and passed me the cigarette.

'Do you agree with him?' she asked.

I took another drag and exhaled quickly.

'I don't know, maybe,' I answered but immediately regretted saying those words. I wasn't thinking. I wanted to suggest going out to buy a pack of Marlboro since I was starting to feel the tip of my fingers getting warmer, and we only had a couple of puffs before killing that cigarette.

'Sometimes our folks say stuff about us as if we were fictional characters or something,' she said, ignoring my hand in front of her and inviting me to take the last draught with a gentle nod. 'You know what I answered?'

I turned to her and she smiled.

'I told him that if you'd loved me, you'd have had the courage to tell me so that morning you stole out the window like a thief,' she said.

Ava was in Kristiansund to sell the property owned by her parents, two chemical engineers who'd migrated to the city at the start of the 1980s. But that wasn't the family's first home in the northern lands. First they'd lived in Stavanger, like everybody else who wants to work in the oil industry. Before trading the Paris of the Middle East for the oil capital of Norway, Mr and Mrs Hajjar had considered emigrating to Brazil or to the United States. The decision was taken, according to what Ava told me, following the massacres that would be known as Black Saturday. At the end of 1975, four members of the Christian right Kataeb Party – also known as the Phalanges – were found dead, and the militias sympathetic to the party totally lost their shit and retaliated, indiscriminately attacking the Muslim population living in the eastern part of the city, the area dominated by Christians. Those who weren't killed were used for ransom. Beirut had always been a divided city, a pressure cooker on the verge of exploding, with Christians and Muslims clashing over control of the city's strategic points (like the hotel neighbourhood). The final straw, at least for Ava's parents, was the Karantina massacre. A Christian militia attacked one of the poor neighbourhoods in the north-east of Beirut, inhabited by Muslims, Kurds, Armenians, Syrians and Palestinians, a place thick with historical symbolism. As usual, the men who were waging war claimed to be struggling to preserve history, but ended up destroying it. The La Quarantaine neighbourhood got its name because it was there in the nineteenth century that a leper hospital for travellers was built at the request of Ibrahim Pasha, son of Muhammad Ali Pasha, governor of Egypt, who at that time controlled Syria and Lebanon.

Ava's parents' choice of Rogaland happened almost randomly. In the week they were getting ready to request a visa for Brazil, they chanced upon a scientific magazine containing an interview with one Farouk Al-Kasim, the Iraqi geologist who played an important role in the exemplary way our oil industry would be set up. The article presented this man's amazing story, how he'd quit his job, a well-paid position in the Iraqi state oil company, leaving a comfortable upper-middle-class life in Basra, the city of his birth, to move to the home country of his Norwegian wife, in search of better treatments for their younger son, who'd been born with cerebral palsy.

On the morning of 28 May 1968, Mr Al-Kasim touched down in Oslo, unemployed and with a head filled with doubts. He knew it would be hard to get a job as good as the one he'd left behind. He didn't even have any idea that the oil drilling in the North Sea had already begun. Not that the information would have been of any use to him even if he had known, since after five years of drilling not a single drop of oil had yet been found. Ava asked me if I'd heard of the existence of this character, if I had any notion that the successful drilling for our oil is thanks, in large part, to the contribution of an Iraqi man, an immigrant. I had no idea, of course. A lot of people of my generation have no memory of what Norway was like without its oil wells, but Ava made a point of setting me straight. 'It was like a gift from Odin, wasn't it?' she said, admitting that her father, Mr Hajjar, believed in these things, and he too felt it was a sign from God. Inspired by that man's story, he left the house on that very same day with the magazine under his arm and went to knock on the door of the Norwegian embassy. He imagined this country as a land of opportunity. If an Iraqi who'd ended up here with only the shirt on his back managed to make it big in his profession, then this was where he imagined living, thriving and raising his children. Of course, the distance between dreams and reality is every bit as great as the 4,676 kilometres separating Oslo and Beirut. He learned this fact no sooner than he had set foot in Stavanger. He was surprised, first, to discover that Mr Al-Kasim didn't have a position in the Ministry of Industry. The post he'd been given was as a 'consultant'. The government needed him, but putting him in a position of power would be an affront to the political system, which was not yet ready for quite that much emancipation.

The plan had been to reveal his presence gradually, in homeopathic doses, so as not to shock the conservatism that persists to this day. Most people who enjoy the success story of our experience with oil have very little idea it's all thanks to an Iraqi. The prevailing narrative is that things happened the way they did due to Norway's exceptional institutions, our national character and Nordic rigour. Within this Scandinavian narrative, there's no space for an Arab hero called Farouk Al-Kasim, a messiah who came from Mesopotamia to deliver the ten

commandments of oil, which were approved by our parliament without much discussion and followed to the
letter by all subsequent governments. Ava told this story with a faint smile on her lips, underlining the irony
of the whole thing. 'Don't you think it's unbelievable it
was an Iraqi who organised the most important industry in the country? Without him, they'd probably have
let the American firms decide what sort of model would
be applied to the oil drilling,' she said. I went even further, telling her that if her parents hadn't come into contact with that man's story, our destinies probably never
would have crossed. She preferred not to think like that
because she'd have to go back even further and admit
that if the civil war in Lebanon hadn't happened, the
chances of our meeting would have been close to zero.
She always thought that kind of supposition was non-
sense. Life happens because it has to. It's pointless trying
to find more whys. I understand, but what can I do. 'If'
has always been my biggest problem.

Later, I snuck out of my grandfather's wake and went
to Ava's house. I rang the doorbell, and as I stood there
waiting, I realised I had never done that before. She smiled
when she saw me. I greeted her with a hey. She replied
with the same hey and pushed the door wide open with
her body to let me through. As I stepped inside, I let my
hand trail behind me, hoping we might touch each other as
she moved hers to close the door. And we did. It was just
the tip of our fingers but enough to bring everything back.
My first kiss, my first time desiring someone. With her, I
discovered sex and love, even if I knew nothing about it at

the time, and it would be years before I understood that Ava Hajjar had been my first love. We had lost our virginity in her bed, on top of those dozens of pillows. Facing the poster of Everything but the Girl's *Idlewild* with Tracey Thorn and Ben Watt, holding a bunch of flowers, and apparently smiling at us, approving of what we were about to do.

Walking through the front door was certainly the first time I'd gone into other rooms of the house and I felt like I were visiting the interior of a country after years of frequenting only the capital, her bedroom. Perhaps an island would be a more appropriate term, such was the contrast between her room and the rest of the house. The large sofa with its back to the wall, a pair of matching twin armchairs, one on either side, a small glass table and on top of it an object likewise of glass, too ornate to be a fruit dish, though it wouldn't have looked odd with a few oranges in it. Three remote controls in different sizes, lined up on one edge of the table. From the angle where I stood, they looked like three skyscrapers reflected in the Hudson. On the walls, framed tapestries, landscapes I think were from Lebanon, men with moustaches and women with mysterious looks in their eyes, peering down on us from their portraits. Ava offered me a coffee, turned her back to me, and walked to the kitchen with an urgency typical of someone receiving guests. And I indeed felt like a visitor, even if everything felt familiar, the smells, the silence. Seeing her at the counter, through that kitchen door at the far end of the living room, it was like we were other people in a life that could easily have been ours. In a house that, despite me never having set foot outside one of its rooms, was identical to that of my childhood, right next door, as well as every other house I'd visited in that city. I know how many square metres each room has. I know that the floor is birchwood, and coats hang behind the doors. There, with the smell of coffee invading every corner of the house, I ask myself what would have happened if she'd followed my grandfather's advice and come to see me in Oslo, if she'd persuaded me not to enlist in the police force. What would have changed? Would we both have stayed in Oslo? Would I have followed her to Beirut?

As I walked into the kitchen, she turned and explained the importance of coffee in Lebanese culture and told me, with all the calm in the world, how it was prepared in the old villages, where families usually roast the beans themselves and grind them by hand. She put the long-handled coffee pot, the rakweh, on the stove and added a teaspoonful of coffee for each cup of water. She then lowered the flame, added a few cardamom seeds, turned to me, and pointed to a cup full of wooden spoons. I took two and held them up to her. She picked the long, slim one to stir the liquid gently until it came to a boil.

'Don't do this at home,' she chuckled as I approached the stove.

She poured it into two cups, but just when I was about to raise mine to my lips, she shook her head.

'Wait a few more seconds for the dregs of the coffee to settle at the bottom of the cup,' she said and pointed to the small kitchen table.

'This is what people drink in social gatherings. Whether informal or for business. In sadness and joy, success and failure,' she said.

'Wow, failure? Are we drinking to that?'

'I think it's healthy to drink to our failures too, don't you think?'

I bowed my head, raised my cup, and we toasted.

'Whenever we have to solve an issue with the neighbours or the family needs to decide which clans to form alliances with through marriage, coffee is always the drink of choice.

'Oh, and one other important detail. Never call this Turkish coffee,' she warned me.

'Yes, ma'am,' I said.

'We roast and grind the beans differently, and the taste of the coffee comes during the stirring process,' she said, smiling with her lips and eyes.

'That's the most delicious coffee I've ever had.'

'I know,' she said with a smirk.

'Where does all this cockiness come from?'

'I have been mastering it since I arrived in Lebanon. It helped me to get closer to my mother.' She pointed to the pot of sugar. I passed it over to her.

'The difference between my coffee and the one my mother makes is that hers is so sweet your teeth would fall out if you drank more than two cups.'

She sat back and laughed loudly. That night ended up being all the more special because we didn't succumb to the temptation to jump on each other. And, God, I don't think I'd ever felt so sober and at the same time so high, like I'd been smoking something. Of course, I kept all that to myself. We rehashed old subjects, we talked about family, about music. She'd become much more sophisticated than me – I was basically still listening to rap. I was captivated by her eyes as if seeing them more clearly, the movement of her lips, her lipstick, pink with light tones of pearl, slowly chewing her words, with a slight accent – I'd forgotten how much more musical it made the Norwegian language sound. Her eyes were lined in black, a frame for her two hazelnut eyes, which fixed on mine and then darted away when I went quiet. The silence became palpable. A familiar look that reawakened a desire that had been long dormant. From her expression of surprise, I was sure she'd recognised it too.

V

I stood up, grabbed my empty thermos and walked to the coffee machine for a refill. Mari was resting her elbows on her knees. The chief inspector was flipping his pen through his fingers, with the back of his chair reclined.

Mari, like me, is the child of a police officer, the difference being that my father has always been present and hers never had. She was born from a one-night stand. She'd told me this in our long hours sitting in the car patrolling the border, in a conversation about what it was that had led to our choosing careers with the police. She revealed that she was born in Oslo but she'd been conceived in Gothenburg, the birthplace of her almost unknown father. That was also where her parents had met. Her mum was an actress, she was in town with a play, and he was a policeman on his day off. According to Mari, her mother said that her father never saw her on stage. The only time he saw her act was on top of a bar table, where the cast of the play were celebrating the end of the run. That was where they'd met. Apparently, he'd been struck by the monologue that Mari's mother had delivered to the highly boozed-up crowd. That same night he went with her to the hotel room round the back of the Stadsteater and they spent the early hours of the morning performing a love scene. The second time they saw each other, nine months later, it was daytime, in the alleyway opposite the police station. Him rubbing his hands nervously, her with baby Mari Gunnhild in her arms, biting her lip to stop herself letting out a shout or a tear. Her mother never married. She did fall in love again, but this time with a much older man and the romance didn't last. He was married. They had a daughter – a sister I've not met, but according to Mari they adore each other.

'My sister's father would take her and pick her up from school almost every day, and I just tagged along pretending that he was my father too,' she said to me once. 'In the summer, he'd take us to the beach, together with his other children.' She learned later about her biological father – when she was on her way out of the Politihøgskolen – that he had married and had more children, though she'd never met them. He wrote this in a long letter to her mother, explaining why he'd never shouldered his responsibilities. Mari remembers arriving home to find her mum in the kitchen, her hands shaking, and the more she read those

words, the more she dissolved into tears. She didn't hold
back, and they cried together. 'That day,' she said, 'I gave
up everything that tied me to that mysterious figure who
was my parent and with whom I share nothing but some
genetic code, nothing else.'

I wanted to knock at the chief's door, but I needed a
convincing excuse to interrupt them. I stretched out my
arms until I heard a click in my joints. What could have
been so serious that he held my partner back for an interrogation? We didn't kill anybody. I've never even fired
the P30, the Heckler & Koch semi-automatic we always
have with us in the car. I don't know anyone who has ever
killed anyone. In 2007 not a single shot was fired. The
previous year there were three shots fired, and just one
person injured. I say this with no pride; there's no cause to
feel that. Guns don't make us feel more just, or more like
men, they're just another tool. We were trained in hand-
to-hand combat and to treat our gun only as a last resort,
when every other option has been exhausted. My granddad used to say that the most powerful weapon a police
officer carries around with him is the grey matter inside
his skull, and then he would move straight on to the metaphor, 'from a distance, a screw and a nail look the same,
the difference is that one of them needs a screwdriver and
the other a hammer'.

'I've never killed anybody.' Those were the words that I
would repeat to myself, whenever the Eritrean girl's song
came back to me. First in my dreams, to the point that
I'd wake up soaked in sweat in the middle of the night
needing to change my sheets or end up on the sofa. A bad

idea, since, being scared of falling asleep and returning to
the same nightmare, I'd always end up sleeping with one
eye open, afraid of going mad. That was when the insomnia started. I've never killed anybody, but that girl's death
squeezed my chest tight – I got this knot in my throat, a
feeling of claustrophobia that was so upsetting that after
a week I called up to ask for a leave of absence. I don't
remember the excuse I gave the chief inspector, but he
seemed to understand and promised to call so we could
talk in two or three days' time. He was as good as his word.
He called once, twice, three times, and I let the phone ring
out and go to voicemail. I never managed to summon the
nerve to answer. The only call I answered that week was
from my brother – I told him I'd taken a few days off,
not giving him much detail, just to reassure him and so
as not to have him break my door down and drag me off
the sofa to some psychologist. I told him I missed him
and we promised each other a night out since neither of
us could remember when we last went clubbing together.
It was him who baptised me into club life, at a time when
most places were still illegal. That's what it was like up
until the opening of Blå and the now-defunct Jazid Club
and Skansen, in 1995 or thereabouts, legendary places that
taught me everything I know about music, through DJs
like Prins Thomas and Strangefruit. Our beginnings were
pretty timid, but club culture in Oslo was abuzz by the
time we were approaching the end of the decade. Every
tiny bar had a decent sound system and a DJ playing some
good house. It was cool, but at the same time, it was the
beginning of the tyranny of house, which castrated the

development of other genres. We were lucky to have DJ Strangefruit on the radio in 1997. Every Saturday night, there were two hours when he was given the freedom to play whatever he wanted, drum and bass, techno, reggae, disco. He was responsible for the musical education of a large part of my generation. He and his partner, DJ Olle Abstract, took the helm and steered us, the listeners, to deeper waters, playing the heaviest dance tracks right through to midnight. They were the 'kings of Norway', a kind of Hot Mix 5 of our own.

The chief inspector persisted in calling me several times, till I ended up disconnecting the phone. What was there to say to him? That it's my fault. If I'd believed the story that kid had told me, she never would have come to that end. My hands tremble just from thinking that her sentence started with the report I wrote and placed in front of the chief inspector inside that fishbowl, who signed the detention order and handed it back to me.

During those nights I spent awake, a question the chief inspector had asked me in his office popped back into my mind. He wanted to know if I ever wondered whether I was really cut out for the force. At that moment, the Eritrean girl's case was all I could think of. The chief could have offered me a promotion or paid vacation: I wasn't paying attention to any of his words. But at home, I had time to retread all the steps I had taken. From the detention to the interrogation, the more I thought about it, the more I wondered if I had chosen the wrong profession. Maybe being a police officer wasn't in my blood the way it was for all the other men in my family. I would say this without believing my own words. I'd spend hours piling up these thoughts only to dismantle them again. Maybe that was the last straw, the sign I'd been waiting for in the three years I'd spent at the Politihøgskolen. Maybe it was time to take off the uniform. I spent my waking nights pondering this question. 'I just need to start sleeping again,' I'd tell myself, 'everything will get back on track, everything will go back to the way it was before.'

I'd travelled through this *before* in my imagination, where it had begun, whether it was the Eritrean girl or some time earlier. If it had started with those looting expeditions by Vikings who brought back spoils that included women. Technically we wouldn't call them immigrants, what with their not having arrived here by choice; they were slaves. Period. Nor would we use the word immigrants to describe those foreigners who came across our borders to marry our aristocrats; royal weddings are not some pro-migration symbol, they happen in order to encourage bonds with other monarchies, to strengthen alliances. So maybe I should channel my anger and look for scapegoats in the Industrial Revolution of the nineteenth century, when Norway needed foreign labour to deal with the demand. We're the largest producer of hydroelectric energy in Europe and dams don't build themselves. This *before* isn't even visible, it passes unnoticed, or maybe it's just that no one pays it any attention any more, unlike the waves of immigrants who arrive here trying to escape from wars. First the Jews from Eastern Europe, the refugees from Hungary in the 1950s and the ones from Chile and Vietnam in the 1970s. And then, in the mid-1980s, I was already witnessing those coming from the Middle East with my own eyes, the ones from Iran, from Sri Lanka and from the Hajjars' Lebanon. I remember it was more or less the time when Jay-Z's 'Hard Knock Life (Ghetto Anthem)' was practically the only song in my life – I'd listen to it day and night. Hundreds of refugees from Kosovo were disembarking in Oslo. Then came the ones from Iraq, from Somalia and from Afghanistan. I know now that they'd been arriving for longer than that, but that was the point at which they became real to me. Maybe because I was spending more time in front of the TV, absorbing everything Eden Harel and Trevor Nelson said. *MTV Select*, The Dance Chart, *The Lick* and MTV Base were my daily bread. The only time they'd be interrupted was when my dad switched to *Dagsrevyen* to hear the world news, wearing his uniform, something we saw him doing for as long I could remember, the uniform later replaced with pyjamas, and *Dagsrevyen* with TV2 Nyhetskanalen. Today his daily dose of news is served up by the duo of Terje Svabø and Mah-Rukh Ali – 'beauty and the bald', as I used to say to provoke him – when I found him with his eyes glued to the TV, barefoot and with his Nøgne Ø Imperial Stout warm in his hand. He paid no attention, he'd just take a gulp of his drink, look at the bottle and add: 'This beer spent a year in oak barrels that used to be used for ageing cognac.' He said this with as much pleasure as if that black liquid, tasting of toasted malt, slightly bitter, with notes of dried fruit, raisins, figs and bits of chocolate, had been packaged by Château Courvoisier and handed to him personally by Busta Rhymes, P. Diddy and Jamie

Foxx, all dressed in white bathrobes and spa slippers.

At the peak of my delusions, I would still turn on the news bulletin to hear Mah-Rukh Ali, a daughter of Pakistani immigrants who reminded me of Ava. It was Ava who'd told me about the book Ali wrote when she was fourteen: *Den sure virkeligheten* – The Sour Reality. I didn't read the book, it was the year of Hova's *Reasonable Doubt* and I was more interested in hearing 'Can't Knock the Hustle' and 'Dead Presidents' than learning the childhood stories of a Muslim girl born and raised in the western part of Oslo. Still Ava did try, joking that the book might be a window into her world. At the time, racism was such an abstract thing for me, it was something I knew about from rap songs – and was thus an American product. I was so far from being able to imagine that both Ava and Mah-Rukh Ali suffered discrimination at the hands of the Norwegians who looked like me, the whites. 'How's it possible that a book about a search for identity can annoy people so much?' asked Ava as she told me, her eyes brimming with tears, about the various threatening and racist letters the author had received at the time. The Norway they suggested seems to me now, not having paid it any attention, more violent, nastier, meaner than most of my compatriots would ever have imagined.

When we spent the summers together, I looked at Ava and saw a Norwegian woman, but she told me that she never saw herself that way, not even if she wanted to. Someone would always show up to remind her that she wasn't from here – not really. They barely recognised her as a Catholic. And all because of her skin. Epidermis and melanocytes as determining factors for each individual's morality, as if it was them that dictated who lied more or less. I couldn't stop wondering whether, if the Eritrean girl had had my melanin levels in her skin, the same blue irises, she'd have been sent to the same place? And in the midst of that agony, maybe her song was a prayer, I thought, a prayer of farewell. Maybe she'd implanted those lines inside me so her name would not be forgotten. After a week without setting foot outside my apartment, I finally went out. Not for long. I just needed some supplies from the grocer's. But along the way, the hallucinations returned. Suddenly I started seeing the Eritrean girl's face in all the black teenagers I passed on the street who had their heads covered in a hijab. I thought I was going crazy. Maybe that was going to be my fate. How could I go back on duty? My career with the police was over, I thought. But curiously, I felt strangely calm.

When I got back home from the shop, my head spinning, I found Mari waiting outside my building. She was in jeans and an old leather jacket. She looked like she'd been waiting there a while. We greeted each other with a hug. 'Sorry to be bothering you at home,' she said, 'but I needed to see you.' I did think about inviting her up, but I remembered the chaos of my apartment and I didn't want her to jump to conclusions about my state of mind. I invited her to come for a stroll. She accepted without acknowledging that we were at the door to my home and yet I carried the shopping bags with me when I could easily have gone up and left them in the apartment. We walked down Ullevålsveien and across Vår Frelsers

Gravlund, with its hundred-year-old trees and modest tombs, aware that beneath those tablets, some of them of marble and the rest, the majority, of common stone, lay the city's most illustrious sons and daughters, like the writer Henrik Ibsen and the artist Edvard Munch. This place, to me, is the mirror of Norwegian society – we're supposed to show restraint and humility even at the hour of our death. I considered sharing this with Mari, but I know she'd just end up agreeing even if she didn't feel the same way. Another of our characteristics as a people: consensus even when we hold opposing views.

We came to Oslo's oldest building, the medieval Aker Church. We turned onto Telthusbakken and went down that narrow slope with its brightly coloured wooden houses that used to be the postcard for Oslo, before we discovered oil in the 1960s. Not many have survived. I thought that if I took her to a bar full of people, my colleague's shyness might mean she'd spare me a really deep conversation. We went into Blå, which was packed at that time of day. We asked for two Nøgne Ø India Pale Ales and sat at the terrace overlooking the Akerselva river.

'Sorry I didn't answer your calls,' I said.

She just smiled, paused, then spoke: 'Yesterday, when I was doing my usual Sunday cleaning – there's no way I can look after the house during the week – I was surprised by a phone call. No one ever rings me on the landline. I even thought it might have been you,' and she paused again, her eyes still fixed on the waterway. I waited for her to pick up the thread of the conversation. 'I answered it. The voice on the other end was familiar, like an old memory

I thought I'd forgotten, a deep voice, excited, like somebody who had a secret they were just about to share. And
so the words sort of tumbled out very fast, not making all
that much sense. I couldn't help myself from asking twice
who was speaking.' Another pause. 'It was my dad,' she
said, folding her arms.

'It was the one thing I've always wanted to hear somebody say,' she continued and, not knowing what to
answer, I kept quiet, listening. 'Not that I still need this,
but it did torment me living without anyone ever having
given me the pleasure of saying, "Child, I'm your father."'
Mari admitted that the phone call hadn't erased all the pain
caused by his absence, but it still made her happy. And I
couldn't help being relieved, having imagined my absence
had prompted her visit. I pressed her on that reunion. She
told me she didn't dare talk to her mum and sister about
the phone call. I hugged her.

We talked for hours about everything and nothing, the
conversation focusing more on her than her father. All the
same, it was some comfort, like a weight had been lifted
off her shoulders, she said, when we were on our second
bottle of wine.

'He called me because it was his birthday,' Mari said,
and I raised the empty bottle to the waiter. She smiled and
continued. 'He revealed things that weren't in that letter
my mum read in the kitchen, which was kind of scary.'
Mari said her father started out by telling her, step by step,
each mistake he'd made since he had left, or rather, since
he had failed to enter her life. The relationships he'd had
and which had since failed. His stormy relations with his

other children, the siblings she didn't know yet but who all the same, when she heard their names, made her feel a bit jealous. He told her the circumstances that had led to his leaving the police force and committing the crimes that had put him behind bars for five years. He ended up saying he had rediscovered happiness by the side of a woman of twenty-one, who he'd saved from prostitution but who he feared would leave him for somebody younger. He asked her advice. 'Imagine my shock. I have an ex-con father and a twenty-one-year-old stepmother.' I said it sounded like a crime novel. We laughed.

That was the first time Mari and I had some quality time outside a work setting. In normal circumstances it would be almost impossible for us to be friends, not because we didn't enjoy each other's company, but because she doesn't like music. It was the first thing I asked her when we got into our patrol car: 'What kind of music do you like?' 'I don't listen to music, whatever's on the radio is fine for me.' That moment I knew our destinies were not likely to cross outside the limits of our professional commitments, and I suspect that, from the look of shock on my face, she deduced the same. Yet there we were, at a bar, drinking and talking about family stuff the way only good friends do, in the hipster Grünerløkka, our very own little Brooklyn that does everything it can to preserve the anarchist spirit that has been slowly fading – even anarchists have bills to pay, we've all got to eat, and if the middle-class kids like to go out for dinner, to drink cocktails or even live in neighbourhoods that until very recently were considered no-go areas, who are we to try to preserve the anarchist spirit which, if we're being absolutely honest, never really stuck, not like in other capitals. But just like Brooklyn, it couldn't hold back the gentrification, and the long-standing residents, the poorest and the oldest, have been increasingly moved out. Signs of the times. Personally, I'm actually grateful, less trouble for us to worry about. I'm only sorry that the music, unfortunately, along with the gentrification, is changing too, and with the exception of Blå, The Villa and Barongsai there aren't many places where you can still hear real music.

That first night of ours unfolded into a dinner. I wanted to take her to New Anarkali, my favourite Indian restaurant, but when we passed in front of Markveien Mat og Vinhus, I mentioned their cheesecake with raspberry sauce, a secret recipe the establishment had been serving for twenty-five years and which has become a local legend. She'd never tried it. There was nothing I could do about her lack of musical taste, but where it came to food it was my responsibility to educate her about the institution that is Markveien Mat og Vinhus. My father used to take us whenever there was something to celebrate. And we did celebrate, Mari and me, we drank wine, we talked more about our parents, I got a few of my pet skeletons out the closet, and when we moved on to the subject of work, I hesitated, but ended up telling her how much the Eritrean girl's death had affected me, how much it had scared me.

'After Eugene Ejike Obiora died in Trondheim, my nerves were still fried. I remember the chief saying that it was crap like that makes heads roll,' Mari said.

'Oh, I remember,' I said to her and admitted I felt that

sermon was specially addressed to me. During our daily briefing right after the Obiora scandal broke, the chief revealed that the force was working to improve new methods. And those of us who graduated before 2006 were being watched closely. He even looked at me when he said – your inexperience could cost us dear. The last thing the police wanted was another scandal involving an immigrant. I didn't think the Obiora and the Eritrean case were related, but I feared they were ready to throw me under the bus. Our training was only part of the problem for the old dogs on top. Experience in the field itself has only limited impact. Mari puffed out her chest and copied the chief's voice.

'On average, a police officer makes one arrest per month. Throwing young agents out onto the street and trusting their service experience to do the rest isn't just an ineffective way of training people. It's also irresponsible,' she said, and I cracked up.

'I had never seen the chief enraged the way he was that day.'

Mari listened in silence, because just like me, she's on the front line, and if one of us is accused of racist behaviour, the whole department will get painted as racist. To the liberals in our society, the Ejike Obiora case sullied our reputation, it lifted the veil covering the rottenness that was festering within our police forces. First because we have double standards for how we deal with subjects who show signs of mental illness. Poor Mr Obiora was not in his right mind, he shouldn't have got worked up in a social services office, and it's true, he shouldn't have resisted arrest. But to go from there to being choked by officers who know very well that lying somebody face-down and pressing on their back with your knee while handcuffing them increases the chances of the person ending up asphyxiated, that's too much. This was exactly what the forensic examiners concluded. Tests carried out on healthy individuals show that a person's lung capacity is reduced by 40 per cent when placed in that position. The thing had already gotten ugly when the report was released. The inspector made a point of having us all read it, since in our unit the chances of us having to resort to force to neutralise a subject is much greater than on a patrol by public security officers. In addition to what was already circulating in the media about asphyxia being the cause of death, there was added internal bleeding of the neck muscles as well as a cartilage fracture. All as a result of the choking. According to one questionable passage, the injuries would have caused the lack of air, but wouldn't alone have caused the asphyxiation and death, which could have been avoided if the officers had known how to carry out the arrest without resorting to the tactic of throwing the subject on the ground.

The situation got even worse when it was discovered that the officer who'd had his knees on Obiora's back had already been involved in another incident in 1999, with a Ghanaian woman, Sophia Baidoo, and some people felt there were similarities between the two cases, and on that occasion there was proof. The incident had been filmed by a security camera in a bank, but the officer was subsequently cleared of all accusations. If you'd asked me, before I had anything to do with a case involving an illegal immigrant myself, I'd have said those officers ought to be convicted, to demonstrate the impartiality of our judicial system. Nobody is above the law, not even us, the police. That would have been the best way of resolving the situation and it would have avoided what happened a posteriori. The band Samvirkelaget released the song 'Stopp Volden' (Stop Violence) in which one of the officers involved in the Obiora case was named. Our federation shot itself in the foot and sued the band in a desperate attempt to stop the CD from being released. The court found no basis for filing a suit. However, it did find the naming of the officer in the song defamatory. The case could have been resolved at that point, but instead of lowering their guard and preserving what was left of our dignity, our Norwegian Police Federation kept on going and tried to sue Samvirkelaget for defamation. The case ended up being decided in favour of the collective.

It's possible that my Eritrean case could end up in the papers too, and the inspector recommended I keep my distance. 'Last thing we need is another song,' he said when he sent me home to rest.

'I should be back by now,' I said to the chief inspector over the phone, as soon as I learned that the girl had been buried and the autopsy results had landed on his desk – that imposing, terrifying piece of furniture. We're all afraid of sitting opposite that pile of rubber stamps, dossiers of open cases, the black telephone that's like an extension of the inspector's ear. 'The autopsy points to suicide,' he'd said in the voicemail message he left me. Just like that, five words that pulled me out of purgatory, five words that allowed me to breathe again. Without the fear of having some blogger sniffing around, trying to expose our interrogation practices. 'I should have felt better,' I said to Mari, swilling around my glass of wine, waiting for all its flavours to open before bringing the liquid to my tongue. 'But the truth was, I didn't. For the first time I thought of giving up, you know, leaving all this, being some other person,' I said, and she interrupted me.

'What other person?'

First I shrugged. 'Someone who isn't just a number on a badge,' I said, but she seemed confused. She'd understood that the Eritrean girl's death had got me down, she understood I needed to rest, travel, take a vacation. But to quit? It sounded ludicrous to her. I didn't try to explain. Instead of going deeper into that particular question, we talked about what motivated us or about the meaning of life. I revealed my plans to visit the place they'd buried her, take some flowers, light a candle, have someone read a few passages from the Quran, as it's quite possible nobody had taken the trouble to read her a farewell prayer. I thought Mari would find the idea ridiculous, that she'd laugh in my face, or even worse, report me to internal affairs. Her reply almost made me choke on my cheesecake. She offered to come with me to the cemetery.

'I don't know any Muslim priests, but we can take her some flowers,' she said with the calm tone of somebody who'd been in this position before. 'What do they call Muslim priests anyway?' she asked. For all I know, Islam might not even have a hierarchical authority like priests, pastors or rabbis – but there is the imam, I replied. But

I didn't dare to travel to Tøyenbekken and knock on the door of the Islamic Centre. Even if I had the courage, how crazy would this look? I could already see the headlines – 'Norwegian policeman asks community to help give immigrant proper Muslim burial.'

VI

When I woke up the following day to the buzz of my intercom, I was soaked in sweat and my mouth was dry. I couldn't remember exactly how I got back to my apartment and why I was wearing my jeans and leather jacket in bed. The curtains were wide open, and since my windows faced east, the early summer sun brightened the entire room, forcing me to reach for a pillow and cover my face. Then the buzzer sounded again, and I felt the noise, painful, inside my head.

'Leave the mail at the door,' I said into the intercom. 'No one steals anything in this neighbourhood.' As I was preparing to drag myself back to bed, I heard a cheerful voice.

'Dude, it's me,' said Mari.

I said I'd be downstairs in two minutes, but it took me seven to brush my teeth, change into a clean T-shirt, shove a couple of aspirins down my throat, and grab my gun and my Ray-Bans.

Downstairs, Mari was waiting for me outside the car, holding a bouquet of white lilies and a large coffee in a paper cup. We smiled at each other, got into the car and drove to Nordre Gravlund. It was right next to the Ullevål University Hospital, the place we used to go with some regularity during our first years at the Politihøgskolen to familiarise ourselves with the secrets of forensic medicine. There, between the statue of the grieving woman holding the body of her lifeless son in her arms, which Gustav Laerum had sculpted, and another of the naked squatting man that the sculptor Odd Hilt had designed in tribute to the twenty-three members of the Communist Party murdered on that spot at the hands of Nazi soldiers during the Second World War; there in the shade of the hundred-year-old trees, on a charmless gravestone, was her name, Kedijah, the young Eritrean who still lives in my dreams. Mari handed me the flowers. I don't know what Muslims offer their dead, but I know Christians believe that lilies are a symbol of the purity, rebirth and light of the soul. This was supposedly the flower that covered the grave of the Virgin Mary, the lily of peace, symbolising innocence. I put the flowers down at the gravestone, trying to find some meaning in that moment, what it meant to be there at that grave. I didn't know whether I was kneeling to ask her permission, or God's, whether I was praying or crying. I opted for silence.

'Why didn't you tell me?' I asked Kedijah. I thought I might have said those words out loud, but my colleague didn't react at all. I asked again: 'Why didn't you tell me? Except that you did, I know it, I just didn't believe you.' I shrugged. 'I wrote the report justifying sending you to that place. That's what I do.' I pulled out my gun and held it in my hands. Mari immediately touched my shoulder, but I just acknowledged her presence and gestured for her to leave me alone. She stepped back. 'In this country, we have a code of moral conduct that says Norway will not allow the sale of weapons to areas where there's a war,' I said as I took the magazine out of the gun, and heard Mari give a sigh of relief. 'Any area under a threat of war or countries going through a civil war.' I paused. 'Fine words, eh, Kedijah?' I put the gun down next to the lilies and looked at her tombstone. 'We all claim to support human rights,' I pulled the bullets out of the magazine and continued, 'but our military equipment still ends up in wars that don't align with our moral codes.' I lined up the bullets next to the gun. 'Last year, we made 3.6 billion kroner exporting weapons.' I paused and turned to Mari. 'It makes no sense.' I couldn't hold back my tears. 'I'm sorry, Kedijah. I'm terribly sorry.' Mari kneeled and put her arms around me.

'I'm starting to feel numb, Mari.' I sank my head onto her shoulder. 'I don't want to be like my dad and his mates, unable to feel pity or pain, indifferent to everything,' I said.

'Let it out, just let it out,' she said, patting me gently on the back.

'I feel I failed this girl,' I said, and Mari frowned as if disagreeing with me even without saying a word. She just wiped my tears with her hands. 'The moment she, who's been stripped of everything – family, land, humanity – came knocking on our door and found us, the police, here to welcome her,' I said, and Mari picked up my gun.

'We're just agents of the law,' she said, and added as she handed it over to me, 'we don't make the laws.' I nodded.

'In this whole immigration debate,' I said, 'I'm amazed there isn't one single reference to the profit made from

armed conflicts in Africa.' Mari just shrugged. I turned to
Kedijah's tombstone. 'We're so quick to point fingers at
ethnic conflicts, civil wars and the ruling despots whose
greed is infinite. But do we really have no words for the
profits generated by the companies or countries who feed
those conflicts?' I said, collecting up the bullets and the
magazine. 'Mari, do you know any prayers?' I asked her,
but she didn't, and nor did I.

'The only verse I remember is Ezekiel 25:17 as spoken
by Jules Winnfield,' I said. Mari looked at me totally
baffled, presumably wondering who the hell this Jules
Winnfield was anyway.

'*Pulp Fiction*,' I said, and she shrugged. 'Samuel L.
Jackson,' I insisted. She grimaced, and I turned to Kedijah's
tombstone.

'Let's just pray in silence.'

VII

I wanted to start the police report on the Angolan like
this:

*I found her standing outside the car, eyes fixed on the E6,
the motorway that connects Gothenburg to Oslo. She was
on the roadside, leaning on the car patrol, her arm on the
bonnet, chin resting on her fist, her eyes and her mind
pointed towards Sweden. The road wasn't too busy, it was
twenty past seven on a Saturday morning. We were on our
first mission of the day, inspecting all the passenger vehicles
crossing the border. Since it was still a few minutes before*

*the first bus came over the Svinesund Bridge to our side,
I'd had time to go over to the bushes to relieve myself.*

*When I came back to the car, I didn't want to disturb
her thoughts. I was about to get back into the car when
she turned to me and noticed I'd brought a bunch of wild
herbs, a habit I picked up from my grandfather on our trips
to see the sea from the Atlanterhavsveien. Whenever we
stopped by the side of the road to pee, my granddad would
come back to the car with a handful of that vegetation
that grew on the verges. I learned to rub my hands with
Saponaria, a natural soap. He'd gather other plants just so
he could look at them admiringly, or to scent the inside of
the car, like Bergfrue and Blåveis. It's the smell I associate
with happy memories, when the world was revealing itself
to me, full of possibilities.*

*'Did you go to pick seven different herbs and flowers to
put under your pillow?' Mari asked me.*

'You honestly think I follow those traditions?'

*'Why, what's wrong with celebrating nature, the
renewal of life, fertility? I'm always catching you staring
out into the void. Maybe you need St Hans to show up in
your dreams to tell you who your future wife's going to be,'
she said, joking now.*

*'First, it's already August, which is too late to be invok-
ing the saint,' I replied, 'and second, look who's talking.'*

The report Mari's being questioned about in the fishbowl
by our inspector doesn't start with this scene, and it makes
no reference to the flowers. I've been keeping the habit up
since I was deployed to the border. I don't like the smell of

the inside of those patrol cars, so I gather roadside herbs and put them in the side compartments in the doors to dispel the odour – heavy with fear – that anyone sitting in the back seat always exudes. Obviously that detail wasn't included either. Instead, I opened the report with information about the time, the location, the bus's registration number, the details of the detained man, the interactions between us in the four hours he was in the police station before we sent him to the detention centre.

Our job when we're interviewing somebody is to obtain information that can be verified, seeking out, assembling and corroborating clues that might establish the likelihood of the prisoner's guilt or innocence. Kalaf Epalanga was the name of the guy we picked up on the bus, an Angolan citizen, with a lapsed passport and a valid residency card issued by the Portuguese Immigration and Borders Service. He communicated clearly in English and said he was a musician on his way to the Øya festival, in Oslo. He'd lost his passport, that's why he was travelling alone, but that wasn't the first version of the story he gave us. When I approached him, first showing him my badge, and then asking him for his papers, he – very confident – handed me his residency card. When I asked him for his passport, he replied, also with a ready response, that it was in his suitcase, in the hold of the bus. In the two years I've spent patrolling the border, every time I met an African who told me his passport was in his suitcase, I knew something was up. I don't know if they think they can insult my intelligence with such a threadbare old lie, or if they just reckon we're lazy. Could they really think,

when they say they've got their passport at the bottom
of their suitcase, that we're going to reply, 'Oh, what a
nuisance – well, there's no way we're going to go down
and check if you do have a passport in your suitcase or
not'? But we did, and, just as I suspected, something was
indeed up. The passport had expired in 2002 and the photograph was completely scratched through. Mari, who
doesn't know anything about music, thought this story
about his being a musician was fake, as the guy didn't
have any kind of instrument with him. I did consider telling her that nowadays you don't need an instrument to
be a musician, but I'd end up wasting too much energy
having to explain to her how music had evolved histori-
cally. I know the festival he mentioned. And so this pass-
port-less individual, travelling by bus from Portugal, was
either telling the truth or he was transporting narcotics to
deal at Øya. There was no way we could let him continue
on his journey without clearing this up. I asked him to
retrieve his luggage and come with us.

Mari didn't believe a word he said. Maybe it was
because the visit to Kedijah's grave was still fresh in my
memory, but I had my doubts. The last thing I wanted was
another musician visiting me in my dreams. So we began
by rummaging through his luggage. A Mac laptop, iPod,
headphones and a few changes of clothes. Our dogs sniffed
around but didn't alert us to any sign of drugs or explosive
materials. We focused on the documents he'd presented.
The name he'd given us didn't appear on the list of asylum
seekers who had been granted entry into Portugal, and we
couldn't find out if he'd committed any crime – domestic

crimes don't appear on the international database. We tried Interpol and the results came back negative. This individual had a cleaner record than a priest. Either we were facing a criminal just starting out who'd had the bad luck of crossing our path, or this Kalaf Epalanga isn't who he says he is.

Exposing a liar is hard, even for trained detectives. A liar can learn to say the right things in a convincing way. And contrary to popular belief, reading body language isn't much help for separating the truth from lies, even if some tricks do exist. One is to see how a group of suspects remembers a particular event. Lying in a group is totally different from lying when we're being interrogated on our own. Since our suspect was travelling alone, the degree of difficulty of dragging the truth out of him was exponentially bigger. For me, group interrogations are more interesting, because they allow us to watch a lot of human behaviour. Gathering the suspects together and waiting patiently always ends up with them unwittingly exposing one another. And even when they say nothing contradictory or reveal only very slight discrepancies in their stories, we always end up gathering more from groups than from one guy on his own. For example, in the case of groups of smugglers, robbers or terrorists, if they are all singing the same litany in perfect harmony, very convincingly, it's because they've rehearsed to death the answers they'd give if they got caught. When you hear something with too many identical details, you should be suspicious. Perfect conformity doesn't sound convincing. That's what amateur criminals don't realise. We always suspect everybody, but especially when the whole group remembers the exact same things. Memory is usually very messy.

This Kalaf could easily be pulling a Keyser Söze, making up this whole story about being in a band that's going to perform at Øya. Maybe he read something about the festival in a newspaper he bought before setting off. Just like Kevin Spacey's character made up this whole plot while he was being questioned by Special Agent Kujan and Jack Baer from the FBI. *The Usual Suspects* is one of my favourite films, I've seen it dozens of times, and I got to like it even more when Jay-Z, in the video for 'The City Is Mine', recreated it with him in the Spacey part alongside Michael Rapaport as the detective.

One of the things that occurred to me at the time, maybe due to the frustration at our not finding anything on file for the individual we had in custody, was the movie's most iconic line: 'The greatest trick the devil ever pulled was convincing the world he didn't exist' – a paraphrase of a Charles Baudelaire line, which I never connected to the French poet till Ava told me afterwards, when she discovered my obsession with the film. Whenever I opened the door to that cell to confront this guy with a few facts, I was unconsciously hoping he'd come out with the line about the coffee, the same one Jay-Z opens 'The City Is Mine' video with, when he quotes the scary Hungarian criminal passing for Verbal Kint, telling the detective that when he gets dehydrated his urine turns lumpy and thick. He not only didn't say it, he never asked for a thing. He behaved very like young Kedijah; he accepted what we offered him and asked for nothing else. The only difference being, when we left him alone, he didn't sing, he kept silent the whole time. He didn't seem worried, as if he knew what was awaiting him. He didn't ask to make a phone call, didn't mention any lawyer. He just kept insisting on his story about the band and the Øya festival. He said the band played this kind of dance music coming out of Angola, a sort of African techno called kuduro. Mari, who'd never been to any iteration of Øya, found this weird. 'Angolan techno in Oslo?' she asked, suspicious, when we were back at our desks.

'What about it?'

'You don't find it weird that Angola makes techno? I always thought African music was made with instruments – guitars, conga drums and maracas – the total opposite of music made with computers.' Mari didn't think the story added up. We didn't find anything incriminating in his luggage, apart from the expired documents, obviously. But something didn't feel right to her, there had to be some other reason for a man to leave Lisbon and travel all the way across Europe by bus.

While she was sketching out theories to try and find a reason to justify what the musician had done, I was asking myself different questions. What was kuduro? Where had it come from? When? Who'd invented it? How had techno reached Angola? Could they also have been exposed to Kraftwerk, Giorgio Moroder and Yellow Magic Orchestra? The same could be said about the music that emerged in the late 1980s, in the heart of the practically abandoned city of Detroit, after the collapse of the automotive industry. In Norway, that genre of music didn't find fertile ground in the capital, it had to travel north, to Tromsø. Our northernmost city, besides holding the title of the city with the most snow in the winter, is also famous for being our insomnia capital. Owing to the high latitude, the twilight is long, meaning there's no real darkness between the end of April and middle of August, so during that time you can't see the city's main attraction, the aurora borealis. Tromsø is in the middle of the 'northern lights' zone, which makes it one of the best areas in the world for watching them. Because of the earth's rotation, Tromsø moves into the aurora zone around 6 p.m., and out again around midnight. These might be the conditions that inspired Tromsøvaeringer like Röyksopp, Biosphere and Bel Canto, and the gang from Beatservice Records and the Insomnia festival, to create the Tromsø techno scene. How did that music end up in Africa? What was the song that woke the minds of the artists who make kuduro? These were the questions I wanted to ask the guy in my cell, not who had issued his residency card. Could it have been Yellow Magic Orchestra's 'Riot in Lagos'? Could it have been Kraftwerk's 'Autobahn'? Could our own *TOS. CD – Tromsø Techno 1994* have made it down there? Might they have dived head first into what Belleville, Juan Atkins, Kevin Saunderson and Derrick May, the figures who were directly involved in the birth of techno in Detroit, did with numbers like Inner City's 'Good Life', Rhythim Is Rhythim's 'Strings of Life'? Or did they drink their inspiration from Jeff Mills's Underground Resistance, or my own absolute favourite, Carl Craig? Our Saturday-night outings always started with meeting up at some friend's house, a few beers, a few shots and the radio on. But the turn of the millennium was disappointing, to say the least. Some of our favourite spots like Jazid and Skansen closed down, and without a place to play, the DJs shut themselves up in their rooms and concentrated on music production. And it was around that time that the world turned towards Bergen with the arrival of Röyksopp's *Melody A.M.*, in 2001, making our Nordic melancholy, a wave that had started in the late 1990s, more appealing. Projects like Kings of Convenience and the music put out by Tellé Records were on the news. Suddenly, we had music to export, which gave the Oslo producers a new vitality, as they took advantage of no longer being the centre of attention to create new music. If you asked me why I became a club bouncer, it was also because I wanted to be close to that scene, and since I have no talent for spinning records nor the patience to be a bartender, looking out for the security of the people and the place was something I could do without too much effort. The only issue was that the nightlife in the city only went on till 3 a.m., which made people more anxious. They were constantly looking at their watches, trying to consume within the space of two or three hours as much alcohol as possible, socialising, flirting, hooking up, smoking, dancing. Just thinking about it makes my armpits sweat.

My brother used to blame these nightlife habits for techno never managing to grow in Oslo. Nobody had the time to wait for a song with a five-minute intro to reach its climax. People wanted to give their all, to live to the max before the club's aviary lights came on and any shame was exposed. Hence, our relationship to drugs like MDMA and ketamine is practically non-existent. Our drugs of choice are alcohol or cocaine, and, for some people, both. Our drinking reaches Olympic levels, and, after my years of living alongside the city's revellers, I'd say the people aren't violent by nature. But the combination of Viking blood, alcohol and cocaine inevitably transformed the taxi ranks into combat rings at the end of the night. Unlike those other cities where there's no obligation to shut so early, making the flow more fluid, our laws force the clubs to kick out a sea of intoxicated people onto the streets all at once. And you don't need to be a genius to know that when six hundred sexually frustrated males are thrown together in a taxi queue, all of them boozed up and high, it's no wonder you get skirmishes.

What's kuduro's relationship to the drug problem? What's the drug most associated with kuduro? Can Angolan society be as conservative as ours? To us, drugs are a sensitive topic. They're illegal and we have very low tolerance for dealers. If we find out that the unfortunate Kalaf Epalanga has any cases related to narcotics linked to his name, he's totally fucked. Our penalties for illegal immigration are light in comparison to how we treat drug dealers. The debate about the decriminalisation of certain narcotics has been going on for a while, but we're far from having a consensus on the matter, and consensus is what feeds this society. Which is why I doubt they're going to be decriminalised. The press tends to pile the pressure on club culture and demonise it, like it was the only thing responsible for the title of European death-by-overdose capital, which was bestowed on us in 2002. The situation's serious, especially in the eastern part of Oslo. The statistics suggest that drugs are behind most crimes in the country, and one of the main reasons why the number of deaths is higher in Norway than in other parts of Europe. All because there are more people injecting heroin than smoking. Not that smoking doesn't end up fucking you over eventually.

I've got a lot of respect for the guys who work in narcotics enforcement. Having worked in the nightlife business myself, I know how the culture of combining cocaine, heroin and Rohypnol with a lot of alcohol is destroying many lives. I'll bet older people must be scratching their heads wondering how come a society with as much money as ours finds itself facing a drug-use problem. If you ask me, it's partly because of boredom. When you think about it, we don't really have problems. I can say this without batting an eyelid because I'm on the front line: I hear all kinds of stories, real nightmares, each worse than the ones before. And when I compare them to *our* problems, it makes me want to laugh. I enjoy fighting boredom by visiting some dark cellar and listening to a Funktion-One sound system blasting Claude VonStroke's 'Who's Afraid of Detroit'.

Shame I can't share this stuff with Mari. Not with her or with anyone else in the station. Maybe only the Angolan we've detained knows and understands it. The VonStroke classic came to me via my brother, by e-mail. As usual, there wasn't a lot of chit-chat, just the subject line that said: 'Drop everything and listen to this one.' I clicked on the link and from the very beginning, when those atmospheric pads come in, I felt chills up my spine. Then that bleepy synth, the deep bassline and the precise beat supporting a surprisingly catchy refrain. And I'm someone who doesn't even listen to dance music outside of the clubs. For listening at home, my scene's always been rap and it still is, but from time to time, mainly when it's been recommended by my brother, I do make an exception. He knows what I like, so much so that I've got it in my Top Five, alongside Model 500's 'Starlight (Moritz Mix)', Richie Hawtin's 'The Tunnel' and Carl Craig's 'Angel', which I came to relatively late when you think he's one of the gurus of the Detroit scene. Before that I was totally addicted to J Dilla's 'Welcome 2 Detroit', until one day my mum turned to me and my brother and said she was going to see a concert by a Cape Verdean singer who sings barefoot, Cesária Évora. She'd asked my dad to take her, but he refused, and since she knows we're our father's children she knew we'd do the same. So she just asked if we could drive her to the airport. On the way, my brother, teasing her, put a song on the stereo and asked if she knew that version. It was Carl Craig's mix of 'Angola', the Cape Verdean singer's song. I didn't understand a word of it, I don't even know what language she was speaking, I could just pick out the word 'Angola' in the chorus. I don't know if that's why I associated her music with an image of my mother shaking her head, but the truth was, from that date on I started to consume everything he'd produced and I ended up at Planet E, where, along with Moodymann, I discovered Innerzone Orchestra's 'Bug in the Bass Bin'.

And my life changed forever. Suddenly everything made sense. All the dance music I'd heard before that moment, mostly the 'broken beats' coming from England, made much more sense. And of what I heard in my brief internet search, I can say with absolute certainty that 'Bug in the Bass Bin' is also in the DNA of the music that the Angolan who's occupying our cell claims is the reason he's come over our border.

Around 1 p.m. Mari touched my shoulder and asked if I didn't want to grab a quick break and pop out for a sandwich. I took my earphones out to say she should head out on her own, I wasn't hungry. If I had been, I'd have eaten right there at my desk. Noticing the sound that was coming out of the earphones, she asked what I was listening to. I passed them to her and she pulled up a chair next to me, maybe thinking I was presenting her with some proof to incriminate our prisoner. She covered her ears with her hands so that no important detail could possibly escape, but after three minutes of that mixture of calypso and electronic beats, she turned to me, disappointment on her face.

'It's just music,' she said, emphasising the obvious.

'It's the music he makes,' I said, and her look of disappointment got even worse. I asked her to put the earphones back in and I showed her a YouTube video of a lad who's lost a leg, dancing frantically on the roof of an abandoned car. The video's had 2.5 million views. 'That's where he's from,' I said, and she seemed more interested. 'Amazing, isn't it?' But she didn't respond, she still had her hands over the earphones. 'The guy in the song is called Costuleta, and they call this music kuduro,' I said when Mari returned the earphones. 'I read that the genre is a by-product of the Angolan civil war that ravaged the country for twenty-seven years.'

She stood up and I followed.

'Where are you going?' she asked.

'Do you want some company?' I smiled, and she grabbed her jacket, checked for her wallet and walked towards the door with me one step behind.

'The music survived the second cold war, between Ronald Reagan's America and Gorbachev's Soviet Union,' I said, and she rolled her eyes. 'They say kuduro is the antidote to mourning, a happy whisper, an absurd dance, that tries to be like the black gold springing from their wells, the most exportable product ever to come out of Angola,' I said, surprised by my own enthusiasm.

'And what does that tell us about our detainee?' Mari's question was a relevant one, but I didn't answer right away. Instead, I pressed on.

'You know kuduro literally means *hard ass*?' She stopped and turned to me with a frown. And to wind her up even more, I offered her another titbit I'd picked up from the internet: 'The kuduro dance style was inspired by one of your favourite actors, Jean-Claude Van Damme. Who'd have thought!' She clenched her right fist as if getting ready to launch it at my nose. And when I was preparing to duck and protect myself, she showed me her middle finger.

'You know what, I would prefer some alone time,' Mari said as she opened the door.

'Apparently, he dances like you, Mari,' I said, laughing. 'And that awkwardness and that hard-as-a-broom ass led to the birth of a whole musical genre,' I added, as she closed the door behind her.

VIII

The lines about freeing someone when we love them that Jay-Z dropped in 'Dear Summer' popped into my head for the second time in a week, when I sat back at my desk. The first time was when I visited the Frognerparken, which, like it did every year, had that distinctive smell hovering in the air of oak and hot dogs cooking on disposable barbecues. The lawn was full of half-naked people, echoing the nudity that Gustav Vigeland shaped in the more than two hundred sculptures you could see around the place. I don't know whether it's because of those figures or the theme that the father of our sculpture chose to represent, but the truth was I always spent hours looking at the figures all stuck on top of one another on that single block of granite pointing up at the sky, evoking our sense of yearning for the spiritual and the divine. And what's even stranger is that the image was accompanied by those lines from the song and an urgent need to see Ava again. I first thought about calling her, but, since years had already gone by since our last meeting at my granddad's funeral, I thought it might be more appropriate to start off with an e-mail, or maybe a letter in which I'd set out the reasons we'd been postponing seeing each other again since the summers of our adolescence until now, maybe not going back so far, maybe since our last conversation, and also explaining why I hadn't asked her to stay around Oslo. I'd start with those exact words from 'Dear Summer', one of the songs Hova had used to come out of his self-imposed retirement and in which, to our delight, he gave us those bars of the purest rap. Calmly, gracefully, he said goodbye to his favourite time of the year spouting verses over a vintage beat produced by Just Blaze, but which could easily have been produced by Madlib, from that jazz soul sample of Weldon Irvine's 'Morning Sunrise'. I wasn't going to bore her with my obsession with Jay-Z's rhymes, but I agree with Jigga. If it comes back, it is because it's here to stay.

I was going to ask if she didn't feel our place was there in Kristiansund, maybe not literally in Kristiansund, but there, looking into each other's eyes, just like we did in her parents' kitchen. Trading stories and drinking Lebanese-style coffee – kahweh, as she'd taught me to pronounce it in Arabic. Thinking about that night made me crave a good cup of coffee. Maybe I should have taken advantage of the sandwich break and followed Mari out. The most reasonable coffee within walking distance is in the actual airport. I should have paid even more attention to how Ava made that Lebanese coffee. Maybe I'll find the recipe online, maybe I should write to her – she'll find it weird, after all this silence, getting an e-mail from me asking for the recipe for that coffee. Maybe I really will do that; when I leave here, I'll stop by Fuglen, that hipster place, café by day, bar and design store by night. I've never checked it out, but I think you can go out at night for a G&T and come back home with a lamp or a chair under your arm.

It's the place of the moment for coffee-lovers. It opened its doors in 1963, and it's a place my dad took me a few times. I didn't drink coffee back then, and I wondered how anyone could like drinking something so bitter. But the establishment was reborn this year with a new radiance. The new management, themselves also the kids of former customers, decided to keep the interior almost completely intact. Visiting it is like entering a time capsule, and the fact they've added a selection of vintage items and furniture, mostly from the 1950s and 1960s, which, according to the experts, was the golden age of Nordic design, makes the place feel a bit like a living museum. My knowledge of design history is limited, but I'm sure Ava would find the place thrilling. Every little corner exudes the optimism and belief in the future that characterised the 1960s in this country. Maybe I really should write to tell her I've found the essence of Norwegian coffee right here in Oslo, a variety of beans originating in exotic lands and prepared according to methods I didn't even know existed: AeroPress, French press, filter, pour-over and even cold brew. And they say the Norwegians are in second place, after the Finns, in global coffee consumption per capita. A lot of my compatriots can't get through twenty-four hours without getting jolted by a shot of java. It's not unusual, seeing them drink one espresso after another, even before going to bed.

Jay-Z's 'Dear Summer' echoes through my brain. He managed to explain why he retired and distanced himself from the microphone, but I can't find the reason to explain the why of our distance. I wonder if we could say that the love for a person can take on the characteristics of a land, a country, and that living far away from them could mean the same as being in exile? Self-imposed exile, in my case. There is a way of putting an end to it: she just needs to want me back, or simply to want me, since I couldn't really say we've ever actually been together, except, of course, those nights when I slipped through the window and then we lived together in that tiny bed. When I went off to the bathroom on that night we spent drinking coffee, I even peeked into her bedroom. All that was left was that same silent bed beside the wall of an empty room, the only real witness to our much-missed summers. Those nights we spent whispering in each other's ears about the albums that had shaped us, we talked about songs, arrangements, composers, about everything, except us. To this day I can't believe her parents never caught us. It would have been harder for her dad, who was mostly away on the oil rigs. But her mum, who slept two doors down from that bedroom, never surprised our naked bodies, my hands caressing Ava's thighs, running across the dip of her stomach as she lay on her back, my fingers combing through her hair.

We spent hours like that, talking about cities we wanted to visit, festivals and shows we'd like to see, without realising – well, really like no young lovers ever do realise – that revealing your desires doesn't mean the same thing as making defined plans. Ava talked so much about travelling that I always thought she'd end up working for Scandinavian Airlines or becoming tour manager for an internationally successful band. You could always hear in her voice, even when she was whispering, that she didn't want to waste a moment of her youth. She had asked me if

I wanted to die in Norway. We were fifteen, the last thing I was thinking about was where I wanted to die. I shrugged and she'd ask me with that big grin of hers, 'You don't want to see what the world out there is like?' Of course I did, but, more than just wanting to see the world, how about if we went away together? I thought about it, but never had the nerve to ask, so I returned to the kitchen and instead asked about her life in Beirut.

'I feel like I belong. My whole life I've been trying to find out what that means,' she said. 'But it's not all a bed of roses. Despite meeting really lovely people and having friends from every social stratum and religion, like most Lebanese people I still live in fear of my neighbours. That's what civil war does to people.' She paused and looked into her coffee cup. 'How can you make a success of your life if you're constantly in the shadow of the ghost of war, the threat of murder, the tension between Israel and Hezbollah, suicide bombs, corruption?' she asked. But she didn't expect me to answer, because, in the same breath, she said she had met a lot of people her age with their suitcases practically ready to go, wanting to get out, this time because of unemployment but it's obviously more than this. 'Who can blame them? The hope for a better future is hanging by a thread. Lebanon is one of the most dangerous areas on earth. That's how people see the Middle East, and that's how they see themselves. The future of Lebanon is linked to the most complex problems in the world. The Arab–Israeli conflict, the balance of power between Russia, China, Iran, North Korea versus the USA and the West. The endless hatred between

Maronites, Shi'ites, Sunnis. They've witnessed more wars, armed conflicts and tragedies than any European could ever imagine. They live in a city filled with adrenaline and schizophrenics. And they only realise how dangerous life is when they're visited by relatives from the West, when they see how nervous they are, scared to go out onto the street. That's when they realise just how serene they are in the face of that amalgam of perfect randomness, which a lot of people call chaos but which, in Beirut, is just life.'

Silence.

'If you don't want to talk about Lebanon, please, I . . .' I said, hesitant, and she smiled.

'How is your life in Oslo?' she asked, and I looked into my empty cup. 'That bad?'

I wanted to tell her about Kedijah, but I froze.

'What are you listening to at the moment?' I asked, and she widened her eyes.

'Eyvind, you're trying to run away from my question?' She smiled and touched my hand. 'Do you need something stronger in your coffee, to help you get something off your chest?' she asked, staring fiercely at me.

I burst out laughing. 'No, I really do just want to know what is on rotation on your iPod!' She shrugged, stood up and went to the living room. She returned to the kitchen, sat down, and scrolled through her music library. She then handed me one of the earbuds and moved closer. I did the same, leaning towards her, our faces forehead to forehead, just a few inches apart.

'It's a song called "Wadih", it's a boy's name and means "alone, one who likes solitude", by Soap Kills, a duo formed by Zeid Hamdan and Yasmine Hamdan,' she said.

'Sound good,' I said, nodding to the rhythm.

'Yasmine Hamdan is like our Beth Gibbons. Let me play you another song of theirs,' she said, scrolling. 'This one's a version of an old Arab song titled "Ya Habibi Taala Lhaeni" – My Love, Come Chase Me.' I smiled. 'This is what I've being listening to lately,' she said. 'Culture was starting to be exciting, but the war cooled everything down.' Ava put the iPod on the table but then picked it up again right away to play me a rock song. '"It's All About Lost Expectations" by the Scrambled Eggs, my favourite rock band,' she said and stood up. I followed, trying my best not to pull the earbud cord out of her ear while she danced. 'I know you only listen to rap, but if you feel adventurous, start with this album, *No Special Date nor a Deity to Venerate*,' she said when the song ended.

'I love the titles they give their projects. It's like they've got some secret message,' I said as we sat back down.

'I can't remember exactly, but Charbel Haber from the Scrambled Eggs once said they did everything as if the world would end tomorrow. The Syrians might come back, Israel might attack, and Hezbollah might start another war. Living in that kind of situation meant you had to do a lot of self-destructive stuff,' said Ava, and I poured more coffee into our cups. 'To them, sex, drugs and rock 'n' roll meant, above all, freedom.'

I asked her about the rap scene, which rappers stood out, and she replied she still didn't know much about the genre, she felt the Arab hip-hop scene did exist but, apart from the odd name like Aks'ser, Kita3 Beirut and this DJ Lethal

Skillz, there wasn't a lot she could add. What she heard – some of them spat better than others – were rhymes about the reality of urban life in Beirut, about social inequality, political instability and life in the Palestinian refugee camps. Nonetheless, on her trips deep into Lebanon, she got in touch with the country's oral tradition. She said I'd enjoy witnessing a zajal, a kind of poetry competition in the Lebanese dialect, which survives to this day in villages in the interior. She gave me a few lines by way of example. It was the first time I'd heard her speak Arabic, she always talked to her parents in French. Strange how a language gives a person a flag, a territory. Until that night she was Ava, my grandparents' neighbour, my little summer girl-friend. Hearing her talk about her other country, in her other language, telling stories of struggle, forced migration and how fragile peace is (that abstract thing we don't know the meaning of until the scales unbalance and, in her case, until Muslims and Christians stop getting along and respecting the native power of representativity), those stories of unnatural deaths, of people exiled, of shame and blind pride, made her feel more alive than ever.

When she paused to take a sip of coffee I asked her: 'If your father had found out about our relationship, what would have happened to us?' That question was more about the present than about the past, and she knew I was asking about now, about how her parents – no, I lie – about how she saw us today. She put down her cup and smiled.

'Improper behaviour in relation to an unmarried girl harms the honour of her family line. Her father and brothers would seek reparation, which could take the form of killing the girl and the man involved, of killing the man or driving him out of the village, or coming to an agreement between the two clans involved. If no compensation was obtained, open conflict between the two families might follow.'

IX

Mari touched my shoulder again. She pulled up a chair and sat down next to me. She'd come back in from the street looking livelier. Must have had a nice coffee, I thought.

'So have you found out yet if our Angolan's telling the truth? Have you uncovered the big secret? So tell me, who invented kuduro?' She laughed, pointing at the computer screen.

'That's our detainee's band, it's called Buraka Som Sistema. The track's called "The Sound of Kuduro",' I said, scrolling the video back to the opening frame, an aerial view of a busy street, with a caption reading 'Angola 2007'. The camera then cuts to inside a car where we see our Angolan declaring in English and, I'm guessing, in Portuguese, 'We made it, we here.' Various pictures of Luanda streets are intercut with close-ups of a man and kids. The sound of a frenetic synthesiser and of the horn of a train announcing its departure, and the voice of M.I.A. inviting everyone to get on board, before coming out with the slogan: 'Sound of kuduro knocking at your door!' And the party starts, several other men appear, dragging themselves along the floor, surrounded by a crowd of curious onlookers. We see the bare torso of another person crawling painfully along the ground. The beat seems to get faster, but it's just the impression we get when we see a man fall to the ground, others spinning in the air, defying gravity and the pain of their fall. We start to notice that these movements aren't random, it's dancing, a dance that, like in that other video of the mutilated dancer, doesn't just use but also kind of challenges the way the body occupies the urban fabric. Pictures of home studios, MCs at a microphone spouting their rhymes, intercut with some of the most interesting, exciting, creative dance sequences I've ever seen. Young people with their feet spinning in the dust, at the roadside, between cars and under a scorching sun. We are transported, by rapid cuts, through street scenes that present an African city without the clichés of beaches or postcard palm trees. We see neighbourhoods that look like Rio de Janeiro favelas, we see traffic, so much traffic; we see a woman walking carrying a load on her head, swaying her hips to the rhythm of the beat. We see a young man, in an acrobatic dance move, launching himself onto a chair, destroying it and getting up again without ever losing his connection to the rhythm, continuing to dance wildly.

'I don't know anything about music, but don't you think it's strange that a member of a band that's apparently successful should be picked up without papers on a bus trying to get across the border? He's obviously come to seek asylum, if not worse,' said Mari, suspicious that our Angolan was hiding something more sinister.

'But he could also be telling the truth,' I said.

'Do you remember what Minister Sylvi Listhaug said?' she asked, and I shook my head. 'She said Norwegian authorities should send a signal to the world that seeking asylum in Norway is difficult.' Mari looked straight at me, dead serious. I couldn't contain a wry smile.

'It would be good if that message got through. It'd make our job easier, but these immigrants, rather than hearing what our minister of the interior said, gather their information from other people who are just as desperate and ill-informed as they are,' I said.

'I'm not joking,' she muttered.

'There's a lucrative market that feeds and exploits their vulnerabilities,' I said. 'The immigration problem won't be solved by locking up everybody that tries to cross the border. There's no point just papering over the cracks.'

'So what do you suggest?' she asked. I shrugged.

'I don't know. I'm just a border agent who's counting the hours to get back home to his computer.'

'Oh, so it's not that easy, is it, Mr Stats?' she laughed.

'I didn't say it was, but I'm not a lawmaker,' I said.

'I just wanted you to admit that,' she said and moved on to another question. 'And you're saying that after spending hours in front of a computer writing reports, you still have the energy to open a computer at home?'

'Why don't you mind your own business?' I said, and we both laughed. I went on to tell Mari about the time I questioned an illegal immigrant, a Nigerian woman in her early twenties who was dreaming of a life in Europe. She'd tried several times to get out of Nigeria. The first time that she paid 500,000 naira – around 250 dollars – for forged travel documents, she got stopped at the airport, still in Nigeria. When I questioned her, I asked how she was expecting to make the money she needed to support herself. She leaned back, raised her shoulders as if she were about to give one of those motivational speeches that contestants in beauty contests use to win over the judges, and I saw her confidence rise up through her graceful neck and face. Her skin was dark black, almost unreal, smooth and taut, her fleshy cheeks shining with sweat and her eyes expressionless. I couldn't tell whether this was because of sadness or if she didn't really give a damn about what our justice system was going to do to her. Incarceration, deportation . . . she had a plan B already. That's the only way to explain why she replied, without blinking, challenging me with her sincerity, when I asked her the question about how she expected to support herself in Europe: 'Sex!' Her voice didn't come out neutral as if she were announcing the death of a soldier to his parents, but as if she were educating me, conveying the secret intentions of this relationship between police officers and prostitutes, actors in the same play that is human misery. 'If you're not ready to be a prostitute, best not to come to Europe,' she'd been told by a woman who had become a prostitute in Italy. After much thought, she concluded that was the only possibility for her to improve her life. The women and men who, she knew, prostituted themselves in Europe, lived like kings when they came back to Nigeria. She made her second attempt to cross Europe's external borders in 2007. The travel costs were paid by a madam in Italy. Along with a group of other migrants, she crossed the Sahara towards Libya. After a few months' wait in Tripoli, she managed to get over the Mediterranean to

Italy, the entry point for a lot of the migrants who end up at our borders. Which is why it was such a surprise today when we got an Angolan, and probably also the reason Mari is condemning him. We know the histories of the ones coming from the Middle East, from Nigeria, from Senegal. But Angola? We don't know anything about them, and not knowing makes us nervous. Might there be more coming? Might there be a new wave of Angolan immigrants and this Kalaf Epalanga was just the fastest getting here? Those are Mari's questions.

She went off to find out what's happening in Angola; I preferred to flush out the truth about the guy's story and so far everything checked out, the band really was slated to perform at 7 p.m. on the Øya stage. Nevertheless, Mari decided to follow her instinct, and when your partner smells a rat, pre-emption is better than cure. Before sending him off to the detention centre I did think that, for the music story to stick better, it would have been easier if he'd been travelling with another member of the band. Someone less suspicious, with their papers in order. Mari laughed at my suggestion. 'Why? He's still presenting the same sketchy documents.'

'But it could give him more credibility if he had some sort of corroborating evidence from someone else,' I said. 'You know how much weight that carries in these kind of cases.'

Mari considered my take before responding. 'Well, it might help, but it doesn't happen like that often, you know that.' I shrugged, and she went on, 'Come on, Eyvind, we both had the same interrogation training, you and me. We both know two people giving the same story is often suspicious. It's the differences between what two people say about an event, *that's* what actually makes their statements more believable. And then, when you take all of the details together and look at them from all angles, it can paint a clearer picture of what really happened, not just what one person saw or heard.'

I leaned in. 'Well exactly!' I said. 'That's why I'm saying it would have been better if he'd travelled with one of his bandmates or the manager.'

She stared at me for a moment, her face unreadable.

'Would you have let him go then?'

I shrugged.

'If the inspector called us into the fishbowl and asked about our night out in Grünerløkka, we'd be constantly interrupting each other, wouldn't we? We'd be like, "No, that's not what we did, we went to Blå first, and *then* we went to try the cheesecake with raspberry sauce afterwards, but before that, we went by the Vår Frelsers Gravlund . . ."'

She smiled but insisted, 'That's not what I asked, Eyvind.' Despite her amused expression, I knew she had asked me a serious question. But I was surprised – unlike some of our colleagues on the force, she did like using group interrogation techniques. And it makes sense. When two people share a similar story but disagree on details, it shows they recall events independently and haven't just fabricated or rehearsed a narrative. Such natural variations show how everyone experiences situations differently, adding depth and authenticity to the testimony.

As she stood up to leave, I called after her: 'Remember,

consistency trumps all other criteria!' She paused
momentarily and turned back to look at me, frowning
now. Before she could respond, I continued, 'Yeah, that's
what my criminology professor used to say. Our criminal
justice system can't understand why people telling the
truth still behave differently. Judges can overlook these
honest discrepancies and deport someone just because
they don't conform to an arbitrary standard.'

She sat back in her chair and crossed her arms, her blue
eyes narrowing as she held my gaze.

'And what about our police intuition?' Her voice was
low but firm. She uncrossed her arms and pointed at me
with a stern finger. 'These immigrants know how to play the
emotional card,' she continued. 'The stories of papers lost
in transit are too common. Oh, come on, you know that as
well as I do.' Her impatience was growing with every word.
Her mouth had thinned into a tight line, and her knuckles
whitened around the armrests of her chair as she tried to
not to snap and just yell at me for my stubborn insistence
on investigating the musical past of Kalaf Epalanga.

X

Four days into my leave of absence, the phone rang. It
must have been about nine in the evening. I was already in
bed. On the other end of the line, my dad. The inspector
must have told him I was off work because of Khadija. I
could feel him breathing down the line and again I heard
those words he had spoken on the day of my graduation:
'If we're going to be good police officers, we've got to learn

to be good communicators, always pleasant and able to work independently. We've got to know how to negotiate, how to solve problems and be in excellent physical shape.'

Now he said: 'It's not your fault.' I didn't answer, I just listened to him talking about the first time someone he'd detained committed suicide, a long time ago, before he'd even become a detective. He was called out to some trouble in a bar, and when they got there they arrested the guy. He was a man in his thirties, with no priors, who'd just had a few too many. Two days later, the man was found in the Oslofjorden, drowned. That death tormented him for some time. If he'd let him stay in jail one more night, if he'd talked to the man . . .

'And when did it stop tormenting you?' I asked, after listening in silence.

'It didn't stop, it developed into one more of the ghosts we have to learn to deal with. I don't want to tell you that time heals everything, but it does bring relief.'

At that moment, and I don't know where it came from, I asked my dad if he'd ever killed anyone while he was on the force. The question must have caught him off guard because he didn't say anything for a few minutes. We both just sat there without speaking, each hearing the other's breathing, and I remembered Jay-Z preaching how to live with regrets. I apologised, I had no right to ask that question, and for the first time I thought he seemed vulnerable. He replied that he had. I don't remember whether we said anything else after this, I don't think so. We hung up promising to see each other soon, which we didn't end up doing.

The midnight sun was piercing the curtains, leaving the room in half-light. I covered my head with the duvet in a search for total darkness. I was in desperate need of a full night's sleep. Jay-Z's voice came to me again, still with my eyes closed, oscillating between sleep and waking. That high nasal voice shook me towards the daytime: the words sounded bare without the instrumental underlay, just a New York accent slowly chewing each syllable, making no great effort, like the mantra of a Buddhist monk. Then a sound rises up slowly, hard to identify at first, it envelops the words, a sound that isn't like the jazzy rhythms that make up the song. The sample of Earl Klugh and Hubert Laws's 'It's So Easy Loving You' is the bedrock beneath the Brooklyn MC's rhymes when he told us the importance of making regrets as part of our learning process. And before those lines have dissipated, a new melody, a human sound, a melody that stretches out without trying to find any words or imitate any instrument. Just a contained cry, the cry of young Khadija chanting that song as sad as the city around me. Oslo had dawned grim, silent. It was raining. The streets were overtaken by silence. I went over to the window and couldn't see a single human soul, not a single umbrella passing across the landscape. The flooded city seemed to have decided to postpone that Wednesday, defer everything to the following day, so sadly had the morning shown itself. At that moment I felt it was time to return to duty. If I left it another day, I might never go back.

I went back.

XI

The first thing the inspector made me do when I set foot back in the station was subject myself to those tests that the psychologists from internal affairs occasionally call us in to do. 'It's compulsory,' he said, when he summoned me to the fishbowl. That might explain why he'd called Mari and not me to present the report on the Angolan. 'People who get the highest scores in the problem-solving tests tend to be the happiest at work,' a colleague said on my way out. While other countries show results suggesting that intelligence tests are one of the best ways of identifying good officers, there's a group of psychologists over here who've got this theory that the most brilliant ones might feel they're not getting much stimulation from work. 'It's only a theory,' he said, 'and you needn't worry, it's not that they want mental retards either, otherwise we wouldn't have 80 per cent of the candidates for this job flunking the first round of admissions.'

Maybe it was time to undo the deal I'd done with Mari, stop looking clever and stop writing our incident reports. I still remember the day I suggested it. The two of us had just turned up at the department and we got handed a victim of domestic violence who, we later learned, had been forced to marry her aggressor. There aren't many jobs in the world that give you the same kind of challenges and variety as the profession of police officer. One day we might be following up clues to dismantle a human trafficking ring, the next we're sitting at a desk, faced with a mountain of paperwork, since 30 per cent of our time is spent writing reports. Being a woman, I thought the victim more likely to talk openly if she was interviewed by Mari, which is what ended up happening. The officers had picked her up off the street; she had hardly any clothes on and her face was bloodied. She'd been pretty badly mistreated. Since she had no documents and said she was Kurdish, they brought her to us. When I saw her, she was pale as chalk. Her legs were faltering. She sat down. Her hands were trembling and we could read her fear in her face, but also her amazement at finding herself in a police station. Her words struggled to come out, as if she didn't recognise the sound of her own voice. Her dry lips trembled while she once again described the events that had put her in that state. It was night-time and there weren't a lot of people around. Her frightened eyes swept across the room. She seemed surprised, maybe because she couldn't find anything that chimed with the image she had of police stations – she must have thought everything was out of a movie. She was the only victim there giving evidence. Mari offered her a cup of our coffee. She held the cup with both hands, so none of the heat would escape her fingers. Still in a state of shock, from the aggression and from having to describe it, she couldn't offer us another word, or shed a single tear. She just nodded agreement, distressed and overtaken by a mixture of denial and a desperate attempt to try to find a reason, an emotional state Mari seemed to understand, this was after all someone who'd just been hurt by the love of her life. She didn't ask a lot of questions, she knew what was going on in her head: wanting to run away, very far away until she had forgotten all about the man in whose arms she was meant to be protected and whose hands were supposed to give her nothing but caresses and support.

She eventually said that for years, she'd feared this situation, being in a police station. The man who'd hurt her in such a cowardly way, more times than she could count, always threatened that if she reported him she'd end up getting sent back to the country she came from. Being back there was her worst nightmare. It was only when she brought her hand to her face and felt the pain from the wounds he had left on her body that the tears started to flow, allowing her to grasp the true nature of what had happened. Yes, it was all real, all too real. She was overtaken by shame. Nothing now could erase the image she still had of her husband's eyes blind with rage, his thirst for blood, his death drive. With all that violence she ended up fearing the worst, and she can't even remember how the police had picked her up from the street. When Mari asked her if she remembered how many times she'd been hurt, she looked down, curling in on herself. What she felt was fear; even now in the police station, sitting with an officer, she was afraid, afraid of the marriage she'd lost, afraid of how people in her world would look at her, afraid of God and of herself. And in a gesture she repeated often, she brought one of her hands to her neck, seeking the shawl she used to cover her head whenever she felt exposed, as she did that night. She must have lost it while fighting for her life. She put down her cup and pulled up the blanket that was protecting her from the cold and covered her head. She began to sob convulsively. For a few moments, walking back to the metro station after the test, when that colleague's words came back to me, I

thought about the possibility of failing. It was the first time
such a thing would have happened to a Nygård. I could
already hear my dad yelling down the phone: 'It's shameful,
your grandfather must be turning in his grave, being a police
officer is in your blood.' It's in yours, Father, not in mine,
I'd answer. They'd be doing me a favour, failing me and
sending me back home. My granddad, at least according to
what Ava had told me on the day of the funeral, would have
been pleased to know I was able to do or to be something
else. I could travel, see Latin America, visit Rio de Janeiro,
climb up the Pedra Bonita and hang-glide off the top,
or if not that then Africa, I've always wanted to climb
Kilimanjaro, that was something my granddad had always
wished he could do, whenever we went up a mountain he'd
bring it up. Not being a technical ascent, in theory anyone
in good physical shape could make it up those 5,895 metres.
Mountains always exerted a kind of fascination for us, and
to our great joy, we didn't need to go all the way down to
Tanzania, as our country's full of them, of all shapes and
sizes. Some of them we liked climbing, like Mount Skåla or
Trolltunga, and others we liked driving through.

Our adventures with grandfather Nygård were like being
inside an episode of *Halvsju*, which in the days of single-
channel TV would have us glued to the screen on many
evenings. When summer came, everything changed. I
don't remember us turning on the TV even once. He was
our own private Ivar Dyrhaug and Erik Halfdan Meyn,
and we were the Brødrene Dal. The things he'd say to
us only made sense to me years later, when we started

to walk the same paths as him. It was him who always said, for example, that if we don't want immigrants, then we've got to stop making them. 'If we don't want them, then let's not sell them weapons, let's not let their Asian children sew our clothes, their Poles pick our strawberries or their Thai women clean up all our shit.' I never saw him defending any specific party or politician, he always said the police are here to serve the people. 'Between me and a city employee who collects the rubbish from our streets there's no difference, we both want the same thing: to live civilised lives in our community,' he'd say. The only time I saw him paying attention to political events was at the time of the 36.9 Ultimatum in 1997. The Labour Party prime minister of the day, Thorbjørn Jagland, announced his government would quit if his party got less than 36.9 per cent of the vote. My grandfather called him selfish and stupid when he quit after a victory of 35.5 per cent, which would actually have allowed him to form a government. When I heard him talk like that, I thought he was a red, disappointed in his party's leader, maybe for having forgotten the 'everyone shall take part' line that stitches together the ideology of the Norwegian left. But no, old Nygård really didn't have any particular political colour, and if he had, he said, it would be green, because 'somebody's got to defend our mountains and fjords'. I, on the other hand, who unlike my brother never got much of a taste for politics, am more pro-Norway, but not like the blue tones of the Høyre conservatives or the FrP progressives. I'm pro-diversity, but I don't feel aligned with Akhtar Chaudhry's politics he promoted at

our parliament either. I followed the back and forth he had
with the liberal Abid Q. Raja when Raja said, 'Once it's no
longer a crime to burn the Norwegian flag, why should
we Muslims have to swear an oath to it?' I wonder how
Chaudhry, being Muslim, deals with the fact that our flag
has a Christian cross at its centre and that our Constitution
clearly states that we are a Lutheran Christian kingdom.
If he really believes that anyone who wants to become a
citizen of Norway should swear an oath to Norway's flag
and Constitution, it's got to have caused an awful lot of
discomfort in our Muslim community.

I mean, I don't blame them, but if you wanted to win
the loyalty of our naturalised immigrants, wouldn't it be
better to teach them to love this country, not starting with
a bit of cloth and a few sheets of paper but with something
deeper, like 'koselig' for example? More than anything,
koselig is a feeling, and one that's hard to translate as it
combines ideas of comfort, intimacy, warmth, happiness
and contentment into a single word. And to reach the
feeling of koselig, you need to have koselig things. Woollen socks and sweaters, candles, warm blankets, hot dogs,
cognac, good coffee and good stories to share with your
friends. With a whole arsenal of popular tales like in *One
Thousand and One Nights*, I'm sure it wouldn't take Muslims long to learn to love our endless winter months, and
who knows if even our next sporting champion might not
be somebody of Muslim origin.

Basically, if we really want these asylum refugees to have
the chance to become Norwegian, we'd be training social
workers in the same numbers as we currently train police

officers. When I see them arriving with all the desperation of somebody who's escaped from hell, I can't help but wonder what good it is us being so prosperous if the world all around us is coming apart. We can toughen our laws, even close our borders, but it's already too late. Europe as we know it is dead, and that's not the immigrants' fault. There aren't enough babies to counteract the 25 per cent made up by the Muslim population in Marseille and Rotterdam, 20 per cent in Malmo, 15 per cent in Brussels and Birmingham and 10 per cent in London and Paris, Copenhagen and Oslo. There are now 101,649 non-Western immigrants here, 18.9 per cent of the total population of the capital. Dear White Europe, if you want to 'save' the old continent, have sex, a lot of sex, reproduce, heed the words of Aloisius Ratzinger, Pope Benedict, and forget about contraceptives. He knows the Christian faith's chances of survival is a numbers game. We don't have enough babies to redress the balance and knowing that this is the beginning of the end has got to be giving our clergy nightmares. There's plenty of talk of tolerance, but when there's a fear of extinction, how can you avoid a current of Islamophobia setting in? The immigrants themselves haven't helped, of course. Most attacks on Norwegian women are committed by immigrants of African origin, mainly Somalis; if the number of forced marriages hits the headlines, you're going to be hearing the slogan 'Throw them all out!' whether you like it or not. Throw them all out before they destroy our civilisation. Numbers, you can't argue with them. Not even the liberals, defenders of the oppressed, have anything to base a counter-argument

on. Even me, someone who leans towards the liberal side
of society – when I look at the numbers, even those of
us with open minds have our hands tied. The Muslim
community needs to answer the question of what kind
of integration they're after. The youngest especially, the
second-generation ones, they've urgently got to start
thinking more critically about their parents' traditions.
One day they'll be called on to make a choice between the
Middle East that's so far away from them and this land of
midnight sun that is their cradle right now.

I know what I wanted to write to Ava, I wanted to tell
her that I feel like I've reached some kind of crossroads
and that I'm scared of my own certainties. It would be so
much easier to give in to ignorance in the name of comfort and my peace of mind. Am I ready to question all
my convictions and give up on something as fundamental
as the right to choose? Sure, choosing's hard work, and
people who know little or nothing seem a whole lot hap-
pier, more patriotic, more devout, so that if I ask myself
what are the values that govern us, I will also succumb to
political correctness. My biggest weakness would probably be the scepticism I unload onto anyone who suggests
an impossible utopia, even if it's based on centuries of
experience, on concrete data left by our forefathers, that
identifies clearly and objectively what caused the decline
of the civilisations that came before us. We have recent
data showing we're headed for self-destruction and our
chance to correct this boat's course is now. It's possible to
make (and we deserve) something better, I'm positive that
dignity isn't a utopian value. 'Peace on earth' sounds trite,

like something from the chorus of an old song, something the sixties generation chanted in the streets of the capitals of the free world, demanding an end to armed conflicts in other distant parts of the planet. But nobody sings those old songs any more. The ones that have survived have become today's elevator music, waiting-room music or, worse, music to accompany TV ads. No one believes peace on earth is attainable, not through poems or through satire, not using prayer, let alone grenades. If some people are driven to blindness by fundamentalism, there are also plenty whose scepticism doesn't allow them to see an ox when it's standing right in front of them.

We are adrift, so certain that we are all dependent on one another, yet suspicious of our neighbours' intentions, of our siblings'. All because we remain convinced that our prosperity as a group can only materialise at the expense of other people's sacrifices and deprivations. There are no miracle solutions so long as there are places on this planet where bullets are cheaper than books – no matter which hemisphere we're in or which latitude we're at, the liberal values we defend are doomed to die.

XII

Jay-Z's 'Lost One', produced by Dr Dre, is one of my favourite tracks from the unloved *Kingdom Come*, the album released after he came out of his self-imposed retirement. And the hook kept ringing in my head as I looked at Mari, who still hadn't revealed what had gone down at the inspector's office. Judging by the way her shoulders were slumped, I'd hazard a guess it was not only about the report. The inspector must have sensed something in me, and maybe those sheets of paper he had in his hands weren't the report on the Angolan but the results of my evaluation. He might have seen that there's something very wrong that needs correcting, before another desperate immigrant ended up killing themselves right under our noses. They aren't prepared for dealing with a wave of suicides – a single one might even go unnoticed, but a second could well set off an alarm, triggering a hunt for scapegoats. And who would be better suited to that role than the individual who arrested them, questioned them, and sent them to jail?

I could have taken advantage of the moment to scarper right now, avoiding getting myself called into that fishbowl. Maybe I should leave all this crap once and for all and go home, maybe even go to my parents' home, not that I'll get any peace there, but I reckon it's time I stopped avoiding the place whenever they're around. Very likely it's time for me to say I feel like I've reached the end of the road, that I wasn't made for this. My dad will shout, I'll shout, my mother will cry, my dad will blame me, I'll rush to console my mum, when really all I want is for her to console me. Sobbing, she'll wipe her tears with the knitted socks she makes every year in the hope of having all her koselig lads around the fire when winter comes, and I'll feel like an even worse son than I do already. I'll smile, this time showing all my teeth, the same smile I always let her have whenever she calls, giving her the answer every mother wants to hear. 'Don't worry, I'm getting by fine.' Always the same response. I don't know if she's ever believed those words. If she didn't, I never gave her the chance to keep questioning me, I always avoid prolonging the conversation and just conclude with an 'I love you' and the promise that next winter we'll have more time to pamper one another properly. I know it's not enough, but that's how it is. I don't remember the last time we had a long talk. It's different with my brother, we never really dwell on things anyway, we don't need a lot of talk, as we always know how the other is, even if we've never said how we actually feel. Regardless of who calls first, we always exchange the same combination of six words in greeting: 'What's up, all good?' followed by a laconic 'Yeah, good . . .' in response. And before launching into whatever the reason for our call, we always ask, 'You spoken to Mum?' prompting the answer – invariably, and in the same tone as the 'Yeah, good' of our greeting – 'Yeah, I did, it's all fine . . .'

It's not easy having your routine as an obligation, a duty you need to get used to. There are days you feel like being something else, because it turns out this routine isn't always pleasurable. When boredom calls, what am I supposed to do – join a gym? Take up a hobby? Learn to practise Buddhism, yoga, or one of those other meditation techniques that help you reach inner peace and accept your duty-bound routine with good grace? Write some haikus and embrace my fate, however tough it might be? On the days when chasing illegal immigrants becomes unbearable, I still prefer shutting myself away at home and making mixtapes for my friends, which basically means my brother, who no longer listens to them, and Ava, who's in damn Lebanon. Only they, like me, who grew up in the 1980s, a time when digital was still a utopia to us common mortals, would understand. To this day, my favourite way of sharing music with someone is using cassettes. I still have the ones Ava gave me at the end of each summer we spent together. I would listen to them and then post her another compilation in response. Like Rob Fleming, the character in that Nick Hornby book, I'm one of that group of people who consider a good mixtape no less than a work of art. I don't underestimate their power, they can rescue or condemn the love-life of those involved, they can easily become a matter of life or death. On a mixtape, each song had – still has – a reason for being. I think my taste in music and poetry was born around that time. And maybe I, like Ava, being very familiar with the secret messages and codes we hide in our tapes, know how hard it would be to classify what we experienced in Kristiansund as 'just a summer thing'. Maybe I should go home and make you a mixtape, except instead of sending it in the post, I'd knock on your door in person, and before you say anything, I'll admit how immature I've been all these years. And I say that with no kind of resentment, that's not my style. Not least because, if we think happiness is something that can't be quantified, I can say that I was happy with you. Even if this happiness was limited to half a dozen summers, and though I never asked you or suggested it to you, I felt like I was your boyfriend whenever I was walking beside you on the street, when you'd sink your hand into mine, whenever our lips met. And since love is not possessed, but enjoyed, I can say we did enjoy love like somebody visiting a garden. I didn't run away from you, but nor did I know how to tell you: for us to experience this, we don't need to have what others have, because we're enough for us. And I hope you'll smile back at me with that child's smile of yours, at this incomprehensibly postponed reunion.

It wasn't easy for me, passing up the chance to say these words to her. Time is less merciful to lovers who want and live in an impasse, in a cautious postponement, the product of an unconscious fear. Even though time is a changeable material and even though it's tiny, with the hunger of desire it'll multiply, leaving traces in the memory, making a single night feel like months. Like the one spent in that kitchen, just the two of us, the coffee in two porcelain cups and the music that played loud but without ever imposing itself. Could she know that in this time-equation of ours, a year together would be like attaining eternity? In that kitchen, my thoughts were filled with ideas and variations on the theme of 'forever', but I didn't share them. I assembled them in silence, while trying, in vain, to catch the secret I used to make time unfold, changing the speed of the hours and making each moment we shared eternal. Never have I been so sure as I was in that moment what it means to want and not possess.

When Mari was talking to the chief, I decided I'd had enough and stood up – I'd taken two steps towards the fishbowl when I saw Mari getting up from the chair and heading for the door. I quickly detoured towards the coffee machine before the inspector saw me and sucked me into that room. I didn't fancy ruining my weekend

answering questions about the Angolan's case. Not that I
have anything planned other than writing all weekend, it's
true, but there's nothing else that can get him released at
this stage. He's not in the system, the only things that show
up are articles about music and he could well be telling
the truth. But Mari, knowing about my rap obsession,
wasn't long in asking how many rappers use music as a
way of covering up illicit activities. I had to accept she
had a point. I genuinely hope this Kalaf has learned some
lessons from the collection of Jay-Z albums he has on his
iPod. When I was rummaging through his belongings, I
made a point of running through what he was listening to.
I still believe a playlist tells you more about a person than
the words that come out of their mouth. The compulsory
Reasonable Doubt was there, the indisputable classic *The
Blueprint*, the unanimously acclaimed *The Black Album*.
I imagine before setting off on the journey that took him
all the way across the continent by bus without papers, to
summon up the courage, he would have put Just Blaze's
'PSA' in his ears. At least, that's what I'd do if I were in
his place, maybe I wouldn't start with *The Black Album*,
but with *Vol. 2 . . . Hard Knock Life*, or possibly even
the recent concept album *American Gangster*, one of
the best motivational albums for someone about to set
off on an adventure that might change their life forever.
The record starts out by telling the story of a young man
without many options for making it in life, fantasising
about how to get into the world of crime, with the early
tracks 'Pray' and 'American Dreamin''. But the young
man does finally make it, and once in, he doesn't hesitate

to celebrate his triumphs with the festive 'Roc Boys (and the Winner Is . . .)'. Until the doubts begin to haunt him and he quickly becomes paranoid. Then comes 'Success', featuring Nas, who appears here in a historic duet, rapping with a rival of his, in a moment of art imitating life. And finally, prison, with 'Fallin''. Even if the Angolan didn't waste quite as much time as me dissecting Jay-Z's lyrical content, I hope he did at least internalise the lines Hova said about committing crimes so none of us would have to do it. As far as I can tell from reading the inspector's expressions, I'm sure that, as far as he's concerned, he wouldn't even be put in a cell before he's seen by the judge on Monday. If in the meantime anything appears that might suggest Mr Kalaf Epalanga is involved in a crime, the inspector will make a point of ensuring he gets immediately deported to Africa. Mari Gunnhild, my partner, came over and muttered through her teeth, 'The inspector's furious.'

I asked if there was anything wrong with my report, and she aimed her cold blue eyes at me. 'Our report,' I corrected myself.

'What the . . . What report?! The inspector got a call from Chief Jan Egil Presthus. He was phoning to ask after the Angolan.' Why the hell would the Special Police Affairs Unit be calling about this Kalaf Epalanga? Either he's the reincarnation of Moses who's managed to get lost someplace on his way through the Mediterranean and made a pilgrimage to our border, or he's got a criminal record bigger than Galdhøpiggen mountain. When I looked into his eyes, I wasn't quite sure what I was seeing in them. He probably wasn't able to take anything from mine either. We were two strangers trying to decipher each other, and it wouldn't have been hard to see that I was the one with the power. I was standing between him and freedom, he necessarily had to get through me. You could understand that as power, having someone else's life in our hands. But I never saw fear in his eyes, it was almost as if he were the one with the power, that until there was proof, he really was the one who had it: the courage that brings us dignity. We might even get caught on the wrong side of the law, and even if the courts condemn us, it's the truth that will help us resist. As a police officer, we learn early on that it's almost impossible to lock up an individual's spirit, you can try to break it with violence, constrain his movements, stick him in solitary and deprive him of contact with the outside world, but truth will keep the flame inside that soul alight. 'The Øya festival's lawyer called to ask us to release the Angolan,' said Mari. 'They want to know everything we've managed to get out of him.'

'Did they ask about music?' Mari replied with a simple no, they must have known about that already, Øya's lawyer must have told them.

The Federation must have panicked and set off every alarm, recalling the Police vs Samvirkelaget case. The risk of losing in court to one of the biggest music festivals in the country, in a case involving a foreign band, must have made them accept whatever terms were offered.

'We're to let the Angolan go.'

XIII

Mari sat down and put her feet up on the table, tilting her chair back. She looked exhausted. 'Why is arresting famous people always so complicated?' she wondered aloud, though knowing I could hear. 'The inspector asked if we need to worry about the Angolan, he wanted to know all the details of the detention and the interrogation; he wanted to know if we touched him. They're scared he might serve us with a lawsuit. The inspector again reminded me of the law and the regulations we are obliged to follow. We should endeavour to arrest subjects without employing unnecessary force. I told him I'm well aware of the risks we're running when we resort to using force. In the case of the Angolan, it was all pretty smooth, we didn't have to insist too much to get him to go with us, it was like he already knew what was coming to him, like he'd been in this situation before.' I agreed – truth was, we didn't even use handcuffs till we took him out of the car to bring him into the station. We aren't part of the statistics of those people who don't know how to put cuffs on properly. The inspector didn't need to pull out the rulebook, we're on the front line, we handcuff more people than a regular public patrol officer, no immigrant has ever complained that their cuffs were too tight. Most of them, poor things, must think the treatment we give them is positively luxurious. When they get agitated, we never draw a gun, we've never found ourselves involved in a situation that needed anything worse than pepper spray.

But once bitten, twice shy – they don't want to go

through the same humiliation again, like in the Obiora case, when the Ministry of Justice and Public Security concluded that, in the case of the three officers involved, there wasn't enough evidence for an accusation. The fourth officer, the one who'd been driving the police van at the time, was immediately cleared.

Mari was spinning a pencil between her fingers as if she were about to perform a magic trick that demanded absolute attention. She always did this when something was annoying her. 'My dad arrested a famous musician in 1968. Jimi Hendrix.'

I laughed. I only realised how loud I'd been when I saw everybody turning towards us, everybody except the inspector, who was on the phone, probably reassuring Chief Jan Egil Presthus.

1968 was the year of all the unrest in Paris, the year our own students, mostly on the left, went out onto the streets to demonstrate outside embassies, prompting our police force to use tear-gas cartridges to disperse them and restore order. The year our politicians, afraid Paris May 1968 might be reproduced in a Nordic version, came to the discussion table in parliament – during the debate on foreign policy – with hot-button topics like the crisis in the Middle East, the Biafra conflict in Nigeria, the Greek junta, Portugal's policies in Africa and the Vietnam War. And after NRK interrupted its programming to break the news of the Soviet invasion of Czechoslovakia, the time for lukewarm debate was over and what followed was one of the most turbulent weeks in our history. My father told us that the radio made a point of constantly playing Czech music. Protests gathered outside the Soviet embassy, shouting slogans like 'Long live Czechoslovakia!!', 'Long live Dubček!', 'No more tyranny!' and 'Soviets out of Czechoslovakia!' And just while the demonstrations were happening against the Soviet invasion of Czechoslovakia, organised by the youth of the Conservative Party, another simultaneous protest was evolving against the US presence in Vietnam, organised by Socialist Youth. The clash between the two youth organisations was inevitable. In Trondheim, protesters played the Czechoslovakian national anthem in front of a Soviet navy ship; they threw stones, ink, rotten eggs and tomatoes. The Soviet flag on the mast was lowered and they attempted, unsuccessfully, to cut the ship's moorings. In Kristiansund, a speech by the mayor, Leo Tallaksen, was interrupted by a violent youth demonstration that went on through two consecutive nights. They attacked a bus, they attacked the police station with rocks, tomatoes and apples. They started a fire in the central square and, amid all this chaos, our prince and future king, Harald V, got married to Sonja Haraldsen, our commoner queen.

1968 was the year of Tommie Smith and John Carlos, with fists raised, in black gloves, on the Olympic podium in Mexico City. The year Yale University opened its doors to female students. It was the year of the *Apollo 8* mission to orbit the moon. The year when *2001: A Space Odyssey*, *Planet of the Apes* and *The Good, the Bad and the Ugly* made movie history. And 1968 will be forever remembered as the year of the deaths of Martin Luther

King and Robert F. Kennedy. All of these being events that have little to do with officer Mari Gunnhild Riisnaes. For her, 1968 will always be a symbolic year in the relationship between the law and fame. To someone famous, the law will always be lenient.

And it all began on the morning of 3 January, when Jimi Hendrix and his entourage took off from Heathrow and two hours later landed at Torslanda Airport in Gothenburg. Him, with a metal-ring belt round his waist, a black shirt frilled in the aristocratic style, a black leather waistcoat under a light cobalt-blue velvet jacket, and over this a white fur coat you'd normally see on a woman, finished off with a sun-shaped medallion and a cowboy hat, adorned with a red sash with badges and birds' feathers, and rings on his fingers. He checked in at the Hotel Opalen, at 73 Engelbrektsgatan Street, in the mid-afternoon, with the sun already fading, and he was allocated room 623. Before he went up to his accommodation, Gerry Stickells, his tour manager, informed him that the journalist Gösta Hanson was waiting for him. The interview was to be published the following day in the *Göteborgs-Tidningen*. That night, together with his drummer John 'Mitch' Mitchell, he went out for a night-time crawl round the city's clubs. They returned to the hotel around 2 a.m. on 4 January, the day scheduled for the first concert in a mini Scandinavian tour – Lorensbergs Cirkus in Gothenburg, Jernvallen in Sandviken, Tivolis Koncertsal in Copenhagen and Stora Salen, Stockholm. Around four in the morning, after complaints from guests about the noise, the night receptionist, Per Magnusson, opened the door to the drummer's room and found the place turned completely upside down and Jimi lying on the bed with a cut on his right hand. There was blood everywhere. Per Magnusson did what any hotel receptionist is trained to do when the situation involves a rock star and a trashed hotel bedroom – called the police. Two officers attended the scene. The first, a veteran, used to dealing with drunk university students, didn't seem particularly impressed by what they found there. After making a note of the items that were damaged, he handcuffed the guitarist and grabbed hold of him. The second officer was a rookie, who even knew 'Hey Joe' already, and whose semen, with true aim, would eventually fertilise the ovum of the mother of our officer Mari Gunnhild, two years after that night, in a single torrid twilight fuck, in a hotel room like the one in which he found himself now. They carried the offender as he lashed out, shouting idiotic things until finally, giving the struggle up for lost, he started to treat his accomplices Mitch, bass player Noel Redding, roadie Neville Chesters and Chas Chandler, his manager, to an unusual line. 'I feel like a bird,' he said as he was led out, first to the Sahlgrenska Hospital's emergency room, where he received stitches in his hand, and then to the police station.

Mari Gunnhild learned from her mother that that had been one of the high points in her father's brief career on the Swedish police force. She was the fruit of a one-night stand that started at a bar. Her mother was there celebrating the end of a season at the Stadsteater, and he was drinking to the soul of Jimi Hendrix, dead in London in the late morning of 18 September. Every year around her

birthday, until Mari begged her mother to stop, Ms Gunnhild would tell her daughter details about that night.
From the bar to the hotel room. Her with her head on
that man's chest, telling him about the theatre company
she was part of, and him pretending to be interested but
with his eyes on the TV set that was on but with the
sound muted. Suddenly he jumped out of bed to turn up
the volume, and on the screen she saw Jimi Hendrix and
his band playing the song 'The Wind Cries Mary' from
the US version of the album *Are You Experienced* recorded for *Popside* on TV. At that moment, she didn't know
he was a police officer, she didn't know his surname, she
didn't know he'd just turned twenty-seven and couldn't
possibly have imagined that nine months later she would
be giving birth to this man's child. But she would keep
that moment in her memory forever because, when the
song ended, she saw that the man was crying as if some
close relative had just died. Trying to console him, she
kissed his lips, his cheekbones and felt the taste of his
tears, she kissed his eyes, embraced him and pulled him
back onto the bed. Mari admitted her mother had named
her Mari because of that song, saying that when she was
born it was one of the few good memories she still had
of him.

'And so where does the Gunnhild come from?' I asked.

'From my mother's maternal grandmother,' she replied,
smiling.

According to Mari, Jimi Hendrix was charged with
criminal damage and the authorities banned him from
leaving Scandinavia, obliging him to appear at a police

station every day at 2 p.m. for a fortnight, while still being allowed to perform his concerts. According to the article that the *Tidningen* magazine published, under Gösta Hanson's byline, the tour's first concert was a memorable one. With his right hand wrapped in bandages, the guitar genius spent a lot of his forty-five minutes on stage complaining about his poor performance and the terrible sound that was coming out of the four speakers behind him. But even not at his best, Jimi managed to be better than most. When he finally appeared at the Gothenburg Municipal Courthouse, on the morning of 16 January, accompanied by a small crowd of fans and journalists, the judge ordered him to pay a fine of 3,200 Swedish kronor and sent him home.

'Our Angolan got luckier,' I replied. She shrugged and turned off the computer, preparing to leave.

'How long have we been working together? Three years and you never remembered to share that story before?'

'We've never locked up an international musician before, and I've never seen anyone committing an offence and get released just because they're famous,' she replied.

'Like Jimi Hendrix, you mean?' I asked.

'Or like O. J. Simpson,' she replied. I laughed. As far as we know he never killed anybody, but like 'The Juice', the Angolan was lucky to have a good lawyer, who not only managed to get him released immediately, but he was allowed into Gardermoen to get a plane back to Lisbon, without a passport.

'They want at all costs to avoid being sued by such media-friendly people, they just want him out of here quickly and with as little noise as possible. That's why the inspector wanted to know if we'd touched a single hair on his head, if we'd creased his shirt or broken so much as a nail. Last thing they want is to hear about court cases. What's the guarantee he won't arrive in Lisbon and immediately bring a lawsuit against us? Or worse – he's an Angolan citizen, he could easily take the case to the courts in his country and make it Angola vs Norway, Europe vs Africa.'

'God forbid,' Mari laughed. 'Commissioner Killengreen would lose her shit.'

'Imagine he came after us seeking damages for the psychological harm caused by his hours under arrest and alleging that as a result the concert at the Øya festival had been a disaster. Imagine around seventy thousand festivalgoers climbing the courthouse steps to bear witness in the case. If it was being heard in Oslo, obviously.'

'That would be almost impossible,' Mari said.

'But imagine it was. Would they fire us? What would you do if that happened?' I asked.

'I don't know,' she answered, batting the same question right back to me.

'I'd write the next *Redbreast*,' I said. She stopped at the station door, the same place where some hours earlier we'd seen the Angolan being escorted away by officers to the detention centre.

'Never pictured you as a writer. You want to be the new Jo Nesbø?' she asked, wryly.

'Yeah, maybe. Maybe I'll move to Kristiansund and devote my life to catching cod.' Mari laughed and asked if I wanted a lift home. I said yes.

XIV

We travelled down the Oslo road without much talk
– driving in silence is something we got used to a long
time ago. I was still thinking about telling her what I've
been mulling over. If I didn't know that she'd laugh and,
most likely, spread it around the whole department, I'd
tell her I actually wanted to be a rapper, but since I had
no talent for it, I'd settle for a career that allowed me to
make a living writing crime novels. I wanted to ask her
what she would like to be doing if she hadn't joined the
force. Did she intend to retire as a police officer? How
long could she stand being the guardian of the privileges
of one group of people at the expense of another? I kept
all these questions to myself, along with the fact that I
had no intention of going up to my apartment. As soon
as she'd left me at the door to my building and I saw
her disappear around the corner, I hailed the first cab I
saw, headed towards Gamlebyen, and joined the crowd
in front of the Vika stage, in the Middelalderparken. And
there he was, the first Angolan ever to set foot on any one
of Øya's stages, singing in a language I didn't understand,
but whose bedrock was the beat, the lingua franca that
any creature with blood in its veins can feel, understand
and communicate without a single word. Just movement.
The beat! There aren't many musical genres that can create
that hermetic bond between body and soul like dance
music, simultaneously incorporating – chameleon-like –
so many other musical manifestations whose emotional
appeal touches the hearts of so many different people.

More than rock or pop, this is the true communal music. The rhythm calls to the listener's heart, transporting him to the very essence of his relationship with the ancestral Africa – even if he's never actually set foot there himself. That bond is genetic, it's spiritual. Hence its being felt like a kind of religious cult, and the experience is only complete when it's shared with one or more other people. At that moment, amid that crowd who were offering no resistance, obeying the watchwords from my Angolan ex-detainee, now reborn, as if he knew what lungs are for, leaping about on the stage like a child who's finally learned how to use his legs, I too felt free. I imitated his movements, and jumped, jumped, jumped, and the second my body rose up, in those brief moments when my body was defying gravity, it occurred to me I had never taken Ava to a concert. In that moment I knew I wasn't going to write to ask her the recipe for Lebanese coffee. I was going to catch the first flight to Beirut and take Ava to the first open-air concert we found, no matter what kind of music it was. I just wanted us to be side by side, shoulder to shoulder, my hand reaching out so she could find it and lace her fingers through mine.

She'll know the meaning of that outstretched hand of mine, she'll know that by lacing her fingers through my fingers she will be responding to the madness of a desire that is so very urgent. No matter what the music or the song. Just like Duke Ellington taught us, so long as something sounds good and feels good, well, then it is.

And that's all we need.

ACKNOWLEDGEMENTS

To all kuduro and kizomba singers, dancers, DJs and producers whose creations are an endless source of inspiration for me. Thank you.